A Few Hours After This

Short Story Collection

Paul Blake

To my darling Helen, thank you for your continued support. I couldn't do this without you.

I love you, and hope you'll forgive the times when I'm in my head plotting and planning the next story.

Table of Contents

Hazy Shade of Winter

Stephen Kemp was walking the dog, Brave, through the thick forest when the first bomb went off. By the time he had returned to the country house he was staying in, boots muddy and nose dripping from the cold, a further nineteen had gone off in major cities across the United Kingdom.

The icy ground crunched underfoot. *We're due snow soon,* Stephen thought, as he reached into his coat pocket for a tissue. *I better not be coming down with a cold.* He could see Brave in the distance sniffing and huffing at a fallen tree.

'Brave! Here boy!' Stephen called, slapping his thigh.

Brave's ears pricked up and with a final look at whatever was under the tree trunk, he bounded back to Stephen.

'Good boy,' Stephen said, rubbing the soft honey-gold fur. 'We better be heading back, now. Mrs Rose would have prepared breakfast for us both and will be cross if it gets cold. You know what she's like.'

Mrs Rose was the housekeeper—cook who came with the country house Stephen was staying in as he recuperated from the wounds he suffered in his last mission. His leg had healed. Fortunately, the bullet had gone clean through the thick thigh muscle rather than into the femoral artery a few inches to the side, however, he was still having mobility issues with his right arm, barely able to lift it above shoulder height. *More physio needed today I think.*

***

As the impressive Edwardian-era country house showed through the bare-leaved trees, Stephen indicated to a panting Brave trotting beside him that he could go, and Stephen watched the dog race towards the house. *Such a beautiful creature,* Stephen looked wistful. *I'd love to have one again, but I'm never home for long enough, it wouldn't be fair.* An image came to him of a young brown-furred puppy with a red bow tied to the collar next to a sparkling Christmas tree and Stephen's parents looking happy and much younger. Stephen smiled at the memory. *In a couple of years, I'll be too old for this work then I'll see.* The smile faded as he saw Mrs Rose rushing out of the house.

'Mr Kemp! Mr Kemp!' she called as she hustled.

'Good morning Mrs Rose, I'm sorry we're late for breakfast… the leg,' he lied, tapping his leg for effect.

'What?' She said as the distance between them closed. 'Haven't you heard?'

Stephen stopped walking and looked at her, her eyes were red-rimmed, her usually perfect grey hair was askew, and she was wearing a frilly robe over a modest nightgown.

'Mrs Rose, what's wrong? What's happened?'

'Oh, Mr Kemp! It's awful, truly awful.' A heavy sob escaped her.

'Mrs Rose,' Stephen said. 'Tell me what's happened?'

'London has gone!'

'What are you talking about?' But Mrs Rose didn't hear him as she buried her face into his chest.

Stephen guided Mrs Rose back into the house and set her down at the kitchen table. He made her a cup of tea and let her cry it out. He put the tea on the table and asked her what had happened.

'I heard it on the news,' she began. 'The BBC in Manchester said that a large bomb had exploded in London. They then showed footage from someone's mobile of large cloud above the city. Then the BBC went off the air. I tried the other channels, but they're just fuzzy.' With that, she started sobbing again.

There were no warning or escalations of tension like there should have been if it was an attack by Russia or China. Could it have been an accident? Stephen turned on the radio sitting on the counter, it was an old-fashioned model, no DAB stations on this antique, and he twisted the dial to see if he could pick anything up. There was just static on the FM channels, he switched to AM and repeated the process. He found towards the upper end of the scale a message playing. He caught it mid-way through the message and waited for it to repeat.

'This is the National Emergency Broadcasting Service. This country has been attacked with nuclear weapons. Communications have been severely disrupted, and the number of casualties and the extent of the damage are not yet known. We shall bring you further information as soon as possible.'

'Oh shit,' Stephen said, his face pale and with a quiver to his voice.

The message continued. 'Meanwhile, stay tuned to this wavelength, stay calm and stay in your own house. Remember, there is nothing to be gained by trying to get away. By leaving your homes, you could be exposing yourself to greater danger. If you leave, you may find yourself without food, without water, without accommodation and without protection. Radioactive fall-out, which follows a nuclear explosion, is many times more dangerous if you are directly exposed to it in the open. Roofs and walls offer substantial protection. The safest place is indoors. We shall be on the air every hour, on the hour. Stay tuned to this wavelength but switch your radios off now to save your batteries. That is the end of this broadcast.'

Holy hell, Stephen thought, what in the world are we going to do?

'Mrs Rose... Mrs Rose!' Stephen shouted to wake her from her pity. 'Fill up any container with a lid with water. Bottles, jam jars, anything. Fill up the bath, we'll use that to flush the toilet. Once you've done that you need to seal up any windows, I'll help you when I return.'

'You're going out? But they said—'

'—I'm going to the village to stock up on supplies, we're in the middle of nowhere, miles away from any major towns so it'll take a while for any fallout to reach us. I'll be back.'

***

Stephen sped into the village in the 4X4, there were a lot a people milling about. Shocked faces and tears were widespread. He parked in a disabled bay outside the village's supermarket. He checked his gun's safety was on and slipped it into his jacket pocket. *You can't be too safe.* He left the car and locked it using the remote on the key fob. He grabbed a trolley beside the entrance and entered. There were queues of people at the tills and a lot of shouting. He headed straight to the drinks section and put bottles of water in the trolley, he then collected several tinned goods, throwing them in the trolley without looking at the contents. The aisle to the fresh meat was blocked with shoppers, so he quickly went around to the household goods sections and grabbed batteries, candles, and tape. He stopped for a second to think of anything else. The house had a good supply of medical supplies, so that was ok. *Shit, Brave will have to eat too.* Stephen went to the pet food aisle and put in as much dried dog food as he could fit. He then retraced his steps wheeling the trolley out of the entrance, avoiding the blocked exit and ignoring the shouts from other shoppers and staff. He loaded the back of the car and got inside.

He was just about to start the vehicle when his satellite phone went off. He took it from the central console and answered it.

'Kemp speaking,' he said.

'Stephen, it's Greg, thank god you're ok."

'Hi, Greg, I'm fine. I've just done a little shopping, and I'm heading back to the house. What happened?' Greg Nolan was Stephen's boss in MI6.

'A complete—fucking—disaster. As far as we can tell nuclear bombs went off in London, Manchester, Birmingham,

Leeds, Glasgow, Cardiff, Liverpool and more... all the biggest cities in the country. Around twenty of them.'

'Twenty? Bloody hell, Greg. Who was it? The Russians? North Korea doesn't have the range.'

'There's been chatter on the internet that it was Iran or an Iran-sponsored terrorist group.'

'I'll just put you on speaker, so I can get back to the house while we talk. The roads will be insane soon if they're not already.' Stephen pressed the speaker button on the phone and put it in the console. He started the engine and quickly pulled out and away. 'Terrorists? How the hell did that happen?'

'We have no idea. We're still trying to gather credible intel.'

'Where are you?' Stephen asked.

'I'm in France, sorting out the mess you left behind, thank God. I would have been in London otherwise.'

'So, in effect, I saved your life,' Stephen said, a wane smile to his lips. 'I'll add it to the slate.'

'Yeah, I'm pretty sure we're about equal on that front. I'm going to go, just wanted to check on you, I'll keep you updated.'

'Bye Greg.'

Stephen closed the call and drove through the narrow roads back to the house.

***

Stephen and Mrs Rose were sitting opposite each other at the kitchen table. Brave was lying on the hard floor beside Stephen, his large brown eyes looking forlornly in the direction of Stephen's plate.

'Mr Kemp,' Mrs Rose said, breaking the silence. 'When do you think it'll be ok?' Shadows over her face danced in the flickering candlelight.

'It depends on how widespread the fallout gets. It could be a long time before it's safe to leave. I should find out in a day or two.' Stephen looked at his plate. He'd barely eaten the gammon and mashed potatoes Mrs Rose had prepared. *Thinking of all those people in the cities all I can taste is ash.* Stephen thought. He placed the plate on the floor.

'Go on boy, at least one of us deserves to enjoy this.'

Brave ate the food with gusto.

'Sorry, Mrs Rose. I don't have an appetite tonight. I think I'll turn in. Goodnight.'

'Goodnight, Mr Kemp.'

***

The shrill ring of his satellite phone awoke Stephen. He answered it, his voice and head groggy with sleep.

'Kemp,' he said.

'It's Greg, sorry for waking you but I thought you'd want to know this ASAP.'

'Give me a sec to clear my head.'

'Sure.'

Stephen put the phone down beside him and slapped his cheeks a little to wake himself up. He blinked a few times then picked up the phone. 'Ok, I'm back.'

'You won't believe this, but the bombs were nuclear fizzles. They didn't reach the optimum explosive yield to reach fission. They still caused a massive explosion in each city, killed many people, disrupted communications and transport, but it could have been a lot worse. Radiation clean-up crews are out there already trying to collect the widespread radioactive material. But it means that there will be no nuclear winter for the UK.'

'Well, that's damned good news, so it's safe to go outside up here?'

'The Lake District? Yeah, you should be fine; the radiation is confined to the surrounding areas around the affected cities. In fact, the other reason for me calling is that we're going to need you to go outside. We have a mission for you.'

'A mission? I better warn you I'm still not 100 percent from Paris.'

'You'll be fine. It's a straight-forward get in, get noisy, get out mission.'

'Who's the target?' Stephen asked, with a note of caution in his voice.

'The Iran Supreme Leader, Ali Khamenei.'

'Oh, totally straight-forward then,' Stephen replied with deadpan.

'There's a chopper coming in twenty minutes to take you to Heathrow. Be ready. Oh, Stephen, when you get to Iran kick the shit out Hosseini from me.'

Stephen laughed. 'Will do mate, will do.'

***

Stephen squinted in the desert heat, the heat shimmering off the asphalt runway in the distance. He was five hundred metres away in the dunes on the far side of the airport. He'd been lying in wait for the past seven hours. Waiting for Khamenei to arrive. Among the sand-flies and scorpions. Hosseini's private jet was due to touch-down in the next ten minutes. Stephen checked his sniper rifle for the hundredth time, brushed grit and sand from the barrel. He had already dialled in the range of where he estimated the plane would stop. The red carpet, steps and honour guard were a big giveaway. He wasn't operating with a spotter for this mission, so he had to ensure he picked up the target quickly with his scope. He was at a disadvantage that the aeroplane doorway would be facing away from him, towards the airport, but this was really the only place he could be. North or South would put him in line with the runway and he'd be covered in sand and shit from aeroplanes taking off and landing above his head. He'd have to catch Khamenei on the carpet; he was elevated so that would help with the shot if Khamenei was surrounded by bodyguards.

Five minutes. Stephen could see at the end of the red carpet a silver Rolls Royce Phantom park up. The driver got out and opened the rear door, so it would be ready for the Supreme Leader. Stephen checked the range to the doorway, the rail-mounted scope on the rifle calculated the distance at five hundred and thirty-five metres. *Well within the rifle's maximum effective range.* Stephen thought. He checked the wind direction by looking at the flags fluttering on the sides of the Phantom's bonnet. He took a drink through a straw from the camelback rucksack he was wearing. *In this heat, it's important to stay hydrated.*

Two minutes. Stephen could hear the plane coming; the jet engine could be heard from miles around. Trying to minimise movement he didn't look for it in the sky. He'd see it soon enough. He went over the plan once more in his head. *Khamenei exits the aircraft and goes down the steps. The honour guard salute him. The Iranian ministers meeting him will stop him and shake his hand for his success in carrying out God's work. I may get a clear shot there. He heads down the carpet towards the car. Another opportunity. Khamenei enters the car, the final opportunity before the door is closed. The tinted windows are probably bullet-proofed and even if they don't withstand a bullet, they will affect its flight making it a lottery. Take the shot, the engine noise will mask or disguise the shot noise. Confirm the kill. Slowly back off down the dune and then head to the jeep hidden in a wadi a mile away. Drive like hell to the rendezvous point and board the helicopter that'll be waiting for me and get the hell out of Iran.*

Showtime. The aeroplane landed and taxied to the waiting steps, the pilot expertly parking it on the button. The honour guard came to attention. Bodyguards exited the plane first, creating a wall between the guard and the Leader. Stephen had the bottom of the steps in his sights. According to the briefing material, Khamenei was one metre sixty-five tall. Stephen raised the barrel the appropriate amount and waited. A cheer went up from the waiting ministers and Khamenei appeared, flanked by three much taller bodyguards. *Damn, no shot.* They stood both sides side and one behind. Stephen could barely make out the man's black turban. Khamenei started forwards. He reached the ministers, and they all bowed their heads in devotion and praise. Then as one man came forward to heap their praise. *A gap, just a two-second one, that's all I need. Nothing.*

Khamenei neared the car. He stopped, turned and waved in triumph at the ministers and the guard. A big smile on his face. *Now.* The rifle shuddered into Stephen's shoulder, through the scope he saw a hole appear in the centre of the Supreme Leader's forehead. In slow motion, the hole expanded and then exploded in a fine red mist. *Fuck you from Her Majesty Queen Elizabeth and the people of the United Kingdom.*

Set Fire to the Rain

I chabod Kilton crossed the street. The muddy ground was rutted by the passing of the steam-powered cars earlier in the day. The unending rain had helpfully filled them, so Ichabod didn't know if he was going to be stepping in a shallow puddle or if his boots were going to be submerged again. He wore leather trousers to keep as much of the water out as he could, but he could feel the mud oozing through the gap between trouser and boot and working its way down to his toes. His vision was hampered by the heavy helmet he wore, sides hanging down to guide the rain to his shoulders rather than to his neck. His peripheral vision was limited to the rectangle of openness in front of him. To see to either side, he had to turn his whole body. Ichabod likened himself to a racehorse during a race, the blinkers focusing his purpose. His purpose this evening, as with every evening, was to light the gaslamps around town before the night crept in to steal away the townsfolk's souls.

Ichabod had been the town's Lamplighter for the past eleven years, he had been passed the job after the incident with Fat Bob. Who'd woken late from a nap after a heavy lunch and in his haste, well as much as someone over two hundred and fifty pounds can haste, had neglected to light a whole quarter of the town. The result had been national news for a week or so, until a similar thing happened to another town, this one closer to the folks in Washington. A city where the lamps never go out. Ichabod had been there once as a child. The city was lit so brightly that it seemed even the rains evaporated before they hit the ground. Ichabod looked at the watch on his wrist, he wiped it to clear the water that had accumulated in the seconds it had been exposed. A half hour before dusk. He was well on schedule. He always started at the furthest lamp and worked in a concentric circle working his way closer and closer to the centre of town and the perceived safety it offered. Other Lamplighters had had their own patterns, and in the taverns, the ideal route was argued, discussed and fought about by the men of the town over many an ale. Ichabod's method was purely designed to keep him away from the outskirts of town when night fell. The forest surrounding the town of Blowing Rock gave Ichabod the creeps, the blackened rotted trunks pointing to the clouds above like dead man fingers, there had been plenty of those over the years, Ichabod thought. Beyond the black fingers, the forest was thriving. The trees and plants drinking their fill of the rain that constantly fell. Blowing Rock was slightly elevated so didn't receive the flooding that other towns did, however on bad days the town was cut off from the world by a lake that surrounded the town like a moat. Bridges had been built but never lasted long, their foundations washed away by the rain, the struts and planks followed quickly after.

Ichabod reached the other side of the road, without incident. His twisting, turning, shuffling walk doing its job as he avoided being run over by the occasional passing steamcar. He walked to the gaslamp, his hand already in his pocket for his piezoelectric lighter. The lamp was twenty foot tall. Black wrought-iron, pitted and rusted from the rain. The light end of the lamp was enclosed in a rectangular glass box topped with a large conical downlighter shade, dubbed by the townsfolk as a 'chinaman's hat.' The shade directed the rains away from the lamp. Well, the straight-down rains at least. The horizontal rain on a blustery day was a thorn in the side of the lamp-repairers.

Ichabod opened the access hatch, at shoulder height on the lamp column. Inside was a copper pipe, valve, and inspection/ignition point. The ignition point was closed by a small metal cover that could be turned to open or close the point. Ichabod turned the cover to the 'open' mark and turned the knob clockwise to open the valve. He removed the lighter as he heard the hiss of gas release. He pressed on the ignition button of the lighter aiming the end at the ignition point. He heard the clunk as the small hammer inside the lighter hit the quartz crystal, but there was no resulting spark at the end of the lighter. He pressed it again. Clunk. Again. Clunk. Again. Nothing. He turned the knob to close the valve. He looked to the heavens, the dark rainclouds making the night come sooner than it should. His heart began to beat a little faster and sweat formed on his forehead. He dismantled the lighter using the faint light from the lamp on the side of the road to assist him.

He thought back to when he was a kid, the lamplighter was a prestigious role. The town had had a Chief Lamplighter and a deputy. They rode around town in a fancy covered horse-drawn carriage which carried any spares parts and tools they may have needed, as well as protected them from the rains. Ichabod was technically classed as Chief Lamplighter, although the deputy and carriage had left the job many years before as the increasing natural gas costs cut into the town's budget. In its way, the job still held prestige, especially among the older folk. Ichabod never had to put his hand in his pocket in the tavern after a shift that's for sure. But there wasn't much interest from the town's youngsters in training up. It's cold, wet, and tiring work.

Ichabod looked at the mechanism, the crystal was there, as it had been earlier when he'd cleaned the lighter, as was the spring-loaded hammer. Before he ventured out each night, he maintained his lighter as carefully as the militia maintained their flintlock rifles. He pressed the button, heard the clunk, and watched as the hammer struck the crystal sending electricity through the thin wires to the end of the lighter. A spark. Ichabod smiled and reassembled the lighter. He turned to the lamp and twisted the knob again. Pressed the button on the lighter. Nothing. He froze in confusion for a second or two. Was that a shriek? Ichabod quickly turned around in a circle looking for the source of the noise, the hood, and rain obscuring his view. His hand pressing the button as he turned. Clunk. Clunk. Clunk. After completing the circle, he stripped the cover off the lighter and pressed the button. Nothing. He turned away from the lamp and tried again. A spark. What the hell? He faced the access hatch again and pressed the button, firmly, carefully. The electric blue plasma crossed the wires igniting the gas.

Ichabod shut his eyes as the bloom of fire reached out to him. The valve had been open too long without a flame, his mind told him as he felt the skin on his face flash burn and could smell the terrible stench of his eyebrow and beard hair singeing. Beside him he heard a godawful screech, like a cross between a wolf and teething baby, that made him leap away, tumbling backward as he twisted to see what it was. Before him was a black and grey figure, their arms outreached. Long pointed sharpened fingers. Ichabod watched as the figure began to disintegrate in the burning light, skin and dank hair floating down to the floor. When the light reached bone, the disintegration stopped, and the skeletal figure collapsed in puddled mud, ashes washed through the vehicle tracks by the rain. Ichabod heard doors open from the houses near him.

"Get me a torch or lamp and be quick already," he said. His voice lacking his usual jovial tone and replaced by the iron coolness of command.

It was too late. He could already hear the screams further down the road.

The Rezal Principle

T he mop bucket weaved along the smooth, white corridor; like a regular in a spaceport bar, drunkenly crossing the dance floor to reach the toilets in time; the small plastic wheels turning in opposing circles as the bucket was pushed along by the mop handle; the erratic path leaving a slalom trail of grey tracks of water as it splashed up against the sides of the bucket with each course correction. Stoddy Rezal, Custodian Engineer (Second Class), lost in his own thoughts, was oblivious to the spillages. Unkempt in a dirty grey coverall, with smears of grease and dirt across the legs and back, he looked younger than his real age of thirty-four; the patchy beard and shiny, oily face making people think he was barely out of his teens. His mind on far more important things than the cleanliness of the, usually, spotless and gleaming corridor leading to the elevator for the Custodian deck.

On other ships, they have custodian robots to do this work. He thought as a scowl flashed across his face. I should be preparing for the interview tomorrow. Not that I'll get it. No one has ever heard of anyone moving from 'The Custards' to crew, it just doesn't happen. Man, I even failed the test for Second Class four times. How does anyone remember which chemicals react violently to each other? On the job sheet it tells you which ones to use why should I have to know it? He asked himself. The air purifiers cleared the examination deck after two days, just fine, the Examination Officer's face was a picture though: nostrils flaring trying to identify a familiar, but rare smell; the panic in his face as his brain finally recognised the peculiar, sweet aroma of the deadly concoction; the shrill "Everyone Out!" as he covered his nose and mouth with his sleeve and hit the button to start the industrial strength air vacuums. Obviously, I must not be the only person to have done that or the safety measures would not have been already in place. Stoddy thought with self-justification. The reaction afterwards was extreme: twenty days in the brig, amongst the malingerers and alien captives. They all had a great laugh at my expense when I finally told them what I was there for. His expression turned sour as he thought of their mocking faces and the hysterical cackles surrounding him; the loud, deep guffaws from the Centuri ape-creature, once the story had been translated into its bestial language, pissed him off the most. Like that stinking brute had ever had a bath! Let alone touched heavy duty solvent for removing brain matter from the teleporter chambers. Stoddy grimaced at the memory of the creature's furry jowls wobbling as its monkey snot dripped uncontrollably from its pig-like snout.

He reached the end of the corridor and absent-mindedly pressed the button to call the elevator; the door whooshed open at a speed that still disarmed him, even after fourteen years of being on board the space freighter *HXN8435*. *Most ships have names that suit their purpose, not this piece of junk, inspirational names such as Intrepid or Endeavour for the ships specialising in exploration and discovering new worlds; or Onslaught or Dreadnought for the warships. Not HXN8435, which sounds like a serial number for a portable vidiscreen. However, when I get a crew position, I'll be able to apply for positions on other, better ships, and ones with more suitable names. This time it will be different, I'm sure.* Stoddy told himself as he entered the small room, reaching for the "Go" button; he tried to psyche himself up for tomorrow. *It's an interview, not a test, and everyone says I'm very personable and affable, I'm sure I'll be fine. I wonder what section they'll put me into? I'd love to be part of the Scouting team, the first ones on new, unexplored planets; or protecting the Captain and his officers as a vital cog of the Security team as they teleport into hostile environments on rescue missions.* As he was thinking these thoughts, there was a small part of his brain trying to urgently tell Stoddy something important, something vital he had missed. *It would even be pretty cool being even part of the Engineering team, messing with the warp drive and giving the ship an extra 10% to escape from pirates and unfriendly aliens.* Just as he pressed the button that nagging voice finally got through. *This isn't the elevator; it's the ship's airlock!* Stoddy automatically grabbed for the handle next to the button as the door opposite him slowly opened and the air in the room was sucked out into space.

***

'Captain, there's an unauthorised airlock release on the Environmental Deck,' Systems Engineer (1st Class) Lomax said with the emotional detachment typical of his species.

Lomax was from the humanoid-feline species Panthera Uncia; his fur was grey with silver specks and black teardrop-shaped markings. This gave him a regal look; which along with the species' characteristic aloof nature meant Lomax was a big hit with the females on board the freighter.

'Thank you, Lomax, can you scan to see who initiated it?' Captain Guthren asked annoyed at the interruption to her daily schedule.

Captain Majoriie Guthren was human; which isn't too surprising as most spaceship captains are human. There appears to be a glass ceiling for non-human species trying to reach a certain rank and it is a hotly contested issue amongst Equal Rights for All Species (ERAS) activists. Guthren came from an impoverished colony on the planet Nacrao, where, due to her impressive test scores as a child she was selected to join the space fleet. The whole colony raised funds in order to pay for her journey to the Fleet Training planet of Kuater; a fact she is constantly grateful for and still sends a sizeable chunk of her pay back to the colony in appreciation. She is almost eighty-five years old and reaching the stage in life where she is looking to start a family and leave the stressful world of space transportation behind her; other officers on the Command deck had noted how in the past few years she had started to take more care on her appearance: her long, golden hair was now brushed and braided instead of just being roughly tied back and she was finally using cosmetics to complement and enhance her facial features rather than being applied like a young girl accessing her mother's makeup collection for the first time.

'It appears to be a Custodial Engineer, ma'am,' Lomax replied. 'A Stoddy Rezal, Second Class Engineer'

'Another Custodial Engineer?' Captain Guthren said with bemusement. 'That's the third Custard in five months that has tried to commit suicide via an airlock.'

'According to his bio: you're interviewing this Rezal chap for a crew position tomorrow,' Lomax said after consulting the ship's computer.

Stoddy's face appeared on the main display screen of the Command deck, along with a very short bullet-pointed list of his 'achievements'. The day Stoddy's updated bio photo was taken, the photos are updated every five years, he'd just finished recovering from a dose of radiation poisoning; brought on by cleaning too close to the ship's powercore, an unknown member of the Engineering crew had removed the warning signs as a prank. His pallor complexion and patchy hair loss were shown in all its glory on the massive screen.

'Well, I can't see that going too well for him,' Captain Guthren joked sardonically. 'Alright, shut it down.' She ordered, still wondering why, out of all the occupations and roles on the freighter, the Custodians were the most inclined to try to end their own lives.

At least this one is using the airlock, instead of trying to kill themselves by sabotaging the ship and risking everyone's life, like the last one. She thought, shuddering at the memory of how close they came to be doing so. The Mechanical crew certainly earned their money that day, noticing and fixing the damage to the shielding system before we entered that asteroid field.

'Yes ma'am, commencing airlock shutdown procedure,' Lomax replied. 'Airlock will close in thirty seconds.'

He pressed a few buttons on the control panel in front of him; his hands moving with a natural grace; like a classical pianist caressing the ivory keys of their grand piano.

***

Stoddy, silently screaming for help, eyes bulging in panic, looked around him frantically for a way to close the airlock door, the flashing red light of the compartment hindering his attempts; the wind tearing at his clothes, trying to pull him through the increasing gap at the bottom of the airlock compartment door; his knuckles white as he clasped the cold metal handled fiercely for his life.

Where's the emergency stop button? Where? Where? Where? It should be next to the start button, surely? I'm going to die! He screamed to himself with terror. The detached part of Stoddy's brain, however, made a mental note to bring the placement of the button issue up at the next ship's safety briefing, along with airlocks that look like elevators. The mop bucket upended itself, spilling its bubbly, dirty water over the floor and thrust its way towards the gap. The metal bucket buckled as it hit the opening, too tight for it to pass; the welded seams burst, and it flattened and flew in space, bubbles and a stream of water trailing behind. Stoddy saw a sign through his clenched-up eyes on the wall to his left, blinking to clear the tears as the pressure around built to intolerable levels, he read "Emergency Stop" and saw the glowing red button below, the glow diminished by the red lights blinking from the ceiling. He stretched out his hand towards the button, it was nowhere near, it was then he saw the mop handle in the same hand. It took him a moment to realise what it was. Why have I still got this? He asked himself and then remembered the mantra from his basic training: 'A Custodian is nothing without his mop. Always keep your mop close. A mop is a Custard's best friend.' Repeated ad nauseam in daily and end of shift briefings throughout Stoddy's career; custodians encouraged to sleep with their mops, to hold them tight and hug them as you would a child woken up from a nightmare. Stoddy drew the line at naming his mop though, unlike some of his colleagues.

He reached out with the mop in his hand; the wind threatening to tear it from his grasp. *Nothing will make me lose my mop.* Stoddy said to himself with a determination that surprised him. The mop head brushed the button, the wet strands of wool leaving a greasy streak across the wall. Stoddy's other hand, gripped to the airlock handle, anchoring him in place, loosened as Stoddy's oxygen levels dropped and he became weaker in the decompressed atmosphere of the chamber.

Just one more try. He thought, raising the mop a final time, like a medieval knight preparing for their ultimate joust. He thrust the mop out towards the button, the sudden action caused his grip on the airlock handle to fail and he followed his mop towards the button at speed. The mop head impacted the wall six inches to the right of the button and the sudden stop caused Stoddy's body to rotate away from the button, towards the widening gap of the airlock door. He could see the dark emptiness of space beyond the ship reaching out to him as he slammed into the door face first. He felt his nose crumple against the smooth, metallic surface; he saw his blood stream out of the gap below him and uselessly scrambled for something to hold onto to prevent the rest of him following. *No, no, no, I don't want to die, not like this, please someone help me! I don't want to die.* He pleaded. Suddenly, the door shut with impressive speed; the gap disappearing as the shutdown procedure finally kicked in. Air rushed in through the vents as Stoddy collapsed to the floor in a mess of blood; his mouth open wide, gasping for oxygen like a goldfish out of their bowl and hugging his mop tight to his body; crying and sobbing like a child who'd lost their favourite teddy in a galactic shopping mall.

***

'Airlock shutdown procedure complete, Captain,' Lomax said mechanically.

'Thank you, Lomax, any news on our suicidal custodian?' Captain Guthren queried, with interest.

'It appears that he failed in his attempt, ma'am.' Lomax replied.

'Excellent, have him checked over by the Medical crew and taken to Psyche for evaluation,' Captain Guthren ordered. 'Oh, cancel that interview for tomorrow too.'

The Rezal Mind

The two doctors stood at the foot of the bed. Machines connected to the patient made a reassuring bleep at reassuring intervals. The occasional hiss from the breathing machine background noise they had a long time learned to block out.

'Any change to our resident Custard?' Doctor Lawrence Guardipee said.

'Nope, he's still rhubarb,' the second doctor replied. He was proud of that one.

The doctors had spent the past week looking up traditional desserts in order to one-up each other in their description of the patient. His condition hadn't changed for the month he'd been in Psyche. The monitors showed that there was brain function, of sorts. The visualiser screen wirelessly connected to the patient's frontal lobes by arcane looking and pulsating mind-leeches showed an infinite black space, the occasional star or whizzing planet breaking up the monotony. One constant on the screen was a diamond-studded mop, front and centre on the screen surrounded in a golden halo.

'That damned mop is still there,' said Doctor Guardipee.

'At least other patients had the good graces to vary their coma-dreams,' Doctor Twillie complained.

Some of the more entertaining dreams had been broadcast on the ships vidichannel for the crew to enjoy. Each year there was an annual competition, The Golden Lobes, for the best coma-dream across the space fleet. It was a huge event. Galactic megastars attended in their droves. Nominated entrants became celebrities in their own right, if they survived the treatment of course. It was considered to be bad taste to nominate coma-dreams posthumously. Coma-dreams of adult nature were supposed to be wiped from the system; however, they usually found their way on to the black market. Some of the more, shall we say extreme, dreams were exchanged for considerable credits.

'Computer, Patient Update,' Doctor Twillie said. 'Patient Rezal, Stoddy, Crew ID Rezal 1. No change. Physical and mental functions consistent. Recommend treatment continued for another week.'

'Notes added to Patient Record Rezal 1,' the gruff male computer voice said. All computers used to have a sexy female voice, but when Captain Guthren joined the ship, she commanded all the voices to be changed to male.

'Yes, the patient is fully spotted dick,' Doctor Guardipee said to his own delight.

Doctor Twillie smiled and with a finger to his forehead, saluted the effort. 'Completely jam roly-poly,' he said.

***

Doctor Guardipee was standing at the nursing station flirting with the robotic nurse. Old habits die hard in that profession. She had just accepted a dinner date in the ship's gourmet restaurant when the doctor's wrist communicator alerted him to a change in a patient's status.

'Adieu mon chéri,' he said with a touch of panache, which was appreciated by the robot's e-motion circuits. She fluttered her eyelashes mechanically in, what her programming suggested was, a suggestive manner.

'Until later,' she said to the doctor's back as he hurried to the Coma ward.

The doctor entered the ward and headed directly to the patient. Stoddy Rezal was lying in the rejuvenation cocoon that had been his home for the past five months. He was covered in a cream sheet. The nutrients and vitamins the feeding tubes had given him had bulked out his natural sorry looking complexion and put some meat on his bones, so to speak. One of the robot nurses finally disgusted with washing his lank, greasy hair had enlisted one of their colleagues from the personal care deck. Stoddy now sported one of the hippest, happening hairdos in the galaxy. One day the curls will wash out.

'Mr Weazel, I'm glad to see you are finally awake. We were beginning to give up on you,' Doctor Guardipee said with a wide reassuring smile on his face.

'W-h-h-h-h…,' Stoddy said.

'You were brought here after the…' the Doctor remembered the Psyche Ward Doctor's instruction not to mention the airlock to the patient. '…incident. You have been in a coma for five months and now are with us again. Your voice will return in a few hours. Well, we're glad to see you've finally come out of it. It looks bad on our monthly figures when patients don't.'

'W-hhh-ee-rr-ee's my…'

'It's okay it's beside you. We couldn't get it from you. You actually bit four robot nurses who tried to remove it. Your teeth were replaced with implants, by the way. Anyway, I have other patients, you'll be moved to a different ward by the end of the day.' With that, the doctor rushed back to the nurse's station.

Stoddy lay there for a while, running his tongue over his new teeth. They feel different. Hmmm, they filled the gaps, and the replacements are all evenly sized.

***

'So, Stoddy, are you ready to share with the group?' Doctor Kessel asked. 'It's been twenty-five sessions so far.'

'I've told you what happened. I was distracted and pressed the airlock instead the elevator. It's as simple as that,' Stoddy said. He looked at Doctor Kessel and shrugged. Doctor Kessel didn't say a word. She stared at Stoddy. *I've told you the truth there's nothing more.* Stoddy broke her gaze and looked around the room for support from the others. There were seven others in the session today. They were in a rough circle facing inwards. Stoddy looked from one crew member to the next. All of their eyes were on Stoddy; some of them had more than two. None said a word to back him up.

They did, however, show support to Doctor Kessel, in their own way, with cries of 'Stop weaselling, Weazal, and just tell the lady the truth,' this request came from Two-Legs Johnson, a man who thought he saw songbirds making love in the ship's air vents, but only on Tuesdays. The rest of the week he was a fully functional quasi-human.

'Get on with it, you curly-haired freeeek,' came from Jimmy Five-Eyes, a female mechanic from the Langan Tanga system. Her name wasn't Jimmy, and she only had four eyes, not five. Her hair was varying shades of chartreuse. Stoddy had developed a small crush for her over the past sessions. Needless to say, it wasn't mutual. She was in the Psyche Ward for dropping a passenger shuttle on her supervisor. Supposedly, he had pinched her bum the day before. He didn't return it until the next morning. She was livid.

Wonky-Face Ferguson called out, '▨⤲♀⟋ ①⊏▨ ♏♀⟋ ▨▨♏≜△〉〉.' But no one knew what he was saying.

Stoddy had complained to Doctor Kessel during his first session at the naming of his fellow patients. 'There is no reason to use a person's physical characteristics to describe them. It goes against the Intergalactic Disability Discrimination Act and it's wrong.'

'You're the one calling them disabled,' Doctor Kessel told him.

'God, Fleeezal, you're such an ableist,' Carrie Droopy-Boobs called out. 'You disgust me. Just because you're such a mess, the orderlies couldn't settle on one name. Fancy hair and teeth can't mask a face that looks like a dog's bumhole.' At this point, she stood up and had to be physically restrained from attacking Stoddy.

He heard later that she'd been released back to the crew, having obviously been cured of whatever affliction had brought her to the Psyche Ward. The naming convention stuck, and the other patients made a point of sucking in their faces whenever Stoddy ventured into the recreation room of the ward or sat near them in the cafeteria, or when looking into the small window to his room as they passed. Stoddy didn't complain again after that.

'There's no point in looking at the other patients for support. They cannot help you. Only you can help yourself,' Doctor Kessel told Stoddy.

'But I'm telling the truth. How many more times do I have to say it? It was an accident. I thought it was the elevator. Do you want me to lie?'

'You are lying, Stoddy. You're lying to yourself, you just can't see it.'

'I'm not. I'm not. I'm telling the truth.'

'Then why the hell are you still carrying that damned mop? It's with you everywhere, even when you are in the shower. We've seen it on the monitors.'

Stoddy looked around, 'What mop?'

'The one you are holding in your left hand. We hear you singing to it at night. Do you want us to play the recording?' She nodded to the orderly who lifted his tablet device and touched the screen.

Stoddy's rasping voice came flooding through the speakers set in the ceiling of the session room. 'This is my mop. There are many like it, but this one is mine…' Stoddy looked like he'd received an electric shock. 'This is my mop, this is my gun. This one is for cleaning, this one for fun.' This repeated over and over until Doctor Kessel nodded again to the orderly. Stoddy's voice slowly faded from the room.

'Needless to say, your "gun",' Doctor Kessel used finger-quotes on the word gun. 'is referring your penis. We have a video of you demonstrating the fact if you want to see it.'

'Erm,' Stoddy said. His cheeks were aflame, and he could feel the sweat flooding down his back. 'There's no need to see that.'

'Now are you ready to tell the truth?'

Just tell them what they want to know, we know the truth, we'll be here forever otherwise, and I have plans for you, Stoddy's mop told him.

'I… er… guess…er… so,' Stoddy said, as he looked at his mop in his shaking hand. His face, under the permanent-fake tan the robot-nurse had applied during his coma, had turned bone-white.

The Evil That Men Do

Director Henry Parkes was engrossed in the 1851 issue of the J. S. Virtue, and Co. published magazine *The Art Journal.* He had read it, and his other surviving issues, many times over. However, the magazine still enthralled him. He was seated at his large Victorian-era oak desk, with its restored red leather desktop. An antique desk lamp provided a homely glow, scattering the dark morning gloom coming in from the window beside him. He glanced out of the window and saw the early mist was still there, above ominous black clouds portended to the weather for the rest of the day. *Will that mean more or fewer visitors? I still can never tell. Even after all these years. Will the weather drive them away or will the shelter of the gallery provide a haven from the elements? I'll find out soon enough I suppose.* The National Portrait Gallery was due to open in just under an hour, at ten o'clock. He returned his gaze back to the magazine, to read more about events in the art world in 1851.

His office phone interrupted his reading about the 1851 Exposition. Parkes put down the magazine with a sigh and picked up the handset.

"Parkes," he said into the device with a bark.

"Director, it's Bev," Beverley Chambers was the Gallery's Curator of the 16th Century to Contemporary Collections. "Have you arranged for any new portraits to be installed on the first floor?"

32

Parkes thought for a second then replied: "No, the last addition was the oil on canvas of Sir James Brooke. What's this about?"

"Can you come to Room 23? There's something here you need to see. It's best if you come and see in person."

"You have me curious now. I'll be there in…" Parkes trailed off as he calculated how long it would take him from his office on the third floor to Room 23 on the first floor. "Five," he concluded.

***

Parkes came out of the lift on the first floor. He walked down the Statesmen's Gallery; it was lined on either side by a series of white marble busts on projecting plinths between painted portraits of eminent Victorians. The statues included Robert Stephenson, the greatest engineer of the 19th century; Arthur Wellesley, 1st Duke of Wellington and British Prime Minister; and George John Whyte-Melville, the poet and novelist's walrus moustache carved in its full glory. The paintings included W. G. Grace, possibly England's most famous cricketer; William Gladstone, Prime Minister and writer; and to show the Victorian era wasn't all about old men, the singer Adelina Patti. Parkes had seen them countless times before. He entered Room 23; this room was dedicated to the Victorian period of expansion and empire. He was expecting to see the oil painting *Florence Nightingale receiving the Wounded at Scutari*. It was always the painting that immediately caught his eye upon entering. Miss Nightingale standing amongst a crowd of soldiers, the artist Jerry Barrett placing 'the lady with the lamp' in a visual spotlight through the use of contrasting darker dressed attendants beside her and by clearly defining her face compared to the others in the painting with their faces blurred with rough strokes. Today, however, in its place was an altogether different piece.

The landscape portrait of Miss Nightingale had been removed from the lilac-coloured walls and placed neatly, standing on the floor leaning against the wall to the side of its original position. Taking its position was an unframed traditional portrait of a British Empire soldier wearing the crimson uniform and the off-white, domed foreign service pith helmet as worn by Michael Caine in Zulu.

Beverley Chambers spotted Parkes at the room's doorway and walked across to him. Parkes' face was a picture of surprise like someone had slapped him with a wet fish.

"Director," she said. "I have no idea how this has happened. I have security checking the overnight tapes, they said they should have some information within the hour."

Parkes walked to the painting, Beverley followed him. "Is there any indication who did this?" he asked.

"There was a card with the painting, Director." Beverley took a card from the folder she always carried and passed it to Parkes.

He looked at the card. It was a simple placeholder, cream in colour with a single line of text in black. It seemed like the same cards the gallery used for displaying information about each piece of work. The line on this card said, 'The evil that men do.'

"The evil that men do?" Parkes said. "That's a line from Shakespeare's Julius Caesar. There is no name on the card, did they sign the painting?"

"There is a signature… of sorts. In the bottom right."

They stood about two foot away from the painting. The portrait was around three-foot-high by two foot wide. Far smaller than the Nightingale picture. Parkes' eyes took note of the work for the first time. It was an oil painting. The brush strokes used were small and detailed. Parkes thought the artist had apparently taken some time to paint the work, befitting the break-in and substitution of the Nightingale.

They had displayed the soldier from his chest up, against a taupe and forest green background as was typical of the time. He looked in his thirties with a moustache and bushy light brown, with slightly darker hues here and there, sideburns. His face was reddened with sunburn but darkened by dirt and shadow. Parkes looked to the bottom right for the artist's signature and was surprised to see, instead of a scrawled name or initials, there was a symbol. It looked to Parkes like the Greek Omega symbol, Ω. *I don't know of anyone that signs their work with an Omega, I'll have to look into it back in the office.* The symbol was covering part of the tunic the soldier wore, Parkes leant in closer and could see a pattern in the red cloth. He moved in and saw, in a shade only slightly darker, were thousands of round circles.

"Sir, if you look through this," Bev passed Parkes a magnifying glass. "There is more than just a pattern there."

Parkes took the magnifying glass with a 'thank you' and looked closer at the painting. Instead of just circles, Parkes could see that each circle was a crudely drawn face, with the stub of a neck jaggedly drawn. Some faces had long hair, others short, or none at all. They were of varying sizes and shapes; however, they were all painted sideways as if they were lying down in stacks.

Thousands of heads piled up against a wall of red. Parkes continued looking at the painting with the magnifying glass, the three gold buttons on the tunic had the British Pound, Euro, and the US Dollar symbols painted on them in an embossed effect to make them look they had been cast like that. The soldier's collar was a dark blue with golden embroidered insignia on each side. The insignia differed from each other: the first was of a cabinet with hinged doors, the artist had painted individual threaded spikes on the interior of the cabinet. The second insignia was of a stool with a pyramid on top. *A Judas cradle?* Parkes thought. Victims would be suspended above the stool and be slowly lowered onto the tip of the pyramid.

Parkes followed the line of the soldier's collarbone and shoulder; there were epaulettes on either shoulder. He examined the right-hand one first. It was painted silver, however instead of the traditional looped rope design Parkes had seen in other paintings of the period, this one was twisted strands of razor wire, the edges red with blood. Parkes looked across to the other epaulette, this one, also silver, was entwined chains with manacles at either end. Roughly made. The links of the chain uneven and irregular in size. *Slave chains.* Parkes glanced at Bev. She nodded at him to continue.

Parkes moved up to the partly exposed neck, the artist had not used any visual or hidden devices, the skin here was pink and coarse, and the occasional brown to indicate stubble of hair. Likewise, the chin: lantern-jawed and strong. The large moustache, however, was made up of figures on poles above bonfires, hints of ginger, and red, amongst the blond, indicated flames. The sideburns descended to level with the earlobe. Through the magnifying glass, Parkes could see figures, their skin dark brown, with what appeared to be car tyres around their necks, the lick of flames coming from the tyre in hues of orange. He moved to the nose, straight and long, ending in a bulb, with large cavernous nostrils. Parkes moved the magnifying glass closer to the nostril and saw diamonds in each, painted ruby in colour.

"This painting is very cleverly painted," he said to Bev. The first words he'd spoken in five minutes. "So many terrible things hidden underneath the surface."

"It doesn't stop there, Director," Bev said, her voice tinged with sadness.

Parkes returned to the painting and worked his way up the long nose, tiny details appeared through the glass as shadows on the skin. Rows of people lined up in front of pits, men, women, and children. The soldier's brow was furrowed, the creases in the skin looking like square bricked chimneys, the billows of smoke rising to form the eyebrows. The shadow covering the forehead below the brim of the helmet looked like ash on a barren field. Parkes looked at the eyes. They were brown with dark pupils. The brown ring within each iris contained hundreds of heads on spiked poles, the faces quite detailed, tales of horror, pain, and decomposition writ across each one. Within the pupil, there was a square of white to show the depth and life of the soldier's eyes. With the glass, Parkes could see a symbol in each square. In the left one was a burning wooden cross, and in the other, the hooked-cross of the Nazi swastika symbol. Parkes noticed in along the bottom of one of the eyes, the artist had painted the partial formation of a tear, the lower lid was redder on this eye than the other, with a watery sheen. Parkes moved up to the tea stained coloured helmet and noted that the helmet had a pattern, which like the tunic wasn't noticeable from a distance. The pattern looked like tusks placed beside each other, some inverted to fill the gaps. The tusks laid out like the walls of an igloo as they went up the helmet to the peak. In the middle of the tusk fortress was a gold coloured regimental badge, with laurel leaves on the outside of the centrepiece and the British Crown on top. In the centre, instead of the usual regiment number Parkes had seen on numerous other paintings from the era, there was a date painted in black: August 1945. Behind this painted as though etched on the badge was the shape of a nuclear mushroom cloud.

Parkes turned his attention to the background of the painting. Even without the magnifying glass, he could see the outlines of shapes on the brown and green backing, painted in colours slightly darker than the background itself. When he looked through the lens, he could see hundreds, if not thousands, of skeletons laid out across the canvas. A mass painted grave. Bodies laid across each other, in rows to the canvas edge. Some were just the bones, others wearing rags of clothes in various stages of decomposition. Some skeletons were whole, others were partial. Parkes handed the magnifying glass back to Bev and stepped back.

"A very interesting piece," Parkes said. "Very interesting indeed. Have it taken to the Conservation studio, for the time being, I'll look into the artist and see what I can find out. Get the porters to rehang the Nightingale." He removed his phone from his pocket and took photos of the picture, the signature and a few of the detailed parts, including the background skeletons, the tunic heads, and the spiked heads from the eyes.

***

Parkes was in his office at his computer. He was on Artistssignatures.com looking for artists that used the Omega symbol for their signature and getting frustrated at his lack of progress. He picked up his office phone and called Beverley to ask if there were any updates from security.

"Not yet, Director," she replied. "It shouldn't be long now though."

"How did they take down the Nightingale without an alarm sounding?" All portraits in the gallery were wired for tampering.

"Hopefully we'll find out. Somehow, they deactivated that system, but only for that one—" Parkes heard shouting in the background as Bev stopped in mid-sentence.

"Bev? Bev?" Parkes waited for her to come back. He could hear talking but couldn't make out what was being said.

Beverley returned after a minute. She was breathing heavily as though she was walking fast. "Sorry about that Director. One of the guys from the Conservation studio came to get me. Something odd is happening with that painting. They were looking at the painting searching for clues to its providence when the eyes started leaking."

"I saw that in the painting, very clever effect."

"No Director, actually leaking. Black oil started running down the picture. I'm on my way there, they said it's still happening, and they can't figure out how to stop it."

"I'll be there straight-away."

Parkes replaced the handset and left the office.

***

Parkes hurried to the gallery's Frame Conservation and General Conservation studio, located outside of the main gallery, on Orange Street. He was met at the entrance and escorted to the holding room where the picture was. In the room was Pierre Mercier, the head of the Conservation Department, and Beverley Chambers. The painting was laid out on a table in the centre of the room. Parkes could see that the surface of the painting and the surrounding tabletop were wet.

"So, tell me what happened?" Parkes demanded.

"We received the painting from the gallery; Ms Chambers explained its unusual appearance in the gallery, so when it came here we put it on the table to examine for clues to the artist's identity. Within a minute of the painting being laid down, oil started coming out of the eyes and covered the painting. The canvas is very slightly raised at the eyes to allow the oil to spread across the surface evenly. We immediately checked behind the canvas to find the source of the liquid to stop it, but there was nothing there. No mechanism or reservoir. Just a hollow space inside the canvas," Mercier explained. "We turned the painting back around and saw the original paintwork had been covered. It's over there."

Parkes walked over to the painting and saw that soldier was covered in a thick tar of black oil. A few features shone through the liquid: the ivory tusks on the helmet, the silver shoulder epaulettes, but the rest was buried beneath the viscous fluid.

"Is there any hope of cleaning it?" he asked.

"We'll try," Mercier said. "It will depend on how the oil adheres to the surface of the painting. We'll begin by blotting up as much excess as we can and take it from there."

"I'll leave you to it; I'm going to keep trying to find out who painted the damned thing."

***

Instead of returning to his office, Parkes decided to head by Security to see what they had captured on the camera footage. He knocked on the door and waited for the guards to open it.

"Anything on the cameras from last night?" he asked the two guards in the small office, one wall of which was covered in monitors, with a large one central.

"I was just going to call Ms Chambers, there is something on the camera from…" The guard looked at the time-stamp on the screen. "Eight forty-six."

That was only fifteen minutes or so before Bev called me. Parkes thought. "Show me."

The guard pressed a sequence of buttons, and a frozen image appeared on the main screen. It showed Room 23. The Nightingale painting was hanging on the wall in the corner of the screen.

"This is the best angle we have; most of the cameras are focused on different paintings. The time is eight forty-five, and as you can see, there is nothing untoward. I'll play the video in real-time."

Parkes watched the time-stamp count through the seconds of eight forty-five and into eight forty-six. He leaned closer to the screen to see if he could see anything. At forty seconds into the minute, a figure entered the frame and walk towards the Nightingale. Without hesitation, it removed the painting from its spot and placed it leaning against the wall.

"No alarm was triggered," the second guard said.

The figure lifted up the Soldier painting and hung it in position. Took one step back to look at it and then left the frame. The time-stamp was eight forty-seven and ten seconds.

"That was quick," Parkes said. "Thirty seconds or so? Rewind to the beginning of the figure entering."

The guard smiled at Parkes' use of 'rewind' and scrolled back to the moment the figure stepped into the screen. Parkes leant even closer. The figure appeared to be male and wearing a form of armour, that glinted in the artificial light of the gallery. His outline was hazy and blurred. One other thing Parkes noticed, the figure's shadow started away from the feet, a gap between the man and shadow. *It's floating?* He kept watching the shadow. It never connected with the body at any point of the recording. Afraid to put his thoughts into words, he stood there, mouth gaping.

Wonderboy

'If it pleases you, your Honour, before you pass judgement. I would like to say a few words in my defence. In the hope, the court shows leniency on me,' Wonderboy said to Judge Gwen Gifford, in whose hands Wonderboy's fate hung and who was leading the trial. She looked at the two judges either side of her, who both nodded their assent.

'We are running ahead of schedule, so we'll allow you a few words,' she said.

Her ten-year-old daughter was a massive fan of his: she had posters of him on her bedroom wall; a Wonderboy duvet cover and matching pillowcase; a Wonderboy lunchbox and flask; Wonderboy pyjamas; and asked for the Wonderboy Annual each Christmas, devouring every page before Boxing Day. Through osmosis, Judge Gifford had become a fan too and was genuinely disappointed that she would have to cast judgement on him and sentence him to life in prison.

'Thank you, your Honour… your Honours; I'll try to make this short.' Wonderboy said.

He thought about throwing a wink in Judge Gifford's direction but decided against it. Best not, he thought, I want my story told, to the people here in the court and to the millions who are watching around the world via satellite and the internet. This is the 'trial of the century' according to the newspapers that are read to me, by the lovely guardians of the maximum-security prison I am residing in and will probably remain, the classic tale of someone who had it all and threw it all away.

Wonderboy produced several index cards from the inside of the suit jacket he was wearing and placed them neatly on the defendant's table in front of him. He picked up the first card and spoke to the court.

'I'll begin at the beginning...'

'... I was born as Wonderboy, well I say born; I mean they created me as Wonderboy. Scientists at SUTECH or SuperHero Technical Labs to give it its actual name, mixed together the DNA of a number of superheroes in a beaker and grew me in a lab. Some clever wit of a scientist there anointed me with the name 'Wonderboy' and it stuck. I am thirty-five years old, with the normal emotional feelings, wants and desires of a thirty-five-year-old man; however, I am trapped in a fourteen-year-old boy's body. My body will never age, and as you know I am indestructible: impervious to heat, cold, poison, radiation, and I do not need oxygen to live. I feel, and I breathe like a normal person, I just cannot die. I know because in the darkest times I have tried. So many ways. It cannot be done. I am here to stay. I will be Wonderboy in my nineties and onwards.

'This is old news to the people here and watching at home and at work, so I'll skip the biographical details, if anyone isn't aware of me, there is a detailed bio on my SuperNet website. You just need to Google it.' He flicked through a couple of the cards and laid them, face down, next to the unread pile. He continued:

'What you all are here for and what you all want to know is why did I turn heel? Why did I turn to the dark side? Why did I become the ultimate Super Villain? And why did I give myself up?

'It wasn't a gradual thing, a build-up of little misdemeanours and misdeeds. I hadn't gone down a slippery slope, down a spiral of criminality. In my case, I went evil because I wanted to, and for a very specific purpose. It's not easy being Wonderboy, loved by millions, adored wherever I go. I know, I know, world's smallest violin playing just for me. I had a life that people dreamed about. People would even kill for a piece of it. Believe me, I know. I had it all, but it wasn't enough. There was something missing. It started off small, little feelings I would get. I brushed them off. I had more important things to do, people to save and all that. But, it got into my head, burrowed deep, twisting and turning, turning and twisting, like an insidious snake wrapped around my brain. It wouldn't stop. Even when I focused on my role: my job. I was saving more and more people, stopping more and more villains, defeating natural disasters; it was still there. A whispering hiss, deep within my ear. A sibilant whisper filled with venom and jealousy. A slithering whisper of loneliness and longing.

'And what was it whispering? You ask. What was the serpent hissing to me? Let me tell you what life is like for me.

'I go to a club and see an attractive woman, she looks at me and I look back. Smiling, I beckon her over, with a gentle come-hither motion. She comes over. They always do. I start the conversation with 'I saw you looking at me,' they invariably respond, 'are you who I think you are?' No matter how I answer this question – 'Yes, I am Wonderboy!' or 'No, I just look like him' or variations on that theme – the response is always the same. The woman will tell me that they loved me when they were young; or their sister, or daughter, is my biggest fan. Some will confess that they had a crush on me. But to all of them, I am still a fourteen-year-old boy. They see me as a child. A fucking – please excuse my language, your Honours – a child. It doesn't help that I'm a little over 165 centimetres, or five foot five.

'Occasionally you get the creepy, crazy one. You know the ones. They're the ones who get caught sleeping with their students, sending them love poems, and revealing pictures of themselves. You see them all the time in the papers. Some are hot, many are not. There is a reason they are attracted to their students. It is because no man would put up with their shit – sorry – no matter how great in bed they are. They're the women who get your name tattooed above their heart after a first date; who move in with you after a one-night stand; who text you a million times a day and get pissed – sorry your Honours, I'll try to restrain from using curse words – get annoyed if you don't reply immediately, no matter if at the time you are saving a family from a burning car wreck, or diverting a hurricane back to the sea. They're the only ones who'll sit on my face.

'They are bat-shit crazy. Total bunny boilers. But they are all I can have, all that will want me. It's not fair. Totally Awesome Man has to beat the women off. He rescues a woman from a burning building, her tongue is already down his throat and she is jerking him off before he has even landed. The Black Cavalier has that brooding, shadowy thing going on and gets hit on all the time. He doesn't even have any superpowers! How is that fair, your Honours? How is that fair?' Wonderboy struck the table with his fists and it split down the middle. He caught his index cards before they began to fall.

'I'm sorry about that, your Honours; my frustration got the better of me. I apologise. Where was I? Oh yes, I remember.

'How can it be fair, for me – the greatest superhero who ever existed, to only get to sleep with the mental ones? Even the hot ones aren't really that hot, but look like an oasis in the desert, compared to their sisterhood. Every normal woman sees me like a child. I get called good-looking, sure, but never handsome, dashing, sexy, rugged, or desirable. Even sidekicks get more action than me. Hell, even the sidekick's sidekicks get laid more. I am stronger than any superhero, have a much higher rescue rate and I even look better in tights. I don't have to roll a pair of socks into my over-under shorts to make myself look like I have a penis. Mentioning no names… Mr Cool, Doctor Devil, and Super Stretchy Man – sorry to disappoint you ladies, he can't stretch *that*, even though he has tried all ways, my favourite time was when he tied *himself* to a bridge like a bungee cord and jumped off. Ha ha ha… Ahem. Sorry.

'There you have it. The reason I changed is because I wanted to get laid by a normal woman. Didn't even have to be a looker, just someone who would see past the outside and see the inside concupiscent me, treat me like the man I am. Did you know I had invisibility powers? No? It's not something I've advertised. It has forced me to turn into a super-peeping tom, the ultimate voyeur, just to see a normal naked woman. I've been in locker rooms, bathrooms, nudist beaches, naturist resorts, changing rooms, art museums, anywhere where I can see a woman's body in all its glory. I'm not proud of it. In fact, I'm downright ashamed of myself. The wankst afterwards is terrible. I am so ashamed at masturbating to women who cannot see me watching them as they wash, or change, or…' Wonderboy trailed off, looking at the ground, tears splattering the broken table.

'I have tried killing myself. Nothing works. Shooting myself into the sun – just burnt my clothes off, I was fine. Diving to the bottom of the deepest ocean – I just surprised some weird-looking fish. Nuclear reactor – not a thing, I deal with them on a weekly basis. Smoking – that just made me smell. Nothing works.

'So, I decided to change. If being the world's best good guy didn't get me anywhere, maybe being the world's worse bad guy would. Ladies love a bad boy, you know. I heard they did anyway. I changed my image. Gone were the canary yellow unitard, and lime green underpants and cape. In their place, was the darkest black costume you could ever have, light was sucked in by that bad boy. I wanted people to know I was bad. Pure unscrupulous ruthlessness... while being ever so attainable. I made it skin-tight to show off my muscles, contoured around the crotch to emphasise my penis and testicles. I had a mask of pure beauty and evil to get the women to want me, but know they shouldn't, but want me anyway.

'My goal was never to hurt anyone, that's not in my nature. I wanted a scheme so dastardly, devious, and sexy it would make women wet just thinking of it. I decided I would steal the Cullinan I diamond or as it is also known, the Great Star of Africa from the Tower of London, where it is kept with the rest of the Queen of England's Crown Jewels.

'I could have turned invisible and used my powers to obtain it. Nobody could stop me. But what's sexy about that? It would be easy; every woman would know it was easy for me. They'd just think I was a jerk. However, if I used criminal cunning, guile and panache, I would be a rogue, a diamond in the rough, if you excuse the pun.

'I won't tell you the details of my plan in case someone copies it and manages to steal the jewels. Needless to say, it would have been perfect. A wondrous heist carried off by Wonderboy. A crime they would be writing about for centuries to come. It would have worked too. It was well underway, everything was going swimmingly, and another minute the diamond would have been mine. If it wasn't for that little girl, outside the tower, who managed to get away from her parents, who within an instant ran into the road in front of the newspaper delivery truck, whose driver was running late getting the evening paper distributed across London, whose foot was harder on the pedal than normal, the truck going faster than usual.

'I had to save her. your Honours. It's what I do. My raison d'être. My sole purpose. Mesmerising traitor in my ear or not. In my haste to save her, I tripped the alarms in the tower blasting a hole through the wall. The Yeomen Warders of the Tower came after me, albeit through more appropriate methods of exiting a building, and arrested me at gunpoint just after I returned her safely to her shocked parents for the scolding of her life.

'And here I stand as Wonderboy, before the court. My alter-ego retired for good. Do you know the name I chose for my evil self? No, not the awful one the papers and news reports gave me, the true one? They haven't told you? Well, it was the Black Stallion. Not subtle enough? I don't know. I had to make it clear I was available.

'I wholeheartedly apologise for my crimes and request leniency from the court and the millions of people around the world I disappointed with my actions. I have given up being a villain, hung up my mask. I am truly sorry. Please remember, your Honours, that for me, life imprisonment really is an eternity.'

***

'This is Tom Witten, at The Hague in the Netherlands, outside the International Criminal Court for the ruling of the Trial of the Century. We have just heard that the judges have made their ruling. The judgement given by Judge Gifford is that the Poisoned Dwarf, also known as Wonderboy, has been released with immediate effect. Judge Gifford cited that the Dwarf's contrite and honest testimony swayed their decision. The Poisoned Dwarf has to attend weekly sex addiction therapy sessions. The judges considered chemical castration to stop his vile urges but realised that his body would withstand the treatment. The Poisoned Dwarf declined to comment. The question we must ask ourselves is: Is it right that a self-confessed, super-powered, sexual deviant is released back into an environment where they have interaction with our children? I'll leave for you, Diane, at the studio to discuss that point.' Tom Witten said. He beamed a gigawatt smile at the camera, waited for Simon, the Networks' director, to say 'clear,' in his earpiece. While he waited, he gazed at his reflection in the camera lens. *That poor bastard, imagine having to live like that. Of course, the children are safe; Wonderboy expressed no interest in children. This fucking job really is the worst at times.*

She Bought a Hat Like Princess Marina

I shuffled along the ledge, barely wide enough for the width of my shoe, the rubber sole scraping the concrete, the black leather uppers with their dull shine, contrasted against the white paint of the building which reflected the brilliance of the moon on this clear night. A mistake on my part, I was expecting the night to be dark enough that the black shoes, black trousers, black V-neck sweater, and a black balaclava, would vanish against the building, hiding me from the security guards below. I even had luminous thread sown into the sweater cuffs and trousers hem to help me see my extremities in the pitch blackness. Instead, I was as conspicuous as a straight-man at Neiman Marcus. My black-gloved palms were pressed against the wall supporting my body as I slowly edged my way to the open window on the third storey of the palace. I froze in place as the powerful beam of the patrolling guard's torch swept below me. I could hear the steady panting of the guard's scary-looking canine companion. I really should have done my homework on this job. A severe dereliction of duty on my part, I'm afraid. The guard moved on following the outline of the building. I waited until he turned the corner. I knew that I had six minutes until his twin, making the journey parallel to him, would appear from the other direction. I knew because I had timed it after being surprised the first time.

The muscles in my leg were aching and my knee was stiffening up as the lactic acidosis level in my bloodstream were elevated from the exertion the controlled ascent up the property caused took. I really wasn't in the right shape for this mission; my preparations were rushed due to the accelerated deadline imposed on me. I started moving again, faster than before, I didn't think my muscles could take another period of stillness. In my haste, my foot slipped off the edge and the following leg swung into space. I overbalanced and dropped to my knee. The impact sent a jolt through my leg to my spine, my hands groped the wall for purchase. I managed to stop the momentum of the fall and recover my balance. I drew my leg back to the ledge and slowly raised myself off my supporting knee. Slower this time I continued my quest. I reached the window. It was a sash window, a foot higher than the ledge and almost six foot in height. The bottom sash window was already raised to let air into the room beyond. I gripped the bottom sash and carefully lifted it up higher, in order to gain entry, it made a few squeaks as it moved up in its frame, but nothing to be concerned about. When it had reached the correct height, I ensured it was secure in place and wouldn't come down on me as I entered. I crossed the threshold backwards, legs first, slowly and carefully, trying to feel out obstacles with my feet as I backed into the room. Now the mission really starts. I thought.

***

'So, do you think you can do it, Nicholas?' asked Francesca Allerton.

'Have I ever let you down before?' I replied.

52

'Well... there was that Chanel scarf,' She laughed, 'I'm just teasing, of course, you haven't. You're the best, a genius.'

'Ha... ha...,' I said, 'watch out or I may take Dior's Summer Collection to another company.' I was only half-kidding; I was in demand throughout the whole industry. My designs were so successful that over the years my fee structure had changed from a modest fixed payment to a generous percentage of sales. Francesca left, and I mulled over the problem she had given me.

***

I suppose I should introduce myself, my name is Nicholas Charmant, I am the most famous fashion designer you have never heard of. World-renowned, my clothes are worn and loved by millions of women across the globe. I do not have a fashion house such as Gucci, Prada and Givenchy; my name is hidden behind the high–street fashion houses of Forever 21, Zara, Superdry, H&M, Miss Selfridges, et al. My clothes are the ones that sell by the hundreds of thousands to ordinary women. I re-design designer wear for a more affordable market. I take the $400 Jimmy Choo high heel and turn it into a $40 heel for Macys; the £250 Armani blouse into a £25 blouse for Next. The skill is in recreating the look, the feel and colour of the original using much cheaper materials while changing enough of the item to avoid being sued for copyright infringement. Anyone can copy something; it takes a real designer to do what I do. People disparage my work, calling them knock-offs or what I do theft, they do not understand the love I put into my creations, the passion I have for my art. It helps that the copyright laws for fashion are for more lenient than they are for other forms of art –

music, paintings, publishing and film. In fashion, the items' overall design is not subject to copyright, just individual parts of an item – the textile print, the clasp on a handbag, and the most important part the logo or name. I can take a Guess jean and as long as I change the small embellishments, such as the back-pocket design or the rivet pattern and do not call my version a Guess jean, then I'm mustard. The skill is in knowing exactly how close I can go before a company or designer can sue. I've been doing this for thirty-four years now and have never been sued, that is an enviable record in this business, and why I can charge so much for my services.

***

The item Francesca bought my skills to recreate, was the most talked about fashion item since the Calvin Klein slip dress in the 90s. It was an item that as far as anyone could tell wasn't available to buy anywhere. No one knew the designer, but everyone knew the piece. Two months ago, a paparazzi photographer took a billion-dollar photo, its subject: the reclusive Princess Marina. It was the first photograph of her for five years.

She had been the most recognisable women on the planet; beautiful didn't cut it as a description. She was the goddess Aphrodite, pale skinned, with a voluptuous figure. Long caramel brown coloured hair, flawless skin, which was always worn natural without makeup, she always looked elegant and regal, she didn't just wear clothes; they wore her. She made even the simplest clothing look like it cost a fortune. However, it wasn't just her physical appearance that enthralled the world; she was also an angel to the poor, the sick and the mistreated. She campaigned for Amnesty International and the United Nations. She visited war zones, famine struck countries, AIDS hospitals, disaster zones. Not just for photo-opportunities and publicity, but to actually make a difference to people's lives, some would call her the true People's Princess. All this changed five and a half years ago when she was kidnapped by Boko Haram in Nigeria. Her plight was watched around the world as nightly footage of her treatment at the hands of the terrorists was uploaded to YouTube and re-broadcast around the world. The beatings and abuse she received were sickening. She was eventually freed by US Special Forces after a mistake by the kidnappers revealed their location. She was never seen again, she retreated to her palace in Luxembourg, hiding from the world. At least until that photo was taken.

In the photo, she was sitting on a balcony at a simple, white wrought-iron table, with a book and a cup of tea. Although the quality of the photo was fuzzy and unclear, due to the distance it had been taken from, you could see she was wearing a white blouse, and a dark brown split leg skirt. On top of her head was the most beautiful hat anyone had seen. It was a small, brimless hat with a trim. It was like a cross between a miniature pillbox hat and a Russian Ushanka. In the photo, it looked like it was the colour of a milky coffee. It had no name; no one had ever seen one before. The internet went crazy. That little hat broke the internet far more than that photo-shopped Kardashian arse ever had. Facebook and Twitter ground to a halt as women everywhere wanted to know about the hat. Who designed it? Where could they get it from? Rumours and hearsay spread across Mumsnet, but no one could find any solid information. The female world was waiting with anxious breath for news about this hat. Of course, Francesca had come to me, poor quality and even poorer designed imitations from Etsy were selling out within minutes. The market was ripe for a Charmant design. The problem was I couldn't make a version that was any better than the Etsy homemade efforts. I couldn't get the right material that gave the hat the shine it had in the photo, the trim didn't look good anyway I tried it. This stupid small hat was the hardest thing I had ever worked on. I obsessed about it for three weeks, catching an hour's sleep here and there; meals with even less frequency. The deadline given to me by Francesca was due by the end of this week and I was no closer than I was at the start. I had never missed a deadline and never was beaten by a task. It had turned into a matter of pride for me and led me to do something reckless, very reckless indeed.

***

I turned around and switched on my small penlight torch, a thin weak beam emanated from it, enough for me to see the room. The room was large, dominated by a queen-size, four-poster bed with white voile curtains draping down, obscuring the bed's occupant. I carefully nudged one curtain to the side and in the dim light could see Princess Marina, sound asleep, her breathing deep and rhythmic. She was partly covered by blankets and sheets; however, I could clearly see her face, especially as I leant closer to look. She looked as perfect as she did the day her life changed. A few slight wrinkles around her eyes the only concession to time. I must admit I wasn't prepared to see her and although I work in fashion I am heterosexual, which has been a boon throughout my career. The sight of her brought forth flashes of romantic lust, and wild proclamations of love, which I struggled to contain. I reluctantly retreated, letting the voile curtain fall back in place and stepped away from the bed, my pulse racing, surprising me greatly. It has been a long time since a woman has affected me this way, if ever at all.

I took a moment to settle myself down and got back to what I was there for. I looked for any obvious places the hat might be — any hat stands, hat boxes, shelves. Nothing. There were three doors leading off from the room I opened the first one, the nearest to me and saw it led to a hallway, dimmed LED spotlights at regular intervals lighting the way. I closed the door, careful not to make a noise and moved onto the next. This door was across the room from the window. I opened the door and saw this was the en-suite bathroom. The hat could be in there I thought. The bathroom was larger than my bedroom, twin basins, a whirlpool bath, separate walk-in shower, and a toilet. Under the basins were a set of six cupboards, I searched them in turn. I only found spare towels, washcloths, and toiletries. Where the hell is it? I asked myself. I left the bathroom and went to the final door. Is this the dressing room and closet? I opened the door and stepped in, immediately the room was bathed in light. The room was a twin of the main bedroom in size, with blazing spotlights in the ceiling, reflected off dozens of mirrored surfaces, there were open-faced cabinets which were all back-lit to display their wares, rows and rows of shoes, handbags, lights replicating on the shiny patent leather. No goddamn hatboxes or hat stands. Where can it be? Amongst the racks of clothes hung by silver hangers on their rails?

I hear a noise from the bedroom, then a voice, 'Who are you? Why are you here? Get your hands up!' The voice sounded heavenly, perfect tones, not too light and airy, a slight husk to it. I could have listened to her speak all night. I raised my hands above my head in surrender.

'I... I mean you no harm,' my voice, in comparison, wavered, like I was going through puberty again.

'Turn around and drop to your knees.'

I slowly turned around, fully aware of how I looked in my balaclava and assassin-black clothes. I knelt, my knees creaking, my heart shaking. In front of me, eyes blazing, holding a very large gun pointed at my head was the Princess. God, she looked incredible.

'I ha... haven't come to hurt you.' I said.

'Remove your mask. I want to see you.'

Carefully I took off the balaclava; a strand of my long grey hair fell in front of my face tickling my nose. I fought the urge to scratch it.

'My name is Nicholas Charmant, I'm not a kidnapper or assassin.'

She paused for a moment taking in what I said and my unorthodox appearance.

'The fashion knock-off guy?' She asked a touch of incredulity in her voice.

'Well, more of a re-designer,' I reply defensively.

The gun lowered, no longer pointing at my head. I liked it even less where it was *now* pointing.

'What the hell are you doing in my closet?'

'This is going to sound crazy, may I reach into my back pocket, just to get a photo, that's all?'

She nodded her assent.

I slowly reached into my pocket and pulled out a folded copy of the famous photograph. I unfolded it and held it out for her. She took it off me and looked at it.

'That's me. Why have you got a photo of me?' She raised the gun again, letting the photo fall to the floor.

'The hat!' I call out, panicked, the gun barrel looking large and vicious, the closet lights giving it another-world appearance, 'I'm looking for the hat!'

'What hat?'

'The one in the picture… I need the hat to copy it; thousands of women want that hat.'

She stood there, a quizzical look upon her face, dropped the gun to her side and laughed at me. 'You come all this way, crept into my room, come within a second of being shot for a hat? A hat? I hate to break it to you, Nicholas, there is no hat.'

'Wh… what? What do you mean? You're wearing a hat in that picture.'

'You see how poor quality this photo is, and how far away it was taken from? The *hat* is my hair. I sometimes wear it that way, if I can't be bothered styling it.'

I felt dizzy and reached out a hand to support myself, 'Your hair?' I looked at her, at her beautiful brown hair, latte coloured, done up in a doughnut bun.

Mob Justice

The Assassin cursed the cold, November weather as he jimmied the lock to the John Marshall Law School building with a short iron bar. He had removed his gloves to maintain sufficient grip and could feel the cold of the metal freezing his hands. The brittle padlock snapped with more noise than the Assassin wanted. He picked up the lock pieces and stuffed them in the left front pocket of his woollen overcoat. The bar he put in one of the two bags he had with him. He rubbed his hands together briskly and took his gloves out of the other pocket and put them on. He heard a noise behind him and turned to see. He saw the faded and brittle front page of the *Chicago Sunday Tribune* rustling in the breeze. It looked like it was from a few weeks ago, the headline exclaiming, "U.S. JURY CONVICTS CAPONE". *Is that an omen?* The Assassin asked himself. He pushed open the door and crept inside. He pulled the heavy door closed behind him, then stopped and listened for a minute. He had already scouted out the building over the past few nights and knew there were no watchmen on guard. He decided to not switch on his Rayovac flashlight, *don't want anyone passing to see the glow of the torch,* and headed to the stairs in the murky gloom. His way was faintly illuminated by the glow from the streetlights outside coming through the leaded windows. He reached the staircase, stole a look at his Elgin-brand wristwatch and saw that it was coming up to midnight, *plenty of time, no need to rush and make noise.* He headed up to the fourth floor, his dark leather Converse All-Stars basketball shoes made the occasional squeak on the marble steps as he turned each corner. Each squeal made him wince. *I should have worn the oxfords, blisters be damned.*

The Assassin reached the top floor and headed for the door that would take him to the flat roof above. He turned the brass doorknob, but the door wouldn't open. He put down the bags he was carrying and took out the lockpicking kit from the inside pocket of his overcoat, knelt and went to work. The lock was quite simple and with his tension wrench and a couple of picks, the Assassin picked it within a minute. He put his hand on the doorknob and pulled the door towards him. The door was stuck in the frame, so he pulled with more force and the door opened outwards with a loud creak. Beyond the door was a set of steps leading upwards. The Assassin walked up them, closing, but not locking the door behind him. At the top of the stairs, another door blocked his way onto the roof. This one was not locked. The Assassin turned the doorknob and pushed the door open. He was struck by how cold the night was and pulled his coat lapels closer together to block some of the chill. The roof was flat with a two-foot-high parapet wall surrounding the edge. The roofing material was asphalt covered with a thin layer of gravel. *That's not going to be good to lay on all night.* He walked across the roof; the gravel crunching under his feet, to the parapet. He crouched down and looked over the edge at the Chicago Federal Building to the northwest; he had an unobstructed view along West Jackson Boulevard; the road bisecting the two. It was as he had expected perfect for tracking the target to the courthouse inside the Fed Building. The Assassin took out two rough blankets from one of the bags and placed one of them on the roof floor close to the parapet in order to block out some of the icy breezes. He then laid on top and covered himself with the remaining woollen blanket.

***

A half an hour's drive away to the south in the Woodlawn district, Judge James Herbert Wilkerson was sat at his desk in his wooden panelled study. The desktop with its green leather top was lit by a brass banker's lamp, the majority of its light aimed downwards allowing Wilkerson a clear view of the court papers and law books piled beside his yellow legal pad. He had spent most of the evening making notes in his elegant Spencerian penmanship. His younger colleagues had moved over to the simpler Palmer method, but Wilkerson preferred the elegance of the older way. *I'm too old to change now.* Wilkerson was sixty-one years old and could feel each one of those years in his bones on this chilly October night.

A knock on his study door made him lift his head for the first time in an hour, the neck joints made an audible crack at the movement. He grunted and rubbed his neck, trying to massage out the stiffness.

'Are you coming to bed James?' His wife Mary asked, 'it's almost midnight, and you have an early start in the morning.'

She walked across the study floor; her white, silk, angle-length nightgown clung to her body as she moved. They had celebrated their fortieth wedding anniversary in August, and Wilkerson was still surprised by how much the sight of his wife's curves affected him. Mary stood behind him, moved his hand and started kneading his neck in firm and deep circles. He groaned in relief as the tension evaporated at her touch.

'I shouldn't be too long now. I have the main arguments down which should refute any objections from the defense,' he said.

'Have you decided how long he's going to get?'

'Since when have you been interested in my cases?'

'It's all anyone at the club talks about. If a had a nickel for every person that came up to me to ask about the case, we could both retire down to the warmth of the Florida sun, away from Chicago in the winter.' She shivered at the thought. Wilkerson could feel the tremors in her hands. 'It is the most famous trial in Chicago since Leopold and Loeb.'

'Oh, if it's for the old gossips at your club, of course, I'll tell you.' Wilkerson said with a smile in his voice.

'What's he like?'

'Capone? Well, he's very well dressed. Wears expensive clothes and jewellery and has a lot of charisma. The reporters and people outside the court love him. But looking into his eyes, it's a different story. He has the dead eyes of a shark. He is quite ruthless, almost intimidating.'

'What even for you?' She laughed at the idea.

'No, of course not.' He said, laughing with her. His laugh died out as he looked down at his pad. At the note, he had left himself. Circled to ensure he paid attention. "Watch your back."

***

Loud backfire woke the Assassin from his sleep. His eyes snapped open immediately. He got to his knees and looked over the parapet. He saw the sleek lines of the black Dodge Brothers automobile highlighted by the streetlights lining the route below, a puff of black-blue smoke came out from the back of the car and he tracked the jerky motion of the vehicle until it passed out of view. The Assassin looked at his watch, the luminous hands showing it was almost three-thirty. *Far too early to be awake.* He backed away from the edge and stood up. He crunched across to the roof door. The door was set into a box structure sticking up above the flat surface. He opened the door and listened for a minute. Satisfied he wasn't going to be disturbed he returned to his makeshift bed. He stretched his back, relieving the muscles from the various aches that had built up while lying on the gravelly mattress. He closed his eyes still hearing the bang of the exhaust in his mind. As per most nights, his brain took him back twelve years, to his time as part of the American Expedition Force in France. The Battle of Cantigny. May 1918. Soissons in July, St. Mihiel in September, and the Meuse-Argonne Forest until Armistice in November of that same year.

Faces appeared and disappeared. Squadmates, men he killed. Friends, and enemies. He could smell the blood and piss of the trenches on the Somme, could hear the screams as his bullets hit their mark, hear his friends as they received theirs. Too many faces. Tears forced their way through his closed eyelids, trickled down the sides of his face into the nape of his neck, salty rivulets of anguish. He saw the mud and the bodies. He heard the whine of the bullets picking off anyone foolish enough to raise their head to look across no man's land. He was celebrated by his comrades, the generals, and the Government. He appeared on posters to sell war bonds. His face and his kill count, side by side. The tally ever increasing. The competition with Herbert W. McBride. Ol' Herbie won with over one hundred confirmed kills. The Assassin not too far behind. Until he stopped. Aimed to wound rather than kill. The faces too much for him to bear.

Returning to America after the war was tough on the Assassin. In bars and on the streets, he kept seeing the faces of his kills staring at him. He was admitted to the Kankakee State Hospital, Illinois, around fifty miles south of Chicago, and diagnosed with shell shock. He stayed there for two years, treated with, at first, deep sleep therapy, where he was given barbiturates to induce a coma-like sleep for periods up to a month. The treatment failed to correct his moods and his hallucinations. In 1920 he was offered the choice to undergo lobotomy treatment, where connections in areas of the brain were scraped away, or electric shock therapy, where electric current would be sent through parts of the body. Both methods had had their successes and some very public failures. The Assassin decided to forego either and hid the symptoms, declaring himself cured. He checked himself out of the hospital a new man. He self-treated his condition with cocaine, marijuana cigarettes, and alcohol. To fund his developing habits, he turned to the one skill that had saw him through the war. He became a gun for hire.

***

Judge Wilkerson opened his eyes. Mary was gently snoring beside him. Rhythmic and reassuring. He looked over at his nightstand. The lightly glowing hands on the oval alarm clock sitting on the

65

cotton doily were showing it was four o'clock. *Too early.* He closed his eyes and searched for the return to the unconscious. Capone's emotionless eyes appeared in front of his eyelids. He felt the goosebumps rise up on his arms. *Enough of that.* He chided himself. He sat up, careful not to disturb his wife. Swung his legs out of bed and his feet sought the slippers on the floor. Once they were clad, he stood up and walked to the bedroom door. He unhooked his robe, put it on and turned the door handle.

The Judge went into his study; he turned on his desk lamp to illuminate the room. The spines of a hundred leather legal tomes on the bookshelves shone in the glow. He walked over to the mahogany bureau, to the crystal decanter sitting on its silver tray. He upturned one of the cut-glass brandy snifters resting on the lace doily beside the decanter. *Mary sure loves her doilies.* He took the heavy stopper from the decanter and poured a generous amount of the Napoléon brandy it contained into the glass. He replaced the decanter on the tray and the stopper. He lifted the glass to his nose, swirled the glass, and enjoyed the cinnamon and vanilla notes emanating from the aroma. He moved the glass to his mouth and took a sip to wet the lips and take away what he knew would be an overpowering alcohol blast that would make him cough. *Waking Mary.* When he was confident his mouth had become acclimatised to the taste, he took a large mouthful, letting it sit in his mouth for a moment before swallowing. The liquid burned his throat and created a warmth in his chest. The flavours of the brandy woke various tastebuds in his mouth and he quickly finished off the rest of the glass. *That's why Prohibition will never work.* Prohibition was a ban on the production, manufacture and sale of alcoholic beverages. It had been introduced in 1920 by the Eighteenth Amendment to the United States Constitution, after a movement by the "dry crusaders", pious protestants and social progressives.

Consumption was not outlawed though. Judge Wilkerson never asked Mary how or where she obtained his liquor, he just wished Prohibition was over. He poured himself another glass and sat in the easy chair beside his desk.

He thought back to his final meeting with Treasury Agent Frank Wilson, where they were discussing the sentence. They were in the Judge's Chambers in the courthouse. Wilson was in charge of the Al Capone investigation.

'Well done, Mr Wilson,' The Judge said when Wilson entered the chambers. 'Your hard work secured that conviction.' The Judge guided him to the long oval table that dominated the centre of the room.

'Thank you, Judge.' Wilson was a quiet man, very succinct with his words. A far cry from Elliot Ness and his "Untouchables". The Judge wasn't enamoured with Mr Ness. *Believes too much of his own press. However, it was a shame that their part of the investigation, the Volstead Act violations, was dropped. It would have made sentencing a lot easier.* The Volstead Act was the informal name for the Prohibition Act; it was named after Andrew Volstead, Chairman of the House Judiciary Committee, who managed the legislation.

'Can I get you a drink to celebrate?'

'A small one would be good. Thank you, Your Honour'.

The Judge walked over to the walnut veneered cocktail cabinet, alongside a long bookcase, filled with thick case law books. He opened the door and took out two glasses. He placed them on top and took out a whiskey decanter. He poured a single measure into one of the glasses and a double into the other. He topped the single glass up with a splash of water from a jug next to the decanter.

'My secretary makes sure this is kept full. I've needed it during this trial.' He brought the glasses over to the table and gave the single measure to Wilson.

'It's ok. Mr Ness is not here now, Your Honour.' Wilson permitted a smile to show on his face.

'So, how can I help you today Mr Wilson?'

'I was wondering how you were getting on deciding about Capone's sentencing and thought that rather than worry about it I'd come here and ask you directly.' Wilson took a sip of the whiskey. He showed his appreciation of the taste by slightly lifting the glass up and nodding.

'I have not made my mind up yet. I am looking into precedent cases that I can use to support whatever decision I make. I will assure you I will not be going light on him. That is for sure.'

'I'm glad to hear that, Your Honour. That is a relief. The team will be very pleased as well.'

'Is there anything else?'

'There is one other matter, Your Honour. You may be aware that while I was investigating Capone undercover, he organised a hit on my wife and I.' The Judge nodded. 'I thought that he could do the same to you.'

'Why would he do that? He has already been convicted.'

'Well, I was looking into it and if anything happened to you before sentencing the case would be given to another judge.

One that Capone could put pressure on or pay off for a lighter sentence. I could see from his face in court that he was thinking about it. He had that look in his eyes.'

The Judge thought for a moment. 'The case could even be declared a mistrial, and you would have to go through all that again. Risking evidence being "lost" or witnesses coerced. Thank you, Mr Wilson, for bringing this to my attention. I will think further on this.' The Judge held his hand out, and Wilson shook it and then left.

Back in his study the Judge shifted in his chair. An uncomfortable itch started dancing in the middle of his back. He downed his drink and placed the glass on the small side table next to the chair. He took a deep breath, stood up and switched off his desk lamp. *Better get some more sleep. I'll need it today.*

***

The Assassin checked his watch, *it's five after seven. If he sticks to his standard pattern, he should be here soon.* The waiting was the hardest for the Assassin. He'd weaned himself from his addictions and had been clean for three years ago. Now, he didn't even smoke. *Cigarettes always made the waiting easier though.* His mind was calm. At Peace. Four years ago, by chance, he met an Indian man in the hotel bar in Boston he was staying at. The Assassin was there for a job. The Indian man, Swami Vivekananda, was in America to spread the word about yoga. He must have seen something inside the Assassin pleading for help as he approached and befriended the Assassin. Over the next few months, they met regularly, and he taught the Assassin about meditation and yoga exercises for relaxation and calmness. The Assassin found his demons easier to deal with. He still had to pay his bills though.

The Assassin picked up the M1903 Springfield rifle that was lying on the roof next to him, his gloved hands not feeling the cold, hard wood. He reached inside his jacket and removed a five-round .03-06 cartridge magazine clip. He flicked the switch on the bolt action up to the "on" position and pulled back the bolt. He then inserted the clip and pushed the bullets into the rifle. He took the empty clip and put it back into his pocket. Then he racked the bolt forwards which loaded a bullet into the chamber. He left the switch in the "on" position, which would give him the use of all five rounds. If he had put it in the "off" position, the rifle would operate as a single-shot rifle, and he'd have to load a new bullet each time. *I should only need the one bullet, but you never know.* He considered attaching a scope to the rifle which would increase his viewing magnification, making it easier to recognise his target, however, due to the close range from the rooftop to the courthouse, he decided against it as the increased magnification would make it harder to track the target. *At this range, I'd be able to look into his ear with the scope.*

The Assassin, satisfied that the rifle was ready, rested the barrel on the parapet ledge. For the shot, he'd be crouched, and the ledge would make a good support for his forearm and elbow to steady the shot. He looked over the parapet and watched the people walking around below. Everyone was hurrying around the large square in front of the federal building. The cold making them hustle. Mainly construction workers in their denim overalls and newsboy style caps, and businessmen in their suits, long coats, and a varied selection of fedora, trilby, and bowler hats. Near the courthouse, the Assassin could see reporters gathered by the entrance, their appearance distinguishable by scruffy looking suits, pork pie and trilby hats. Interspersed among them were smarter dressed men, wearing sleek looking suits and wearing homburg hats, the Assassin smiled at their preening. *Obviously, gangsters waiting for Capone.* Three police wagons stopped on the road that ran parallel to the federal building. The Assassin saw the herd of reporters make a beeline for them as four cops exited from each of the first and last vehicles, Winchester M1897 shotguns in hand and at the ready. They walked to the middle wagon and spread out, facing outwards in a defensive position. The man closest to the wagon banged a fist on the side panel, two, three times. Two officers got out of the vehicle and walked around the back of the wagon. One drew his sidearm and aimed it at the wagon as the other unlocked the doors. The Assassin watched on as Capone shuffled out of the back of the wagon, his hands bound by cuffs. He was wearing a black suit, waistcoat, and a brilliant white ascot hat. The courthouse gangsters wished they looked as sharp as he did. The officer helped Capone down from the wagon. The protective cops formed a moving corridor either side of Capone and the two escorting officers. Shotguns aimed outwards. The reporters shouted questions, flashbulbs popped from their cameras. The Assassin forced his gaze away from the spectacle and scanned the area for the Judge. He knew the Judge parked his vehicle a block away and walked to the courthouse, picking up a paper from the newsstand on the corner. The Assassin watched the newsstand while keeping the Capone sideshow in his peripheral vision. Capone and his uniformed entourage entered the federal building, and the hubbub died down. The Assassin picked up the rifle, ensured his grip was secure, and waited.

***

Judge Wilkerson hurried along the pavement. He pushed past throngs of commuters from all walks of life. *That damn truck.* He had hoped to be in the courthouse before now. A truck had broken down crossing an intersection and had blocked traffic until some good Samaritans helped push it out of the way. He stopped at his usual newsstand and bought today's issue of the *Chicago Tribune.* Capone's expressionless face stared at him from the front page. He folded it in half and tucked it under his arm which was carrying his beat-up red leather briefcase. He crossed the square, noting the built-up crowd by the entrance.

***

There! The Assassin saw the Judge cross the road and walked on to the square. The red briefcase shone like a beacon. The Judge's pace slowed as he looked at the federal building entrance. The Assassin tracked his journey, biding his time. *Now.* He pulled the trigger. The rifle shuddered as the gunpowder in the casing exploded, and the bullet left the barrel. The Assassin automatically pulled back on the bolt to expel the spent casing and readied a new bullet.

***

The Judge felt the passage of the bullet as it jostled the air behind his head. He then heard the crack of a weapon. He instinctively ducked at the sound. He then heard a metallic clatter behind him and then the sound of something heavy hitting the ground moments later. He spun around, and his eyes widened at the sight of the wicked-looking Bowie knife gently spinning on the floor, with its dulled steel blade and wooden handle. He then saw the large man in the double-breasted suit with a bullet hole in his forehead, his eyes glazed and unfocused, slumped on the ground.

The Judge looked across to the John Marshall Law School and up to the parapet. He nodded to the Assassin, and then hurried to the federal building entrance against the tide of people coming the other way.

***

The Assassin tipped the brim of his fedora hat and waited until the Judge was safely inside the building. He ejected the four remaining bullets from the rifle and put the rifle down on the roof. He picked up the bullets and the empty casing and dropped them into a pocket. He then picked up his bags and walked towards the roof door, leaving the rifle in position. *It would be too conspicuous walking out of here with that. The Judge has paid me enough I can get a new one.* He started thinking of his next mission in Honolulu, Hawaii, protecting the defendants in a rape case from the local white population so they could face a fair trial.

(Nothing But) Flowers

I see the body on the ground and it takes me a moment to realise it is mine. I look around for my head. There it is, on the bonnet of that blue and now, very red Toyota Qashqai. It seems to be in a good shape. It's a shame they don't sell a neck protector made out of the same material as the helmet I was wearing. My face is facing the driver of the Qashqai and if this had been a comedy, no doubt the driver would have received a severed-head wink that the audience would have loved; instead I see her behind the wheel, mouth open in a frozen smile of horror, her eyes open wide, the white visible all around the dilated pupils, involuntarily taking the scene all in. I look with sympathy at her and see the empty child seats in the back seat. Not what you expect to see on the school run, at least the kids weren't in the car. I reach for my head to put it back with my body and find that I cannot lift it. I strain harder and harder, the cords in my neck looking like a ship's rigging, my cheeks puffed out, I give up, it's not moving an inch, I can't even turn it around to spare the driver any further sight of the wild expression on my face. I look like Ed Miliband eating a bacon sandwich while having a hairdryer blasted in his face, all quivering lips, bared teeth and nostrils flaring. Not the best look I have had, it even beats my driver's license picture, and that was blown up and displayed in my work's HR department office for the first four months of my employment before James, my boss, finally showed me and it was taken down to expressions of dismay amongst my colleagues.

It occurs to me that nothing around me is moving: the lady in the car; no one rushing out of their vehicles to come to my assistance or take photos of the macabre event; the scared-looking girl who caused me to swerve my motorcycle into the oncoming lane by rushing out after a raggedly old tennis ball; the balding, pale yellow tennis ball itself; the truck whose wire metal cage containing sofas, mattresses and other unwanted items was the reason for the separation of my parts; my body certainly isn't moving; the back wheels of my motorcycle. Everything has stopped, frozen in time and this moment. There are no sounds apart from an irregular, muffled thump of vibration, like the distant bass of a wannabe gangsta's souped-up speaker system in their Corsa, which travels its way up my body and nestles in the top of my head, flexing its presence.

I am surprised at my lack of emotion and even that surprise feels false, like I think I should be surprised at what little I am feeling and am trying to live up to that feeling but failing. I seem detached from what has happened and not just from the neck up. I have a physical form and can feel the touch of my clothes against my skin, the movement of my muscles, and the ache in my hands from the effort of trying to lift my head off the bonnet. I realise I am not wearing my helmet or my biking leathers like my twin on the floor, with the absurd bikers back patch, displaying a bandanna-wearing skeleton holding a bottle of JD and the motto 'Born Free Ride Free', that I picked up in a rundown store in America during a Route 66 biking experience I did a few years ago. Instead, I am wearing smart dark, almost black trousers, black leather shoes with a mirror shine I can see my face in and a white shirt that wouldn't look out of place in a Meatloaf video, all flounce, frills and new-romantic fashion. Normally, I would be appalled but for some unknown reason, it feels appropriate.

The womp... womp... womp... of the bass is annoying me now and I circle to locate the source, I find it is stronger depending on the direction I am facing and at its peak, a compulsion comes over me to head towards it. I follow the urge as there doesn't seem like there is much else going on in frozenland to hold my interest. I walk past my embedded motorcycle in the truck's grill, force myself to ignore the instinct to kick the cursed tennis ball as I pass. I follow the pulsating sound down unfamiliar streets, the identical houses blending into corridors of conformity, bland walls of a maze with me as the mouse searching for the cheese.

The intensity of the pulse feels as though it is reaching its zenith and I have to walk on my tiptoes to contain the powerful tremors. Suddenly it stops as I see the church ahead of me. The sudden silence gives the church an ominous presence and I wonder if this is where I state my case to St Peter to avoid going to hell. I reflect about my life and feel quietly confident that I haven't done anything bad enough to warrant eternal damnation. A thought quickly strikes me that at least I'd find out if music piracy really is theft or not. The building is in the typical grey stone colour, as I get closer the sheer size of the building begins to impressive itself. The main doorway could easily accommodate a double-decker bus and I am dwarfed by its magnificence. In the doorway, there is an ornate solid looking oaken door, and it opens smoothly in front of me, welcoming me, ushering me in.

Inside, my eyes slowly adjust to the relative interior darkness and I begin to be able to pick out details, the large main hall, three or four stories high, a giant font at the entrance adorned with sculpted faces with expressions of joy and ecstasy, leading to, what I kind of remember from Sunday school as, the nave with rows and rows of chairs, not the expected and traditional wooden pews, but wooden chairs, all with cushions on the seat that I assume is to be removed to kneel upon when praying. There are enormous stone columns on either side of the nave, separating the main hall from the rest of the church, with colourful and cheerful banners displaying images of God and Christ hanging from them. There is a statue of Jesus on the cross in the centre of the hall, just before the nave is cut-off by a wooden arched frame, leading to the chancel, which from my teenage years onwards always seemed like the VIP area of a club, only for the most believing of attendees, the most devout, the most generous, which was far from being me.

The statue of Christ is over-proportioned and expansive in its magnitude, it stands on a plinth and the statue itself is over nine foot tall. Even from the entrance the face of Jesus is terrifyingly detailed as his anguish and pain on the cross was etched in grave detail and realism. I am staring at the statue when colourful light from the stained-glass windows around me strike the statue; the colours swirl and undulate, covering Jesus, the light intensifies and becomes too powerful to look at. As I tear my eyes away from the incandescent statue, I see the aisles of the nave slowly open outwards away from the centre, the imposing columns appear to be changing as they move away, changing from stone to some sort of organic material, looking like fallen giant redwood trees. Ivy and vines start whipping across and under the surface, like dark green and brown varicose veins. The wooden chairs start to dissolve into the carpet they are standing on, the carpet changing from a deep red velvet to a mossy, fern green, here, there and everywhere small plants and flowers and colours shoot up, from where I am standing at the entrance to the great hall I can see the wooden archways stretch towards the high-vaulted ceiling, twisting, turning and curving, flowers bloom across its body in a riot of colour. The light around the statue at the apex diminishes and I see the statue of Christ has gone and in its place is a cavernous fissure in the wooden structure, an opening, almost oval in shape, with beckoning pink rose petal-like folds surrounding the introitus.

A voice from the heavens, with a rich, deep, but feminine, earthy tone says 'Come, my wandering seed, your time here is finished, return to your mother, return to me… to Gaia.'

I take an unhesitating step forward. I push past the large yielding petals. The sap covering the fronds is sticky to the touch, like clear honey. I enter the darkened cavern, the faint light from the church guiding my way. The ground here is soft and springy like walking on rubber. The light slowly fades as I get deeper inside. Delving further into her. Moving closer to her centre. I don't know at what point the church became Gaia in my mind. Maybe it always had. Maybe it wasn't and I was imagining it. That's what it feels like though. I know I don't care though. I just have to continue, get to the final destination.

After what feels like days travelling through narrow tunnels in pitch blackness, using my hands to guide me. I come to a large chamber, lit with a gentle pink pulsating light. Standing in the middle of the chamber, waiting for me, is Her. She is wearing a simple tunic, held in place by a rope belt that accentuates her curves. Large breasts, wide hips and extended middle. Her long is long. The colour of cedar, with streaks of deep red running through it. Her skin is a rich pine shade of brown. My fingers ache to touch it. To run my fingertips across the surface. Feel the warmth from within.

'Welcome,' she said. 'You are home now.'

I cross the space between us. Not feeling the ground below me. Not feeling anything but desire. Sexual. Nutural. Natural. Pure desire to be with her. To give my all and to take it all. I get to within an arm's reach and she raises her hand. It stops me in mid-stride as it presses against my chest. It burns. It freezes. It feels incredible.

'You must answer this question first,' she said. 'Do you submit freely to my will?'

'I do,' I said, without thought, just longing.

'You need to be sure. There is no going back. No changing your mind. You can either be with me forever, or the Other Place.'

I hear a grating sound behind me and turn. From the floor a great stone wall rises up. In the centre of the wall is a pair of pearl-white gates. The metal had been shaped into figures of angels and cherubs. I feel a pressure from the other side of the gates that envelops my mind. The pressure gives me feelings of peace, of calm, of love. I look back at Gaia and feel the pressures shift inside. Love and peace competing with desire.

'He and I came to an agreement. We each take a turn to guide your decision. However, you must choose your path freely. There is no wrong answer.'

I look again at the gates, and they start to glow.

'There's no third option? The Bad Place? Where all the rockstars and politicians go?' I ask.

'There never was another place.' The voice behind me has changed. Gone were the rich, honeyed tones of Gaia. In their place is the voice of ultimate authority, but kind and gentle with it.

I spin around and there is nothing there but a white mist, undulating and billowing. From the mist emanates a sense of purest love and affection. The weight on me as the mists surround me brings me to my knees. The feeling of absolute peace resonates throughout my full body, causing a sense of complete security and assurance. A sense of joy and exhilaration. I feel swept up in the calmest waves of tranquillity.

'You must choose,' the Voice of God speaks inside my brain.

Gaia reappears as the mist parts to allow her access. The tendrils of calm and love changes to hot desire and back again. Over and over. Like a battle of the senses. They continue to assault me. My mind changes as often as the feeling. I feel dizzy with conflicting desires: Love. Want. Blessedness. Yearning. Beloved. Need. Peace. Sex. It continues for what feels like eternity. I watch as Gaia slowly unknots the rope of her tunic and drops it to the floor. All confusion stops in an instant. And I choose.

The Battle at Kilburn High Road Station

B
eth Hudson walked down the steps to the platform. Her head down, being careful of her footing on the concrete stairs, much to the annoyance of the businessman behind her. She could hear his sighing with every step, along with tinny EDM beats coming from the earphones. Her four-inch heels clicked and scraped with each downward step, the platformed outsole slid, ever-so-slightly, on the wet footprints from earlier commuters. Her aquamarine ASOS pencil skirt restricted her stride. She had one hand on the stair railing, the other held her oversized Louis Vuitton knock-off purse and her large Costa cappuccino. The purse was from her girlie holiday last year to Sunny Beach, Bulgaria. Beth was looking forward to next month when the girls would be heading off to Paphos, even though her best friend Jen wouldn't be coming. She had hooked up with a fella at her office Christmas party and was currently four months pregnant. Beth frowned at the thought and then at herself for the frown. Both women were twenty-seven, and Jen had always wanted kids. Beth just wanted a man first.

She reached the bottom of the steps, and the businessman pushed past her and headed to his favoured spot on the platform. Beth looked up at him and tutted. She took the time to check him over though. *Not bad,* she thought. His arse looked good in his tailored suit. Tall and slim, dark wavy hair, and a battered but chic cracked leather satchel briefcase in one hand, his own travel coffee mug in the other. She headed in the man's direction and stood four foot away from him, standing slightly forward so she'd be in his eye line. They were about halfway down the platform. *He's much better looking than my Tinder date last night. Attitude about the same though.* She thought about the date. How Chris turned up at the bar wearing obviously the same clothes he'd been wearing all day at work. A wrinkled suit and a shirt with a barely cleaned ketchup stain down the front. One drink and he was getting restless. Talking about going back to his 'pad'. *The Lothario.* Well, when he was not on his phone that was. She could see him swiping left and right. *More right than left. Creep.* Beth excused herself to go to the toilet, walked past the toilets and out the door.

Beth looked across the tracks to the other platform. The same faces she saw every day. Yawning. Coffee drinking. On their phones. On their own. It's not a time for families. In her peripheral vision, she watched the tutting man drink out of his travel mug. The way his head lifted exposed his tanned underjaw and muscular neck. *Hmmmm.* Beth purred to herself. Over the platform's tannoy system the female voice with its odd phrasing gaps announced the arrival of the next train.

'The train now approaching Platform... 1 is the... 07:20... London Overground service to... Euston.'

Passengers started shuffling forward in anticipation of the train's arrival. Beth held back waiting for the guy to choose his carriage. *It's not stalking. It's just nice to have something to look at instead of all the travel insurance and vitamin posters on the train. Guy candy.* He moved to the yellow line at the edge of the platform, Beth stood slightly behind him to the left. He looked in the direction the train would arrive from, she followed his gaze. A minute's wait and the train came into view. The bright yellow and blue driver's cabin lead the way. The train slowed as it travelled along the tracks, the occasional brake squeak disturbing the air. As the front of the train came level with Beth and the businessman she heard a commotion occurring further down the platform and Beth stood into tiptoes to see what was going on. Waiting passengers were moving down the platform towards Beth but looking at the roof of the carriage. Beth followed their stares and saw two men on top of the roof, getting closer as the train slowed to a stop.

Both men were facing each other about four foot apart, legs wide for balance and arms in a wrestler's' grapple stance. The train came to a halt, and the men swayed at the sudden loss of momentum. The man closest to Beth had his back to her. She could see he was a beast of a man. Muscles bulged through his tight, grey knitted jumper. Shoulders, far wider than his waist. He towered above the other man by a foot or more. The other man wore a black dinner suit, with a burgundy cummerbund, and a perfectly tied black bowtie. He was devilishly handsome. He had a chiselled jawline and a kind, but strong face. Looking at him Beth felt her heart flutter, and any thoughts of the businessman in front of her disappeared as though they had never been there.

The beast stepped forward, having regained his balance quicker. He reached with his tree trunk arms for his quarry. As he did his foot slipped on the metal surface, and his leg went out from underneath him, he fell to one knee. His weight carried him forward and to the side. Beth gasped. He grabbed the jacket of the other man and pulled him with him as he slid off the roof. They landed in a heap on the platform four foot away from Beth. She heard the thud of impact in tandem with the hydraulic hiss of the train doors opening. The smartly dressed man struggled to his feet, elbowed the bigger man to the side of the head as he rose. The beast grunted. Beth saw a trickle of blood from his left eyebrow drip down his face. His face was a grotesque mask of scars, crisscrossing his cheekbones and forehead. He pushed the smart man away from him, to give himself a chance to get to his feet and shook his badly shaven head. His head was a mammoth square. Cords stood out in his massive throat. He got to one knee and then the other and stood. *He must be seven foot tall.* His dark and emotionless heavy-set eyes were focused on the other man. He pushed the tutting businessman, whom Beth had been admiring earlier, out of the way. His face struck a pillar, and he crumpled to the ground. Beth gasped. The colossus roared and charged the dinner-suited man.

The suited man heard the challenge and dodged the charge at the last second hitting the beast in the small of his back as he passed. The brute stumbled a few feet into the crowd that had gathered. He regained his balance and then turned to face his urbane opponent, whose positioning had put him next to Beth.

'Kick the ugly fucker's face in!' a voice from the crowd shouted.

'Watch out Bigfoot, you're in for a pounding!' another jeered.

The brute spat to the floor, 'Come on Alessandro, give yourself up,' he said. His voice was like nails on a blackboard, high-pitched and squealy. Someone in the crowd laughed. Then another. A domino effect of laughter rang around the platform.

Beth heard the announcer over the laughter 'The train about to depart from... Platform 1... is the... 07:20... London Overground service to... Euston calling at... South Hampstead... and... Euston.'

Alessandro said to the beast, 'Davor, you're going to have to try and take me.' His voice soothed Beth like poured chocolate and warmed her insides like a shot of whiskey. She could see the smile on his lips. He smelt of sandalwood: masculine and powerful. *Is that Bleu de Chanel?* Beth felt her body reacting to the smell and the closeness of the man.

Davor walked forward, slow and glacial. The ground didn't shake in response, but Beth thought it wanted to. Alessandro looked at Beth and, with a smile that lifted her heart, asked 'If I may?' He took the coffee from her hand. She gave it up powerless to resist. Davor got within striking distance. In one fluid motion, Alessandro removed the plastic lid from the cup and threw the scalding liquid in Davor's face. The smell of freshly pressed beans hit Beth's nose as Davor screamed. Alessandro moved forward and launched a series of rapid kicks at Davor's shins, knees and thighs. Davor's legs gave way as Alessandro pushed him through the open train door and on to the train. The crowd cheered as the doors automatically closed and the train moved off. Some wit started singing 'Nah Nah Nah Nah Hey Hey Goodbye.' But faded in isolation and embarrassment before the second "hey".

Alessandro turned to Beth and said, 'Thank you, my dear. I think I owe you a coffee.' He offered his hand to her with a beaming smile. With hesitation, Beth took his hand, and he led her to the steps, and they ascended. They exited the station and Alessandro hailed a black cab. As she entered the taxi, she didn't see Alessandro reach into his pocket and retrieve a small mobile phone. She also didn't see him send a prewritten text message and replace the phone. He entered the taxi and told the driver to head to Soho.

'There's a great little café on Wardour Street, which serves the most exquisite coffee.' He told Beth as he reached for her hand. As they passed Edgware Road station, with her heart pounding in her head, Beth didn't hear the explosion a mile or so to the east. Alessandro did though, and his smile grew wider.

A Letter to Elise

Elise Miller got into her bed and clapped to turn off the lights. She was looking forward to putting this day behind her and having a good night's rest. The light clapper was a birthday gift from her dad. She remembered hating the present when she first opened it; she was hoping she would be given some Urban Decay makeup like Gwen Stefani uses. However, on nights like this, she was glad for the convenience. She moved around on the mattress, throwing a couple of scatter pillows on the floor until she was comfortable. She closed her eyes.

Barely a minute later she heard the 'ding' of her phone as a notification came through. She opened her eyes and reached for the phone, the screen light making it easy for her to find it. In her hands, the phone's light went off, and she pressed the side on switch to turn the phone on again. The glare hurt her eyes, she blinked a few times to clear them. She placed her finger at the top of the screen and dragged down the notification bar. *It better not be Candy Crush telling me I have full lives*, she thought. It wasn't. The notification said that Chad had tagged her in a Facebook post. He's probably apologising, she thought. He was a jerk today, and he knows he's made me pissed off with him.

Elise clicked on the notification and waited for the Facebook app to load. It's taking longer and longer to open, I'm going to have to get a new phone. Dad is going to go crazy, I only got this one six months ago. Eventually, the app loaded and it took her directly to the post. She was expecting to see a long grovelling post from her boyfriend so was surprised to see just a YouTube link. No message, no emoji, no preview picture. Curious she clicked on it, and the phone took her out of the Facebook app to the YouTube app. The video was titled "For Elise", and a black screen appeared with the familiar rotating circle of dots. She turned up the volume on the side as the video loaded. The dots finished their tricks, and the screen changed. Elise could hear Beethoven's 'Bagatelle No. 25 in A minor' playing in the background. She smiled, it was her favourite piece of music: 'Für Elise'. She could see Chad sitting in his gaming chair in his bedroom. This is where he does his pathetic gaming videos for Twitch and YouTube, wanting to be the next DanTDM or whatever his name is. Chad was looking directly at the camera, his eyes were red, and there was a mark on his cheek. I hope he is not getting spots, not this close to the Prom, Elise thought.

"Dear Elise," Chad said. His voice was hesitant and wavering. "I wanted to say I am sorry for the way I acted today. I don't treat you the way you deserve. You are a goddess, so beautiful and full of life."

He looked up towards something off camera. Elise could see his bottom lip quivering. I've really upset him. Good. He was a total jerk today. I only told him about that guy asking me to the Prom as a way of making him jealous, making him spend more time with me instead of those silly games. I didn't expect him and his stupid jock friends to humiliate the guy in front of me.

She thought back to that morning when she was standing by her locker with her girlfriends. She was taking out the books

88

she needed for the morning's classes when she heard a cough and a voice say, "Errr…Elise."

She turned around and saw Matt-something, he was blushing furiously and had his eyes fixed on the ground, she could see a couple of flakes of dandruff in his hair. He was in her Trig class, she had noticed him staring, then looking away quickly. He was kinda cute in a nerdy, greasy sorta way.

"Matt isn't it? What's up?" She said.

Still looking at the ground, "Ummm… I was wondering… um… if… er… if… ifyou'dgotothepromwithme. I know it's stupid."

He turned and walked away quickly before she could answer. She felt a little thrill, it was nice to be asked. Chad hadn't asked her yet. And although she was definitely going with him, they'd been going steady for five months, he should have asked her. It's tradition. She'd invited him to the Sadie Hawkins dance. At recess, she told Chad what had happened. She might have indicated that she was considering the offer, seeing as no-one else had asked her. She didn't expect Chad to react the way he did. He raised his voice and told her that there was no way she was going to the Prom with that 'fucking geek' and how dare he even ask her. His attitude angered Elise. *How dare? How-fucking-dare? I'll show him who fucking dares.* She stood up and walked across the schoolyard to where the nerds hung out staring at the girls and discussing, well she didn't know what they talked about. She saw Matt sitting in the corner, his back to her, talking to his fat friend with the crazy hair. She went over to him and bent down to tap him on the shoulder, she saw his friend try to look down her top as she did. She straightened up and folded her arms across her chest.

"Matt, I'd love to go to the Prom with you."

He turned, still refusing to look her in the eye, "W-w-what?"

"The answer is yes. I'm wearing dark purple so you can match the corsage. I look forward to it. I hope you can dance."

With that done, she walked off giving Chad the bird as she passed his table.

During Study Hall, Elise was in the library, doodling on her pad as she thought about the morning's events. That Matt, although painfully shy, could be quite cute. He'll have to wash his hair and maybe wear some decent clothes. No one listens to grunge anymore. I'm fed up with being treated as second best by Chad anyway. We never talk. He's either playing his games or trying to stick his hands down my panties. I'm sick of it.

The doors of the library banged open, waking her from her thoughts, then the sound of laughter, dozens of people laughing at once. She looked towards the commotion but couldn't see past the ring of people there. She got up from her chair and walked over, curious. She pushed past a couple of the crowd to get to the front. Once there her mouth opened in shock, her hand came up involuntary to cover it. Lying on the floor, naked, tied in duct tape, was Matt. He had 'Nerd', 'Loser', and 'Faggot' written on him in marker pen. *Is that his penis?* She thought, surprised. It was limp, shrivelled and surrounded by hair. She looked up and saw Chad there, surrounded by his football friends. A wide grin on his face.

"You still want to take him to the Prom?" He asked.

She turned and fled, Chad's laughter echoing behind her.

In the video, Chad was no longer laughing. His head was down, no longer looking directly at the camera. A tear, then a second, a third, trickled down his face.

"I don't d-d-d-deserve to live in the same world as someone like you." He continued. Elise thought his voice sounded strange, robotic as though he was reading from a script. "I don't deserve to live? What?"

The gunshot made her jump, its loudness distorted through the phone's tiny speaker. She saw Chad slump out of his chair, causing it to spin slowly around. There was near silence in the video, just a faint, rapid breathing sound. As the chair made its rotations, Elise could see blood on the wall behind. It was obscured by the backrest of the chair, there, then gone, then there again. Her hand shook, the tears in her eyes made the video blurry. A hand grabbed the chair and turned it, so it was facing the right way. Matt sat down. He looked straight at the camera. Elise noticed his eyes were a piercing grey-blue. She could feel them staring at her. Her skin began to crawl.

"Elise," Matt said. "That piece of shit didn't deserve you. I don't deserve you. I love you so much. I have done for years. Watching all the undeserving jerks, you let put their hands on your perfect body has made me sick. They will never love you the way I do, they will never love you more than me. How can I show you? What can I do to show you I love you more?" He paused. Elise managed to breathe, she didn't realise she had been holding her breath. Her breathing was rapid, little gasps of air.

"I love you, Elise," Matt resumed. There was a look of determination on his face. "I love you so much no one else will ever touch you again."

His hand reached out and pressed a button on the keyboard. The video stopped. There was silence in her bedroom, then 'ding', 'ding', 'ding'. A symphony of notifications made her phone sing. With her, still shaking, hand Elise brought down the notification bar, her friends commenting on the post. She touched on one of them, bringing back the Facebook app, in all its aching slowness.

"OMG! Elise."

"Call the Police!"

"What a freek."

"Call 911."

"Now Chad is out of the picture…"

"911 now!"

"Get your dad's gun."

Elise heard the doorbell ring downstairs.

***

'Who's ringing the doorbell at this hour?' Robert Miller asked his wife, Mary. They were in living room, in their recliners watching the latest episode of NCIS.

'It's probably Chad, for Elise.'

'I don't know what she sees in that guy. In my day someone who loves video games as much as he does would never have a girlfriend. We called them nerds and they knew their place.'

'I remember you getting very excited when the video arcade got their first Pac-Man game.'

The doorbell rang again. Robert placed his bowl of popcorn on the table beside him and pressed the button for his recliner to close. The leg rest lowered and the back straightened. Robert lifted himself out of the chair when the chair's action was done.

'That was different. Those were real games with a challenge.'

'Ok granddad,' Mary laughed. 'Go answer the door before he wears the button out.'

Robert mumbled underneath his breath as he left the room.

The doorbell rang again.

Robert called upstairs, 'Elise, are you awake?' as he slowly made his way to the front door. He wiped popcorn crumbs off his t-shirt as he went. Before opening the door he stood up straighter, puffed out his chest. Making himself look bigger. *Goddamn nerd.*

He opened the door.

'You're not Chad.'

***

Elise heard the door open, it always stuck to the frame so could only be opened with a jerk, which shook the rest of the house. Two gunshots sounded. Loud and violent. Elise dropped her phone on the coverlet, which was still dinging away. She swung her legs out of bed and sat up.

Another gunshot echoed up to her. *Oh God Mom!*

She stood up, her whole body shaking.

She heard footsteps coming up the stairs. Getting louder. Tears started to fall from her eyes. She heard a knock on her bedroom door, quiet and hesitant.

Articulated Dreams

The armies stood facing each other, across a flat landscape of various hues of browns, swirls of green and pink breaking up the patchwork fields. They had agreed to fight outside the city to protect the innocents. The ancient rules of engagement in place. The terrain flat, offering no advantage to either side. The rules were fair. There is no honour in a victory gained by unfair advantage. This battle, like many others, would be fought with strength, guile and willpower.

The castle loomed over the battlefield. The city beside it. The castle was built out of a mountain, the rock a strange blue-green hue. The castle with its imposing skull, carved into the front. Its open mouth the only entrance. A simple horned helmet atop the skull's head. The castle was the goal of the invaders. Its mythical powers the prize.

The two armies were lined up and stoic in their stillness. The lines of men interspersed with heroes and champions. Three, four times taller than the troops. These would decide the outcome of the battle. The fate of the Sorceress in the castle in the balance.

The home troops stood at attention. Their dark green coloured uniforms ripped and torn. Covered by dirt and blood. Theirs, or their enemies, they did not know. It stiffened the cloth and chilled the heart. Faces rigid with determination. They would do their duty. They would either die this day or be celebrated for eternity. The champions paced between the lines, anxious for the start. To, again, prove their mettle against their foe. This could be the final battle. The end of the war. The invading tan army had been repelled many times. Each time at great cost to both sides. The general of the assaulting army had been killed in the last battle. Crushed by a passing giant, oblivious to the slaughter going on around them. The loss of their leader, rather than weakening the army's morale, merely increased their resolve. Increased their determination to defeat the hated 'Greens'.

"Soon the power of the Sorceress will be mine," said the newly installed leader of the 'Tans'. "Then I will be free to conquer the universe, and reap my revenge on Hordak," his evil cackle carried across the battlefield. Hordak was his former master, trapped in another dimension. Hordak still living was an open sore in the leader's festering soul.

"When will we begin?" His ginger-furred right-hand Beast Man asked.

"When I tell you to. Beast Brain."

Beast Man's cheeks coloured, he clenched his powerful fists around the butt of his whip but remained silent. *Now is not the time.* He told himself. *Patience.*

"We await your command, Skeletor," Evil-Lyn said. A smirk on her face as she enjoyed her rival's chastisement.

Further down the line of troops, the red-cloaked, demon priest Mumm-Ra was discussing the elevation of Skeletor with Starscream.

"Either of us should be there," he pointed with a bandaged-wrapped arm at Skeletor and his henchmen. "We are both more qualified, and more ruthless."

"I agree. Skeletor has had his chances in the past and failed every time," Starscream said. "As much as I hated him, Megatron was far more worthy than—" Another cackle came from the centre of the army. "That laugh," he shuddered.

"It is grating," Mumm-Ra said, his red eyes gleaming. Megatron had been a useful pawn. Capturing the castle would have been my chance to rise up. Mumm-Ra, the Ever-Living. I will deal with the hooting skull the same way and anyone else that opposes me.

"Optimus, do you think we'll win?" Lion-O asked the robot standing next to him. They were looking across the field at the forces against them.

"With Megatron, it would have been easier to judge. He would have sent their troops straight into battle. No guile. Their new leader is an unknown quantity," the giant robot replied, his electronic voice sounded reassuring despite his uncertainty. "Prince Adam has had dealings with him before."

Optimus Prime called across to where Prince Adam was standing, deep in conversation with his mentor Man-At-Arms. Teela, Man-At-Arms' daughter and the rest of the Royal Guard were in the castle as a final line of defence. Prince Adam came over.

"How can I help Optimus?" he asked.

"What do you know of this Skeletor?"

"He has mystic powers, is cruel and delights in wreaking havoc. He is devious and unpredictable. We will need to be on our guard with him. The ancient accords may not be enough to restrain his deceitfulness. What is our plan?"

"I will send in Grimlock and his Dinobots first, our troops will fire from a distance. Grimlock is spoiling for a fight, and he and his band are a useful distraction. I'm going to hold our four amphibian friends in reserve. Their skills and agility will be essential against a tiring opponent. I'm just worried about the Autobots. Since the Tans took the Energon facility, our supplies have been running low. I'm not sure how long we can maintain our maximum effectiveness. I think it would be best for you Eternians and," Optimus looked at Lion-O. "you Thundercats to follow the Dinobots. By the power of the Matrix, we will succeed."

"Soundwave, start the battle cry," Skeletor told the dark blue and silver robot, as he mounted Panthor, his purple panther companion.

Soundwave opened his chest compartment and called Laserbeak down from his vigil in the air, scouting the Green's formation. As he neared Laserbeck transformed into his cassette form and flew into the compartment. Soundwave converted into his cassette deck form, and a cacophony of noise blasted out of his speaker. The Tan troops started marching in formation towards the Greens. Behind them followed Mumm-Ra and his minions, Slithe and Monkian. Mumm-Ra raised his arms in the air and incanted "Ancient spirits of evil, transform this decayed form to Mumm-Ra, the Ever-Living!"

Starscream transformed and took to the air in his jet form, while the Constructicons changed into their construction vehicle form and moved towards the enemy. Finally, Skeletor's minions followed. Beast Man, Mer-Man, Evil-Lynn, Trap Jaw, and Tri-Klops headed into battle. Skeletor released his trademark cackle and spurred Panthor forward.

When Soundwave's signal reached across the battlefield, Optimus Prime called his Autobots to transform. He ordered the Dinobots forward first. Grimlock, the leader of the Dinobots, said to Prime as he passed. "Me, Grimlock, want to munch metal."

The Dinobots moved towards the approaching Tan army in their dinosaur forms. They were followed by the Thundercats, and the Eternians, Man-At-Arms, Ram Man, Man-E-Faces, Mekaneck, and Buzz-Off. Prince Adam raised his magic sword and said: "By the Power of Grayskull!" Sparks flew from the sword and lightning flashed across the battlefield. Prince Adam transformed into He-Man. He then called out "I have the power." He pointed his sword at his shaking pet cat Cringer. Cringer changed into the fearsome armoured Battle Cat. He-Man leapt into Battle Cat's saddle and raced to the battle.

Optimus Prime watched his allies head into battle and sadly said: "And so it begins."

He ordered the Green troops to fire upon the advancing army. The sky was filled with bullets and bazooka shells, many hitting their mark on the Tan troops. From the sky Starscream and his four Deception jet subordinates fired lasers into the Green troops causing devastation to the soldiers. A brave few bazooka sporting men fired at the jets before being taken out. Four of the five jets sustained hits and retreated back to their lines. Starscream seeing his wingmen defeated fled behind them. A cheer sounded out among the remaining soldiers.

From behind Optimus Prime came a roar. He turned and saw the Turtle Van speed past him. The four turtles and their master, Splinter, wise-cracking as they went.

"Not yet!" Optimus called. "It's too soon."

His cries went unnoticed as the Turtles let loose their battle-cry of "Cowabunga" and fired towards the enemy. As the van approached the Tan soldiers, it skidded to a halt, and the four Turtles jumped out kicking and spinning the men. Splinter followed close behind mopping up any they had missed. As soon as it looked as though they would make a difference to the battle, Soundwave released his mini-cassettes Ravage, Frenzy, and Rumble. They took on the Turtles, and it was soon a battle to the death.

"Simon!"

"Simon!"

"Time to clear up your toys! It's almost dinner time!"

Simon looked up from the battlefield, in his hands were Rafael and Ravage. "Mum, I'm not finished yet," He shouted to his mother in the kitchen.

"It doesn't matter, you can play again tomorrow."

"But Mum."

"No buts, clear them up."

Simon looked down at the epic scene in front of him. The living room carpet was covered in soldiers laying together in heaps. Henchman against heroes. Robots against robots. *Maybe tomorrow I can include the Star Wars toys. The Millenium Falcon will make mincemeat out of the Deception jets, especially that coward Starscream.* He reached for the plastic boxes and started putting away his treasures.

***

Simon looked across the front room at his children on the sofa. Their faces reflected in the electronic glow of their tablets.

"Why don't you go play with your toys?" he asked them.

"Boring," his eldest, Michael replied.

"Yeah so boring," James, the younger child added.

Oh, how little you know. I wish mum and dad hadn't thrown away my toys when I went to university. It's not like they took up that much space in the attic. He thought back to that final battle. Of course, it wasn't the final battle. The war was still ongoing… *Rumble banged his fists into the ground knocking the Turtles to the floor. Ravage leapt upon Leonardo, his jaws snapping at the air in front of the turtle's face. An inadvertent swipe of Grimlock's tail knocked Ravage away before he could draw blood. Ravage leapt again…*

Sleep Now In the Fire

The train sped across metal tracks flanked by barren fields, crops withered and dead, farming equipment left to rust and die as the oil and petrol had run out. The rattle of the carriage and the wheels a welcome counterpoint to the screaming and crying from the passengers around me. I had fought for my place beside the window, the slight gap allowing in the wintry air, providing sweet, cool relief from the sweltering bodies around me. Air conditioning had long gone, too expensive to run, unnecessary for these passengers. In the cramped confines, it had become survival of the fittest, the strongest, and the ones most willing to take what they wanted. That's what it has always been about. Will. Ours, Yours, Theirs. The Will of the People. Our will to survive, Your will to obey and Their will to lead.

I could see the clouds in the sky ahead, a dark grey, and a forbidding portent of what was to come. They obscured the weak December sun behind us, casting a shadow far and wide. Beside me, Steven collapsed to his knees, I lifted him back up. He had helped me gain this position, any weakness and we would be back in the heap, on top of the already dead, already rotting from within as the heat of the carriage sped up the decomposing. We were in the camp together. In his other life, Steven was a journalist. We spoke occasionally, but like most in the camps, we tended to keep ourselves to ourselves. In the carriage of death, we decided early on to team up and get the best spot.

"Steven, stand up for God's sake!" I spat into his face.

"Mark, I can't… I can't," Steven said. His eyes glazed and half closed, his voice weak and wheezy.

"You have to, for both our sakes."

Steven didn't respond, his face slackened, his muscles drooped, his badly shaved head rasped against my cheek as his head dropped. I found I was supporting all his weight, I looked around me, at the faces of some of my fellow passengers, no one was looking, their eyes downcast, lost in their agony and fear. I stood up straighter, expanded my chest and pushed Steven up with all my might, as he came back down my fist connected with his face, I heard the crunch of the nasal cartilage break, the sickening pop as his optical socket broke, his right eye bulged as the air from the sinus cavity tried to escape. I pushed him towards the centre of the carriage, where his corpse tripped over another's outstretched leg and tumbled over, the skull made a nauseating shattering sound on the hard wooden floor of the carriage, the blood mingled with those already passed. No one said anything, no one dared, they were just looking to survive, to end this journey, to get off this meat train in one piece.

How had it come to this? I was a college professor; I had a doctorate in Medicine; I wrote books; appeared on television shows; I played Rugby Union for England; I voted Remain. Yes, that was it. I voted fucking Remain. It had been ten years and six months since that fateful rainy day in June when seventeen million people voted to leave the European Union because of …

I don't know. There were a thousand 'reasons', none of which stood up to the slightest scrutiny, a thousand lies, untruths, rumours, hearsay and bullshit. This was compounded by the government deciding in all its insanity to crash out of the EU with no deal and no plan. Crashing out to cheers across the tabloids and social media with Mr Farage's reptilian grin plastered across every television channel and paper. He soon buggered off though, didn't he? His work done: his pockets full of EU money. The Prime Minister, Theresa May, was ousted by her Senior Ministers before the ink was even dry on the Exit document. A vicious leadership battle took place between Boris Johnson and Michael Gove, which only ended when footage appeared via WikiLeaks. Of course, it would be that Russian propaganda machine. Footage of BoJo at a party mocking the people of the UK, calling them gullible spastics for believing in his lies. His crazy hair and zany antics were soon missed as Gove, free of restraint and full of power in the top job used the Henry VIII powers to suspend General Elections, in the National Interest, of course. We mustn't have anything disrupt the Leaving process. Labour and the other political parties, were forcibly disbanded, with 'Oh! Jeremy Corbyn' locked in Belmarsh Prison, along with other traitorous members of Gove's own party, Clarke, Soubry, Morgan and others. The House of Lords was abolished, they had tried in vain to prevent the No Deal approach and it destroyed them. The People were sick of these unelected free lunch bastards trying to take away their sovereignty, or so they were told.

Every trade deal the UK attempted after Brexit was rebuffed, The US, India, New Zealand, Canada, Japan, China, even Micro-fucking-Nesia. The Commonwealth countries that were supposedly aching to join the UK turned their backs on their former masters, in some cases publically, laughing as they stuck their fingers up. A result of the Boris School of Charm no doubt. No one wanted to be associated with the 'Nation that cut off its own nose and then stuck it up its own arse.' These were all told to the People as successes, the UK standing up for the People, carrying out their wishes. Oh the People, what happened to them? Well, we became poorer, much much poorer, the new Government abolished the minimum wage and the working time directive, which in turn removed holiday pay, maternity leave, the maximum working limit, night work limits, rest breaks. Brexit turned the UK into a little sweatshop of horrors, all long-term contracts were dissolved and everyone put on zero-hour contracts, so they could 'choose when to work', their employers just took the logical step and chose people that were willing to work any and every hour, if you didn't then you were not chosen. The disabled and on benefits were made to work, if they didn't they wouldn't get any money, if they couldn't, well it was simply a matter of Will really, they weren't willing to work and the People weren't willing to continue to pay for scroungers. Homelessness, food banks, prostitution, betting shops, pawnbrokers all increased, as did bankruptcies, repossession, suicide, crime. Inflation rose as did interest rates, borrowing became more expensive, the grocery shopping far more expensive, luxury shopping was reserved for the Upper Class, in shops barred to lower classes. To combat the rise in crime and disorder the army was deployed on the streets of England and Scotland.

Ireland was left to fend for itself. The British government was unwilling to pay to maintain any border between Northern Ireland and the Republic and left them to battle amongst themselves and then swept in when violence spread to the mainland. Good Friday Agreement? It was more like Pancake Day for the Irish, on both sides of the border. Ireland is now a Celtic ghostland, and eventually, people will be able to safely go back there. Our Government told the world it was an accident, a plane carrying a nuclear warhead, or maybe more than one, a computer error, or maybe it was a submarine, I can't remember. Winter started early over there, the sky over Ireland a mass of dirt, soil, ash and Deoxyribonucleic acid.

GDP growth slowed to zero and then crashed under. The Pound collapsed to pennies against the Euro. The People were reassured that it was okay as it meant we could export more, however, no one wanted UK goods. The EU and the US found you could transport cheaper, better quality, and less controversial goods from China, Taiwan, Vietnam, Thailand, Somalia, North Korea. The Service industry collapsed, the majority moved abroad, bankers to Germany, insurers to Belgium, creative industries such as fashion, film, advertising who were sick of the intolerance, the racism, homophobia, transphobia they saw across the unfettered Right-wing papers moved to sunnier climes. Farmers couldn't get enough workers to pick their crops or buy their goods. The fishing industry died as seas were polluted in the name of Sovereignty. The government changed the way the media was controlled The Guardian newspaper was closed for printing anti-Brexit propaganda, along with The New European, Metro, Evening Standard, and Daily Mirror. Headlines shouted out and denounced them one by one, screaming Traitors, Mutineers, Enemies of the people, Saboteurs, Defectors, Judas', and more. I admit they were very creative in their synonym usage. The BBC was closed down and heavy regulations were imposed on broadcasters, what they could or couldn't show, most just decided to show repeat after repeat of old comedies as they were cheap and easy to procure. 'Till Death Us Do Part' and 'Love Thy Neighbour' were the nation's most-watched shows. The internet was filtered and then filtered further; the range of sites allowed narrowed and narrowed until there was no point in it. VPNs and encryption were banned, which led to a breakdown in the remaining banking industry as anyone could easily hack into their systems, and did.

Within two years of leaving EU Citizens fled the country in droves as after a campaign from the Brexit-supporting press the Government decreed that all EU Citizens had to register online and wear the yellow stars of the EU on their chest so U-Kingdomers would know not to hire them, and know to avoid them. In their absence public services ground to a halt due to a lack of doctors, nurses, officers, and specialists, it was the final nail in the NHS and it died, replaced with an insurance scheme copied from the Yanks. Replacements were brought in from the Middle East, as they were only ones willing to come: Syrians, Iraqis, Afghanis, and Yemenis. They came because of promises of a land of plenty and plenty for everyone, these promises were soon found to be as empty as the shelves in shops; as dirty as the rubbish-strewn streets; they were left as abandoned as the cars on highways thirsting for petrol their owners could not afford. They left as fast as they arrived, gangs of indigenous white men, aided their decision, viciously and fatally in some cases. The Sun called them the 'Red, White and Blue Shirts' and 'we're proud of their Bulldog spirit.'

Upon the ten year anniversary of the referendum, with the country starving, unemployment rife and murmurings of dissent amongst the rulers it was decided that The People needed someone to blame, there was an obvious choice. 48 percent of the country would free a lot of hungry mouths from the meagre resources left, and who better than those that talked the country down, that spread Project Fear and fake news, the snowflake Remoaners, going against the Will of the People, dissenters, conspirators, renegades, and rebels. Social Media and television archives were scoured for any Remain-centric content, that's how they got me: I was a vocal supporter of Remain and highly critical of the Government before and after leaving. My apparent 'celebrity' status made the crimes even worse.

And that is how I ended up here on a train from Newcastle to Godknowswhere, from holding camps in Gateshead, and the North and South Shields for the past four months among my fellow betrayers, men and women, vermin and cockroaches. I looked out of the window at England's shit-brown and unpleasant land, grey-clouded hills, and satanic sweat-mills. A tear streaked down my cheek, followed by another, and another, my shoulders shuddered and shook and I started coughing, a rough, and hacking cough. When it had subsided I saw flakes coming through the window. The train began to slow. Through the window I saw Battersea Power Station in the distance, its four chimneys spewing great dark clouds, the orange glow of the fires beneath lighting the clouds in the gloom. I saw the buildings and streets around the station covered in a blanket of dirty snow, as we passed them. The streets deserted by people.

The train pulled into the station and the carriage doors were unlocked. I saw signs saying 'Victoria Station' and 'Detainees This Way' arrows pointing in the same direction. We were pulled from there by men with no necks and tattoos of the Saint George's Cross, their emblem. We were marched in pairs past black cab pickets of screaming fanatics, shuffled past cries of "traitors", "scum", ironically "splitters" was a popular chant, which made me smile without humour, and from one particularly venomous patriot "Merry Christmas you cunts!" We crossed the Thames over Chelsea Bridge. The Thames, never the clearest and cleanest, had slick rainbows of oil shimmering on the surface, churned by the waves; the smell was nauseous, of rotten meat and spoiled fish, with a lingering aroma of charcoal.

I could see we were being herded towards the power station, hazy in the wintery air, obscured by swirling wind-blown flakes of... well, of course, the old ideas never disappear, do they? They circle and bide their time, waiting for the right moment to come swooping in. The analytical part of my mind informed me dryly that there's no denying it isn't an effective method, proven to work. The emotional part screamed at me to run and to run fast. I listened intently and I pushed the women next to me hard into her escort making them both stumble, and set off at a tangent to our line of quislings. I ignored the shouts telling me to stop and pushed my legs harder. The long train journey and malnutrition in the camps were making this more difficult than it should be. It felt as though I was running through thigh-high waves on Britain's now polluted and toxic beaches. Hands reached for me and I swatted them away as I ran. I pictured myself at Twickenham heading for the try line, ball in the crook of my arm. I surged forward. Ahead, I saw the wooden fence ahead of me. The panels looked weak. I saw a barren urban wasteland through the gaps. An upturned shopping trolley, a beer crate, a broken wooden pallet, black bags, white bags, the thick dark green bags, all piled on top of each other. Bags torn by rats, birds, scavengers, their contents spilt. I hit the fence with my shoulder and it cracked, I pushed further, deeper, harder, using the power of my legs and broke through. I tumbled to the ground; someone tumbled over me, cracked my head with a knee or elbow in the melee. I pushed myself up as more hands grabbed me, clawed me and dragged me back down to the ground. The world went bright and then black as I was struck once, twice, more. I lost count and stopped caring, I saw through one bleeding eye the chimneys above me and the thick clouds of swirling twisting eddies, and I suppose, Kevins, Michaels, Thomas', Annas, Jennifers, and all, too.

Give the Anarchist a Cigarette

The wheel of the wheelie bin was wedged against the lip of the driveway edge. Simon heaved upwards and it freed itself over the obstacle with a startling momentum, he stumbled backwards with the bin lid flipping over towards his face. He quickly raised an arm to block it. *Shit, that'll leave a bruise,* he thought, angry with himself, *come on a little more panache, please. You're supposed to be a professional.* He replaced the heavy lid carefully and straightened the bin, there were a few cardboard boxes, flattened as per Council guidelines, scattered on the driveway. *Number Eighteen eats cornflakes, do they? I would have thought they would have been more exotic: something like granola or Cinnamon Grahams. The way they carry themselves, dressed in smart, office attire, leaving at the same time each morning, a chaste kiss on the cheek before getting into separate cars. Hers playing Heart FM, his Classic FM, as they drive off in separate directions, I definitely wouldn't have thought of them as own brand cornflakes eaters.* Simon picked up the dropped boxes and placed them in the bin. *Mustn't litter, as Mum always told me, well, at least before I killed her, she did.*

He dragged the grey bin off the drive and wheeled it round to number Sixteen. Did you know the colour of this bin is in the achromatic grey spectrum? The official name of the shade is Davy's Gray. He told himself, I wonder who Davy was? I'll have to look that up when I get home. He placed the bin adjacent to number Sixteens and reached for their bin. This one was easier and he managed to move it out without incident; exposed spiders scattered in the sudden sunlight. He moved Eighteens into the gap neatly and with a couple of minor adjustments stepped back to consider his handiwork. Very nice, they'll never notice the difference until they go to put something in there, then that own brand cornflake box will stand out accusingly. I wonder if they'll have a row about hiding food from each other again, that would be delightful. He remembered the occasion from a few months ago well, a shiver of pleasure tightened his scrotum as he recalled the horrified tone of the woman as she screeched at the man:

'You've been eating peanuts again. You know you're allergic to them, why the hell would you do this? Do you want to kill yourself?' and the initially confused, and then angry voice of the man as he rebelled against the harridan in front of him, 'I can eat whatever the hell I want. I might even go down the pub and eat a packet of dry roasted. That'll show you.'

Simon wheeled number 16s bin back to number 18s with a bounce in his step, filling the gap between the green and brown bins like a dentist bridging a missing tooth. He felt a small, hard lump in his trousers pocket. *Maybe soon they'll have replaced that dust cap.*

***

Cap, keys, wallet, glasses, all set. His hands patted each pocket of his jacket in turn; an ingrained habit; a physical, reassuring comfort.

'Come on love, we'll be late,' Arthur called, reaching for the front door handle.

'We can't go yet.' His wife, Eileen, answered from the living room, 'He's out there again.'

What's he doing this time?'

'Come and have a look, it's hilarious.'

Arthur entered the room, his face questioning. He saw Eileen with a big smile on her face, the net curtain parted in front of her; its off-white colour showing its age, *And ours, I suppose.*

'What's Simple Simon doing this time?' He said.

The smile turned to a frown, 'Don't call him that, it's not his fault, you know,' she admonished, 'he's just taken the bin of that nice couple opposite, you know; the posh ones.' The smile returned, 'It was hilarious,' she repeated. 'He yanked the bin over that border edge so hard; the lid flew up. I thought it was going to smack on the head, and the bin fall on him. Luckily, he got his arm up in time and blocked it.'

'I bet that will give him a bruise; those bin lids are quite heavy, you'd know that if you ever took the rubbish out.' Arthur said in a deadpan tone with a sparkle in his eyes.

'That's what I've got you for,' she retorted, her laugh warm. 'I would have dumped you years ago otherwise.'

'That's not the only reason why I'm still here.' His eyebrows jumped up and down suggestively.

'God! You're disgusting, thinking those thoughts at your age, you're lucky you're good at least one of those tasks,' she admitted.

Arthur walked to the large window and lifted the opposite end of the net curtain. He peered out, wondering whether to put his glasses on so he could see what was happening better.

'He's just put that nasty woman's bin in the posh ones driveway. I can't stand her, how that man puts up with her; I don't know. He must be a saint; you can hear her screeching from here sometimes,' Eileen said, screwing up her face like she had just stepped in something.

'Is he touching himself through his trousers? In broad daylight? I'm not having that.' Arthur left the room in a hurry and threw open the front door.

'Oi!' he shouted and watched as the figure legged it down the street.

He came back in with tears running down his face, out of breath he gasped laughing, 'Did you see him run… Oh my god I've never seen anyone run like that… his legs were all over the place, like Bambi at the beginning of the film. Oh I have to sit down.'

'That's not funny, Arthur. You know he's been like that since the accident,' Eileen said; her arms folded across her chest. 'It can't be easy on him losing his parents like that; so suddenly. It's bound to affect you… mentally.'

Immolation

'Wretches disperse, or face punitive action!'

The horde ignores, there's no visible reaction.

Pounding on the metal, looking for weakness,

Their desperate species, reduced to such bleakness.

He raises his rifle, viewing through the cross-sight.

His vision enhanced; images fuzzy and green in the night-light.

Women and children, filthy and worn, surrounding the core,

Preventing him targeting the stronger males attacking the store,

A wall of flesh; young and old: political suicide.

They'd be hell to pay; the headlines will read 'genocide.'

The radio crackles, 'Captain, state current situation.'

'Stockpiles are being assaulted, but there is a complication,

Targets are surrounded by a ring of protected wretches'

There is a pause, a slight hesitation, time stretches...

A loud, guttural cheer, as one of the containers is breached,

Contents spilling out: grain and fodder being leeched.

'Command, the wretches have gained access to one of the stockpiles.'

The Captain pauses, waiting instruction, it takes a while.

'Captain, please contain situation with extreme force.'

He blinks, suddenly unsure whether to continue this course.

He sees in his mind how this will be played out on the newscasts,

That's one way to make your mark; there's no denying that infamy lasts.

'Control, please repeat order' He temporises, hoping to delay,

'Captain, I repeat, contain with extreme force. Make those wretches pay!'

'Order confirmed.' He says, his voice full of subdue.

'Squad, we have to stop this' He states to his crew,

'Orders are to end this situation with lethal countermeasure.'

They voice their excitement, faces glinting with pleasure.

'Damn wretches', 'Gonna make them dance', ''Bout time too; filthy scum'.

He winces at their glee; their hateful grins displaying their gums.

'On my mark, commence firing!' He commands with a bark.

Feeling sick inside, he starts the countdown, '3… 2… 1… Mark!'

The crowds start to scream, wretches collapse into heaps.

As his crew methodically carry out their sweeps.

The Captain does not join in with the slaughter uncontrolled.

He stares with tear-filled eyes as he watches the horror unfold.

The Captain's dedication to advancement: his only goal.

His life's path all mapped out, obliterated by 'Control'.

The choice of court-martial or notoriety,

A martyr for maintaining the order of society.

Break Up, Break Down, and Break Face

"No," she said.

It took a moment for the words to sink in. This wasn't right. That's not how it goes. I opened my mouth to say something. Anything. Nothing came out. I closed my mouth. Opened it. Closed it. Like a fucking Hungry Hippo. Grasping for the right words. The plastic pill to change her answer.

"Get up. You're making a scene. And put that thing away," the disgust on her face was plain to see.

I looked down at my hands. Shaking in misunderstanding. The diamond ring, beautiful and mocking. I became aware of the people at the tables around us. The laughter and the embarrassed silence. The maître d' behind me with the three-hundred-pound magnum of champagne already opened, the naturally carbonated fizz leaking out of the bottle into the night like my dreams. I lifted my knee off the carpet and slowly rose. I kept my head down to avoid the stares and the pity and her. My heart was beating round my ears, its rhythm matching the pulsating throb in my temple. An aneurysm? I hoped, wishing for release from this world.

"Sit down, Stuart."

I numbly followed her order and sat on the chair, unconsciously pulling it in closer to the table, erasing my earlier exuberance of pushing it back with force as I leaped up to deliver my fool's errand. I stared at the plate before me. The half-eaten cheesecake with its blood-red coulis smeared around the plate like my future. The maître d' placed the bottle beside my plate and exited without a word. Condensation dripped down the bottle to the tablecloth, darkening the material. I placed the ring in the wet patch. It glittered in the low lights of the restaurant like the diamond it was.

"I wish you hadn't done that," her voice was tight. Strained. Like she was struggling to contain her anger. "I was going to tell you."

My ears picked up on that, and I glanced at her. So beautiful. So cold. I looked back down.

"It's over between us. It has been for a long time."

But we'd just bought a house together a couple of months ago. My mind protested. Why would you do that if you didn't love me?

"I'm in love with Marcus. No. We love each other."

Marcus? A thousand images of my oldest friend, my best friend, my would-be best man. Us together. Since forever. From the earliest schooldays to this year. He had been my one constant. The only one, apart from her, who knew me.

"He is going to move in. You will need to find somewhere else. I'll pack your stuff over the next few days, and you can collect it," she stood up and walked past me. She accidentally nudged me as she passed. No apology.

I slumped in my seat. My elbows on the table and in the cheesecake. My face cradled by my hands. The restaurant faded into blackness as I closed my eyes.

***

"Stuart, there's something I want to tell you," she said. I could see she was excited but trying to hide it. The corners of her perfect mouth kept rising and falling. Her hands were behind her back.

"Go on then," I said. "Tell me."

"Let's go over to the sofa." She skip-walked across the living room, past the cardboard boxes strewn around the floor to the salmon-pink leather sofa under the window. She practically jumped into the seat and patted the cushion next to her.

I walked over and sat beside her. Her summer dress had risen, showing her toned and tanned inner thigh. I reached out to stroke the soft skin, and her hand came out from behind her back and slapped it away.

"Later," she said with a smile.

I felt a draft of chilled air hit the back of my neck. I shivered as the goosebumps popped up along my arms. She noticed   and   squealed,   "You're   excited!"
"The suspense is killing me." I smiled.

"Okay, close your eyes and hold out your hands."

120

I did as she said. The draft was still there. Colder now. With a damp tinge to it. Her hands were warm. I felt her fingertips run across my outstretched palms, then placed an object in my hand.

"Don't open your eyes yet. I want to get a photo."

I felt her cushion rise as she got off the sofa. She ruffled my hair as she passed and then planted a light kiss on the top of my head. I heard her go into the kitchen. The temptation to open my eyes was immense. I wouldn't though. She wanted to see my reaction. I wanted her too as well. Anything to make her happy. The chill air hit me again, this time it ran down my back, along my spine. It was like iced water. I kicked out in surprise. Still balancing the object on my palm. My foot hit one of the boxes on the floor. It made a thumping noise, but the box did not move.

"You didn't peek, did you?" she asked as she came back in the room.

"I wouldn't dare. Cross my heart."

I heard the leather cushion beside me squeak as she sat down. She put her hand on my knee and gave it a stroke.

"You can open your eyes now."

I opened my eyes, blinking a few times to adjust to the exposure of light. I heard her phone make its camera shutter sound. Another blast of icy wind hit me from behind.

I looked down at my hand, and there was a white plastic stick, with a little window and a blue case covering one end. I looked at the window and saw three lines, two on one side and the other under the word 'pregnant.' Her phone kept making the shutter noise. I could feel my mouth start to make an 'O' shape of shock which I quickly changed to a wide smile, all teeth, and happiness.

"We're pregnant? That's incredible." I stood up and then picked her up. I swung her around the room, being careful to mind the boxes that surrounded me. Her laughter was like little bells.

"Stop! Stop! I'm getting dizzy," she said in between laughs.

I slowed and stopped. I placed her gently back on the sofa.

"I'm going to have to fix where that draft and get rid of all these boxes. My study is going to have to be a nursery I suppose."

"What draft? What boxes?"

***

Something rubbed against my cheek. Stroking. Gentle. Maybe she was awake? I lifted my hand to stroke hers. I felt something soft and furry. It nipped at one of my fingers. I sat up with a sudden jerk. Vomit rose in my throat and I fought the urge to shit. Why is it always rats?

I looked around but my bedtime companion had scampered off. Shivering. I felt a tightness in my chest. Here it comes. I began my usual waking routine. I coughed. A nasty full-bodied cough. Another. Another. Tears streamed from my eyes.

Another. Another. Trying to loosen whatever evil was in my lungs. It felt as though I couldn't breathe. Eventually the cough finished. My throat was raw. I reached for the bottle I had managed to save for. The cheapest. The strongest. The foulest. A mouthful left. I swallowed it gratefully. The alcohol burn soothed the rawness of my throat and numbed the pain.

I placed the bottle neatly against the wall of the bridge I lived under. I lifted my wrist and looked at my watch. The broken dial told me the same time it always does. I should throw it away but it was a present from her. *I guess it's time.*

I pushed myself to my knees and then to my feet. The joints ached from the cold wind that came from the canal that ran through the bridge. The canal, or as I call it my bath, my toilet, was a murky brown with a rainbow patina of oil. I bent down, ignoring the agonies in my back and folded my cardboard mattress and duvet into a neat pile. I lifted the bundle and left my home. I placed my belongings at the entrance to the bridge in a shady nook, covered from the rain and set off on my way.

"I didn't mean to hit him. Officer," the man said. "He surprised me, and I thought he was attacking us."

The man was next to the doorway of the restaurant, his girlfriend? Wife? beside him hugging him. The blue lights of the police car kept sweeping over the pair. Blue. Blue. Blue. Blue. Like the world's worst nightclub lighting system. Fuck, that punch hurt. I could feel the blood tricking through my beard. I was sitting on the kerb next to the police car. I wrinkled my nose trying to see if it was broken. For a change I couldn't smell myself, so that's one good thing. What the fuck am I doing, she doesn't even look like her. They never do.

"It's ok, sir. This man is known to us. He does this at least once a week. Not always at this restaurant. He did it to a couple at Nandos the other month."

"He should be locked up, you people should do your job, disgusting letting perverts like that on the street," the girlfriend, of course.

The Police Officer, to his credit, paused a moment before answering. "For surprising people? Ma'am if we did that, Jeremy Beadle's career would have been a lot shorter than it was. He's harmless. We'll take him back to the station. Get him a hot drink and a warmish bed. Much better than cardboard city, over by the canal, where he normally sleeps. That is if he decides he isn't pressing charges, of course."

"He press charges?" Her voice rose.

"He's the one who was assaulted, ma'am," I could hear the smile in his voice. "Your boyfriend might be lucky, Stuart's never done so before."

I started to feel funny. Not funny ha ha, but like I'd drunk a ton of bad wine funny. My vision started to blur, and it felt like I was swaying. The police car lights became too bright, and I closed my eyes. The after light burned on my eyelids looked like a shining blue diamond ring. A blinding pain struck me just behind my left eye. I slumped against the car. Everything went black. And stopped.

Watching

Today is the day, I know it. I see him standing on the platform. He is there each day at the same time. In the same place. Today he is dressed in a sharp navy-blue suit, pale blue shirt with the top button undone, no tie, grey rucksack hung over his left shoulder, only the faded green Adidas Gazelle trainers spoil the overall look. Maybe he ran to the station or has to walk a while to his destination. Perhaps I'll find out soon. I sit on a bench behind and to the side of him as I usually do, the cold metal seat is uncomfortable, but I bear it. He is standing there, content in a world of his own, the white cord from his perfectly shaped ears leading down to a pocket inside the suit jacket. His foot tapping in time to the music, I listen for the faint, tinny beats coming from his earphones, trying to recognise the song. I love it when I do, it feels like there is a connection as I silently sing along in time.

I've never had the courage to approach him before. Something always held me back, always given me pause. The obnoxious woman speaking loudly on her phone about the guy she met the night before. The golden, happy, family going on holiday with their suitcases and pram, excited and so full of joy and laughter. The putrid body odour of the middle-aged man in his crumpled shirt and bloodshot eyes wafting down the line. The stern-faced businessman tutting at the delay, pacing like a thoroughbred at the start of a race. They would have spoiled the mood, the sense of occasion, the sense of providence, so I held off my advance. I want to savour this moment, a day I'll never forget, etch each precious sensation deep inside this memory. I hear the clack, clack, clacking of the high heels echoing down the stairs; the scraping of a handbag next to me as it is placed upon the ground. I smell hot coffee in the hands of those waiting; that modern-day morning aroma pungent in the air, tainted by the faint, sweet miasma of decay wafting up from the tracks as stale air is pushed through the tunnels by the trains.

I see the rustle of a dozen newspapers as their readers turn the pages, reading about the latest scandals, gossip, and lies. I see the woman stood nearby him absorbed in her book, her thick-rimmed glasses overtaking her face. The man with unruly eyebrows, playing on his phone, gazes over at her, his look of wistful longing quickly replaced by passiveness as he checks around him to see if anyone caught him staring. I see the train lights far in the tunnel approaching us at speed, blazing like cat's eyes at night illuminated by a torch. I wipe my hands on my trousers, the sweat of anxiety making them damp. I feel the rough cloth texture on my fingertips and palm as it soaks away the fear. I stand and make my way behind him. Taking in as many details as I can to remember this for all time; the colour of his hair and the way it shines in the artificial lights; the neckline is looking shaggy, he is due to get a cut soon. A few stray hairs on his shoulders glisten in the lights. He is taller than I thought, not enough to make a difference. I can smell his subtle cologne with notes of exotic spices, and I utter an inaudible sigh of pleasure. The music from his earphones is louder now, I recognise the tune. This is a sign, a message from above, that this was supposed to happen.

I reach out my shaking hand and tap him gently on the shoulder, a shiver runs up my arm as he turns around and looks at me. His eyes widen with recognition, a hint of a smile forms on his lips. He has noticed me after all! As he reaches up to remove an earphone and starts to say 'Yes?' I place my left hand on his chest; feel the muscle under his shirt, slightly yielding but still firm. I push him backwards with all my might and slowly walk away. Away from the screeching wail of brakes as they conjoin with all the screams, a delicious reverberation of noise, that perfectly finishes this memory and fills me with eagerness and anticipation of the next.

Out of Space

Arcs of electricity illuminated the darkened cabin. Purple and blue sparks rained down from damaged circuits onto the steel floor. A monotonous robotic voice announced its garbled warning through one of the speakers. It stopped, and an ear-piercing squeal followed until the speaker blew. An underwhelming wisp of smoke came from the plastic case in the sudden silence. Major Michael Pitman opened his eyes. He winced at the sight before him: steel support beams from the ceiling crisscrossed the cabin like a snakes and ladders board; bundles of cables dangled above his head, knocked from their racks; various steel rods and other debris littered the floor. He reached down and undid the clasp of his safety harness. Once free, on shaking legs, he crossed over to his co-pilot and Commanding Officer Kellie Traynor, she was still. Strapped into her chair. Her neck at a wrong angle. He felt her throat for a pulse, noticing the skin was cold to his touch. *Damn.* No heartbeat. *Damn. Damn.*

Must contact base. Pitman looked on the floor for his headset and saw it across the cabin by the airlock door. He picked it up and moved back to his chair in front of the centre console. The electronics looked dead. No blinking lights. No illuminated dials. No video display. He plugged the headset connector into the slot on the console and pressed the "talk" button.

'This is Major Pitman for Houston Base. Come in. Over.'
Nothing. No static. No atmospheric hiss. He pressed the talk button harder and repeated the phrase. Again nothing.

'If you can hear me, Houston Base, we have suffered an unknown event. Commander Traynor is dead, and the craft is damaged. The diagnostic system is down so I will attempt to determine our condition and report back.' *I hope they're receiving this.*

He removed the headset placing it on the console. Behind him, a fire started from one of the sparks on a wall panel. Pitman grabbed the CO2 extinguisher from its place by his feet, pulled the safety pin as he walked towards the fire. The cabin was only ten metres by twenty metres. He aimed the nozzle at the wall panel and pulled the trigger. The CO2 gas bloomed out engulfing the orange tongues of flames. He swept it from side to side until he was sure the flames had extinguished. He put the extinguisher on his chair. The emergency lights overhead flickered but remained on. Pitman crouched down by the centre console and looked for the hard reset switch. It was tucked underneath to prevent accidental activation. His groping fingers reached it. The switch was similar to the one Pitman had at home on his fusebox. A selector switch with a lever that pointed to on or off. Pitman twisted the switch to the off position, and the cabin went dark. He counted off ten seconds in his head and twisted it back. Nothing. *Damn.* He repeated the process, and the second time the overhead lights came back on, and the console kicked into life. Different systems and functions bleeped their readiness like a chorus of electronic birds in the morning. Pitman stood up and picked up the headset. He pressed the "talk" button and repeated his earlier message. He was rewarded with a blast of static in his ear, then, '... Roger..., we hear you. What is the status of your ship? Over.'

Pitman breathed a sigh of relief. 'It's good to hear your voice. I have restored electrical power to the console and will be opening the front shield to see if I can see anything. There is no engine noise or vibration, so wherever we are, we're dead in the air.'

'Ok Pitman, keep us informed. Over.' The line went dead, and Pitman removed the headset.

He reached over to Traynor's side of the console and pressed a button. The craft shuddered as the reinforced metal plates of the front shield separated into halves and exposed the seven inch thick, triple paned, aluminium silicate glass and fused silica glass windows. Sunlight streamed into the cabin making Pitman close his eyes at the sudden glare. The afterglow behind the eyelids was intense, and he raised his arm to shield his eyes until they recovered and adjusted. *Sunlight? We were headed away from the sun.*

After a few minutes, the glow faded, and Pitman slowly opened his eyes, still behind the arm. The sun's light was still penetrating, so Pitman pressed the button to close the shield. The plates slid back into position with a clang. *That's not going to work.* He turned to the video display and popped the keyboard out of its slot below the screen. He tapped a few buttons to look at readings from the sensors dotted around the exterior of the craft. Expecting a temperature of around 2.7 Kelvin, or -270 Celsius, Pitman was astonished to see the temperature was close to positive 28 Celsius, similar to a balmy summer's day back on Earth. What the hell? He pressed a few more buttons to take a sample of the outside atmosphere. Less than a minute later the screen displayed the result. Largest proportion was Nitrogen, then oxygen, and argon. There were trace amounts of gases like carbon dioxide, nitrous oxides, methane, and ozone. *That is not possible.* The chemical composition of space is made up of hydrogen and helium with tiny traces of other elements such as carbon, oxygen and iron. Pitman shook his head in disbelief. *Let's see if I can get the computer's track up before jumping to conclusions.* The track contained details about the craft's journey and how it actually compared to the set trajectory.

Pitman stood up and went across to Traynor's side of the cabin. 'Excuse me,' he said automatically as his knee hit hers. *Damn.* As CO she had the computer that contained the track. Pitman powered it up and went straight for the track's location on the system. They had been in space for seventy-five days out of their planned 15-month journey to Venus. The two-person mission was to see if it was possible to colonise the planet's upper atmosphere. According to probes that had been sent out, the surface of the planet was determined to be a write-off. An atmosphere made up of 96.5% Carbon Dioxide was too toxic for humans, practically total greenhouse effect and the planet's surface was thought to be highly volcanic and have an atmospheric pressure equivalent to a depth of 1km under Earth's oceans. The Upper Atmosphere was supposed to be more promising and could help alleviate the growing population concerns back on Earth.

The track came up, and Pitman traced the craft's journey. They had remained on course as planned, as he had known they had. However, for some unknown reason, the craft had veered off course in a trajectory that looked like a preschooler's drawing of a pig's curly tail. As far as Pitman could determine the spaceship had travelled four hundred thousand miles off course until it had come to a stop for the past three days. *What the hell happened?*

He returned to his chair and picked up the headset. 'Houston Base, this is Pitman. Over.' He waited for a response. His mind whirling.

'Pitman, this is Houston Base. We read you,' the voice on the other end of the headset wire said. 'What have you found out? Over.'

'For some unknown reason, the ship went off course about four...' He did the rough calculations in his head, '... no, five days ago. We're currently four hundred thousand miles or so off course. Over.'

'That tracks with our systems here. We have you on course and then lose you five days ago. There had been no signal from your craft until we spoke to you. We can now see where you are. We're working out a solution to get you home. Do the engines still work? Over.'

'I don't know. They're not on now. I'll see if I can ignite them,' Pitman said. 'I'll be back.'

He removed his headset and returned to the main console. He called up the Engine-Start-Up Process on the main computer. Before trying to ignite them, he decided to run a diagnostic test. He pressed the appropriate icon on the screen and waited for the computer to return the results. It took less than a minute and indicated that the right engine was showing a fault. However, the left engine appeared to the computer to be operational. Pitman pressed the screen again to delve deeper into the reported fault. The system reported that there was a fault on the sensor that tracks the amount of fuel passed through the main fuel valve. *Damn.* There were spares parts for everything on the ship and Pitman had been trained on maintaining all the systems and parts. The main fuel valve was outside the ship.

Pitman returned to his chair and gave Houston the news.

'While I'm outside, I'll gather some samples for you,' he said.

'Be careful, out there,' the Houston controller said.

'Of course. Over.'

Pitman looked at Traynor. There was sadness on his face. 'I'd better make you more comfortable.'

He undid her restraints and she slumped forward. Pitman caught her before she fell. Her cold face rubbed against his. Her lifeless body heavier than it should have been if she was alive. He lifted her on to his shoulder and he took her to her quarters. He hit the door open button with his elbow and the door slid aside. He stepped in to her room and carried her to her bed. He laid her on the bed, supported her head to the pillow, and lifted her legs on to the bed. He took a blanket and covered her with it. He kissed her forehead and then covered her face with the blanket. *Damn.* They had worked together the past four years, or so. They had been close. Pitman had been to her house, met her husband, and had met her two young kids. *Damn.* He wiped the tears from his eyes.

***

Pitman put on his 'outside gear' as he liked to call it. The air in the helmet, from the life support unit, had a faint antiseptic aroma to it that Pitman initially had disliked, reminding him of hospitals, but over time he had grown to feel reassured by the medicinal hiss of the air. He walked to the airlock and checked the parts, equipment, and tools on the remote-controlled wheeled trolley beside him. *Don't want to have to come back for a screwdriver or a nut when I'm clambering above the engine.* Satisfied that he had everything, including sample bottles for soil, and fauna he may find. He pressed the airlock button. The door behind him closed and the chamber began to depressurise. Within a minute the green light on the airlock command panel turned on. Pitman took a deep breath and pulled the handle down to open the airlock. The airlock doors opened, there were two doors that were powered independently from each other, forming an additional fail-safe, and Pitman saw the 'planet' for the first time.

The ground consisted of a fine brown dust, interspersed with large grey boulders. Small funnels of dust kicked up in a spiral, and then floated down slowly when the wind found its next patch of dust to disturb. Pitman waited in the airlock compartment watching this new world in front of him. The dust funnels danced as dark clouds in the far distance glowed and flashed with lightning. He couldn't see anything living moving around. No creatures with five mouths and teeth as sharp as piranhas. No flying dinosaurs hunting for wandering humans to take back to their nests for their dragon-like chicks.

Pitman walked forward, his stride bouncing in the planet's lower gravity. Dust clouds bloomed with every step. He jump-walked to the back of the spaceship. There was no external damage to the craft. He saw a large gouge in the dust from the spaceship's descent to the surface. The planet's wind was already carrying armfuls of dust to cover the scar in the ground. Pitman looked up at the engine. He sighed at how high up it was. The engine had a diameter of two-point-four metres. On top of this the engine was two metres off the ground. *I better get started. I don't know how long the daylight will last.* Pitman took out the trolley remote and directed the trolley to his location. He avoided most of the dips and bumps on the surface and the trolley reached him without harm. He removed the extendable folding ladder first and set it up against the spaceship. He tested the stability of the ladder against the planet's surface by standing on the lowest rung and hopping. The ladder dug into the dust and stabilised. Pitman next removed the tools he would need from the trolley and placed them in the specially designed tool bag for the spaceship. Most of the tools were similar to the ones you could pick up in a hardware store but modified by NASA engineers to suit the rigours of space and dexterity problems caused by the astronaut's suits. Pitman finally removed the replacement sensor. It was lightbulb shaped with a screw fitting for easy removal and installation. He placed it in the tool bag and started his ascent up the ladder.

Pitman made it to the top of the engine without incident. He located the panel the faulty sensor was under and began to unscrew the bolts the panel was held down by. After a few minutes the four bolts were removed. Pitman could feel sweat dripping down his forehead and into his eyes, in spite of the cool air circulating through the spacesuit. The effort of working in a lower gravity environment taking its toll on his body, as he had to restrict his movements to maintain control of his position on top of the ladder. He unscrewed the faulty sensor and placed it in his tool bag. He removed the replacement and installed it in place. *This better work. I don't want to do this again.* He fitted the panel and securing bolts, closed the tool bag and descended the ladder. As he reached the second step from bottom he missed the rung and his foot stepped onto nothing. The unexpected momentum made him lose his grip on the ladder. Pitman fell backwards on to the floor. He landed flat on his back, the life support backpack system he wore reduced the impact of the fall. The tool bag went flying out of his grasp. Around him clouds of dust shot up blinding his vision through the helmet. Damn. Pitman struggled to flip onto his front. His backpack did a great job at hindering his efforts. Finally, with a lot of exertion he managed to turn around. He got on to his knees. The dust was starting to settle around him. He lifted his head and for barely a second he saw a dark shape out of the corner of his eye. *There was definitely something there.* He carried on watching the rocks where he had seen it. The rocks were about fifty metres away from him. They looked to be about twenty foot high and probably thirty foot wide. He hadn't managed to see any details of the something. Just a shape that was there standing out against the brown rock and then not. Pitman stood still watching the rocks. Nothing. He moved closer to the rocks, away from his spaceship. He couldn't hear anything over his own breathing. The hiss of the life support system. He rounded the rocks looking for whatever he had seen. His heart was beating stronger. Faster. He reached the back of the rock. He looked all around him. There was nothing. No strange and exotic creature. No dust plumes indicating something had been there momentarily. Nothing. *Maybe it had been a shadow of a cloud or something.* Pitman stood watching the rocks for a minute then turned and made his way back to the spaceship. Every so often he'd turn around, just in case. Nothing. As he was coming closer to the spaceship he saw a build-up of debris in front of the ship. He went over to check it out. The front of the ship was buried under two feet of sand, rock and dust. *I'll have to clear that before I leave. Damn.*

***

Pitman returned to the spaceship. He was breathing heavy from his exertions outside. He manoeuvred the trolley into the airlock and closed the hatch. He pressed the button to pressurise the chamber to match the air inside the spaceship. When the light turned above the button switched to green. Pitman unclipped his life support and removed the backpack. He removed his helmet and gloves and wiped his face. He wanted to lie down. *Work to be done first.* He made his way to the console and started the engine diagnostic program. All clear. Pitman breathed out in relief.

He put on the headset and toggled the on switch. 'Houston Base, this is Pitman. Over.' He waited for a response. As he waited he sat in Traynor's seat. His limbs weary and weak.

'Pitman, this is Houston Base. We read you,' the crackly voice on the other end said.

'The engine is up and running,' Pitman told Houston. 'There is debris in front of the craft I'm going to have to clear out in order to attempt lift off. Even with the equipment on board it'll take me a few da—'

He stopped as he heard a noise coming from the airlock area. It sounded like a high-powered welding torch.

'Pitman, are you there?'

'Yes, I'm still here. I can hear a noise coming from the airlock area. I'm going to check it out. I'll be back. Over.'

Pitman put down the headset and walked over to the airlock hatch. He looked through the thickened Perspex viewing

137

window, and his eyes widened at the three figures he saw emerging from the fissure in the airlock door. Tall, much taller than Pitman. Wearing a dark hooded garment. One of the figures looked at him, and Pitman screamed at the visage he saw. Black reptilian eyes that showed his own petrified face in the mirrored surface. Steel-grey skin leading to a mouth with a shark's smile. The figure stepped forward.

Pitman scrambled backwards, his left foot stepped onto a fallen rod that rolled under his sole. His arms flailed about trying to correct the overbalance. He fell backwards, still looking at the airlock door. The back of his head came down, along with the rest of him and bounced off the steel floor. Once. Twice. Pitman saw the figure at the window peering in as his world went black.

***

Pitman came to. Confused. Disorientated. An image of the figure from the airlock flashed into his brain. He gasped and tried to sit up. He found he was restrained. Unable to move his limbs. His blood ran cold and then warm and then cold. It rushed to his head and then left. He slumped back down, eyes closed. His breathing ragged then slowed.

***

The pain in his side woke him a second time. An intense burning inside him. Pitman opened his eyes in shock. The glare of artificial light making his pupils contract and his eyes water. He blinked away the tears as he cried out. He struggled but to no avail. He couldn't move.

His heart hammered in his chest. His vision cleared, and he could see he was in a bright, laboratory-like room, he looked to his left and saw Traynor on a metal table. Nude. Her greying skin dulled and dead. A figure standing over her with a sharp knife.in its hand? *No that's not a hand. There are claws instead of fingernails.* Pitman looked at the figure. The hooded cloak had gone. In its place was what looked like chain-mail over olive green skin, which rippled with muscle. The lizard eyes and shark mouth had gone. Replaced with small pig-like features. Small, hidden eyes. A snout and tusks. *W-w-what?*

Another tear in his side, this time on the other side brought his attention to what was happening to him. His raised his head as high as he could and saw two creatures, similar in appearance to the one beside Traynor. One held a wicked, sharp knife. The other. *Oh my god is that a probe?*

Shaddap You Face

Katie Hopkins

From Wikipedia, the free encyclopedia

Katie Olivia Hopkins (born 13 February 1975) is an English media personality. She first came to notice in 2007 as a reality television contestant and later became a columnist for British newspapers, initially *The Sun* (from October 2013)[1] and later the *MailOnline* (from autumn 2015 until 2017).[2]

Hopkins has been accused of racism by journalists, advocacy groups and politicians for her comments about migrants. Her role as a presenter for the radio station LBC was terminated in May 2017 following her comments on Twitter about the Manchester Arena bombing.[3][4]

In 2016, *Mail Online* was forced to pay £150,000 to a Muslim family whom Hopkins had falsely accused of extremist links. In a 2017 libel case, Hopkins was required to pay £24,000 in damages and £107,000 in legal costs to the writer Jack Monroe after making defamatory remarks on Twitter. Later in 2017, *Mail Online* was forced to pay substantial damages and legal costs to a teacher about whom Hopkins had made false claims. A day before, in late November, it had become known Hopkins' contract with the media outlet had not been renewed.[5] Her final column was published on 5 October 2017.[6] She joined the Canadian far-right website The Rebel Media in January 2018.[7] She continued to court controversy and in

November 2018 it was revealed that she had accepted money from the Russian government to stir up the British population [8] to induce civil war. Following these revelations Hopkins was the first British citizen to be subject to the 2019 Gagging Order for hate speech and sedition.

The 2019 Gagging Order was a controversial measure brought in by the British Government to limit the growing rise in hate speech and sedition of the masses [1]. It is not to be confused with the term Gag Order (or super-injunction) which is designed to limit or restrict information or comment being made public.

Background [edit]

The 2019 Gagging Order was an Order introduced by the Parliament of the United Kingdom. It officially became law on 24th April 2019 after an unprecedented rise in hate speech reports and the Cambridge Academia scandal [2]. It is said that the increase in hate speech came after Tommy Robinson and Katie Hopkins visited Speakers' Corner in Hyde Park, London on the 18th March 2018. Race crime and violence soared after the event [3] and online became a battle of colour, race and religion.

Passage [edit]

The United Kingdom Parliament, after a heated debate, decided to vote on whether to introduce a new Order to drastically reduce the spread of hate messages throughout the country. The vote was taken on 23rd November 2018 and the motion was passed 410 to

220. 20 MP's abstained on the vote. Boris Johnson, the UK Prime Minister, said after the vote, 'This is an important result in the battle against hate of all kinds. I welcome this result and look forward to seeing the people of our country getting on with each other, like the Hippalectryons and Odontotyrannos did in Ancient Greece.' [4] Jeremy Corbyn, the Opposition Leader, said, '[The Order] is a tyrannical device that belongs in the Dark Ages, just like most of the Conservative Party's policies.' [5]

Controversy [edit]

The Order was highly controversial and criticised both domestically and internationally, from groups both on the right and left of the political spectrum. A 50,000 strong protest march was organised for the day after the vote was passed [6]. The march erupted in violence, resulting in five days of riots which caused an estimated £150m worth of damage to businesses and properties in London, and an estimated £3b worth of lost trade [7]. The riots finally ended when the Government brought in the Army to police the streets and imposed a curfew of 8pm.

The Order was discussed in the United Nations and the European Court of Human Rights. The United Kingdom had sanctions imposed on it for the breach of Human Rights.

The First Gagging Order [edit]

The First Gagging Order was given to Katie Hopkins due to a tweet she posted on Twitter, and later deleted which said 'All White Britons should rise up against the Blacks and Muslims and take Our Country Back.' [8] She was arrested for Hate Speech and at her trial in May 2019 she justified the tweet by saying that it was posted as 'a satirical take on the words of the United States President and was not meant to cause offence' [10]. She continued 'that she had hoped that Britons would have been intelligent enough to see the nuance'.

On May 15th 2019 She was sentenced to five years Gagging.

The Gagging Process [edit]

There were two proposed methods of Gagging.

The first method 'Drug Induced Gagging' was equivalent to the chemical castration process where the 'patient' was curbed of their propensity towards spouting hate speech via selective serotonin reuptake inhibitor drugs which changed the brain's chemical makeup.

The second method 'Electronic Behaviour Control' where the patient was Gagged by having an electronic behaviour chip inserted into the amygdala of the brain. The chip controlled the electrical impulses in the brain to deaden emotional highs and lows. The outcome of this method was that the patient was far less likely to think extreme thoughts, or take extreme actions. A secondary action of the Electronic Behaviour Control was that it curbed all criminal behaviour. Researchers at the Department of Criminology at the University of Pennsylvania, who had previously determined that certain kinds of criminals had deformities in the amygdala [11], tested the chip in patients who displayed psychopathic behaviour and noted a dramatic change in behaviour. This research made the Electronic Behaviour Control the preferred method for the Gagging Order and Katie Hopkins was fitted with a chip on 10thDecember 2019, coincidentally the International Awareness Day of Human Rights [12].

Based on the research by the University of Pennsylvania, on 20th February 2020 the United Kingdom government expanded the Gagging Order program to reduce the prison population [13]. Fitting prisoners with an Electronic Behaviour chip who wanted an early release on their sentence. Only prisoners with a history of sexual or violent crimes were eligible for the program.

Notable Gagged Persons [edit]

Nigel Farage, ex-MEP and Leader of UKIP was gagged on 1st April 2021 for equating Jews with Rats [14]. He was sentenced to 3 years.

Tommy Robinson, Founder of the English Defence League and ~~wannabe~~ journalist, was gagged on 15th July 2019 for including the phrase 'Kill all Muslims' on a Youtube video [15]. He was sentenced to 10 years.

JK Rowling, Author of the Harry Potter series of books, was gagged on 10th September 2020 for retweeting a post which depicted all Brexiters as a 'wall of gammon' [16]. She was sentenced to one week.

The End of the Gagging Order [edit]

The Order was rescinded on 30th June 2022 after the 2022 General Election. Labour won the Election with 56% of the vote [17]. Leader Emily Thornberry said in her victory speech 'this result is a victory for free speech and an end of the oppression from the Conservative party.' The Conservative Party came in third behind a resurgent Liberal Democrat party, with 23% of the vote.

Outcomes of the Gagging Order [edit]

In total 264,767 people were served with a Gagging Order in the three years the Order was active, with sentences ranging from 3 days to eleven years. 23,124 were prisoners afforded an early release. [18]

Instances of Hate Crime and Hate Speech drastically decreased while the Order was in operation. When the Order was rescinded these rose to levels around half of what they were before the Order and then decreased as the slogan 'Sticks and stones make break my bones, but words will never hurt me' increased in popularity and proponents of Hate Speech and Hate Crimes were no longer given a platform to spread their views, due to a new Order – The 2023 Gagging Order banning them from Social Media, public gatherings, television and radio.

Sanctions against the United Kingdom for the 2019 Gagging Order were lifted on 15th July 2022. [19] The sanctions were estimated to have cost the United Kingdom 25% of GDP. [20]

Dream Academy

The television studio designed as an auditorium went dark as I waited in the wings for my mark, hands shaking, my left leg twitching. Suddenly the giant screens burst into life, a swirling graphic of red and silver, which transformed into letters as the announcer's voice boomed out my name over the dramatic, pumped to the max, chorus from O Fortuna. The audience started cheering, screaming and clapping as the displays changed into an idealised, stylised, version of me, excessively made up, flattering lighting and expensive post editing effects. To be completely honest, I thought I looked great up there, like I belonged, like a goddamn star.

The screens changed as the pre-recorded segment began:

'This week we are going back with the contestants to their hometowns,' the narrator announced. 'First up is twenty-two year old, Benjamin Harrison from Kirkhead, in Rochdale.'

The image changed to one of screaming crowds as the camera whizzed past them, all of children and adults doing the 'X' symbol with their arms crossed across their chests, looking like the party members in 1984 screaming at the black and white image of Emmanuel Goldstein during the 'two-minute hate'. I saw signs, held aloft with my name and face on them, crude hand-drawn pieces, sometimes spelt correctly, with pictures of me cut from a magazine, stuck roughly to the signs at oblique angles. Then I saw me emerging from a silver stretch Humvee, looking ridiculous and cool in pop star clothes: hipster tight jeans; a natty graphite grey waistcoat over a striped collarless shirt, sleeves rolled up to the elbows; a tatty, blood red scarf that wouldn't look out of place in a group of female foreign exchange students walking along Oxford Street in summer; and a sequined trilby on my head to top the look off. The screaming from the crowd intensified and they swarmed me, touching me, kissing me; a million arms around my shoulder and the flash of a million camera phones as the whole world tried to capture a picture of us together for their friends to 'like'. I saw a glimpse of myself standing in the midst of mayhem, my eyes wide, my face drained of colour underneath the fake tan, my shining, cosmetically whitened teeth bared in a snarl and the setting changed to me knocking on my own front door to 'surprise' my mum and Carl, my step-dad. They welcomed me with their arms wide open and hugged me like I had been lost at sea for years and led me and the camera crew into the front room, they described how they felt about me being on television and how they thought I would do in the contest:

'He'll win for sure,' Carl said, with exuberant passion. 'He's the complete package, the voice, the looks and the sex appeal for the girlies.'

The audience, back in the studio, screamed at this in approval, I felt my cheeks start to burn. Thankfully, it was dark in the wings so I didn't think anyone noticed.

The video on the screens changed to familiar, individual faces of people I knew: Mr Jackson, my drama teacher, his hair a lot greyer and thinner than it was when I at school six years ago,

147

and Mrs Spencer, the headmaster with a wide smile on her face gushing my praises; Linda, my boss at the supermarket I worked, looking like her idol Bet Lynch from Coronation Street, faux fur, false tan, and fake jewellery; Granny Pam from the café next door wearing a new, clean blue apron; Hannah, my co-worker and part-time girlfriend, who constantly nagged me to enter the competition after hearing me sing Milk and Alcohol by Dr Feelgood, while mopping up a massive milk spillage, which always reminded me of the Great Boston Molasses Flood, after jugs of milk had been opened and poured down all the aisles of the supermarket by the local gang in retaliation to Linda blocking the youngest of the gang from buying cigarettes. I don't know why she thought a nine-year-old should be denied the right to smoke; and Kevin and Michael from school, still as tough looking as they did back then, now with tribal tattoos and too-tight shirts to display their muscles. Each person said something flattering about me, how they always knew I'd make it; how I was going to go all the way; make Kirkhead proud.

The studio screens started showing clips of my auditions and previous rounds building up, a crescendo of intensity, each clip shorter than the last, slightly louder and then a sudden stop, the music ceased, the screens turned black, the producer gave me a microphone, and the announcer's voice boomed 'Rochdale's finest, Benjamin Harrison.' The studio erupted in screams and light as I strode to the mark on the stage floor; I placed the microphone on the stand as the accompanying music started.

'In this dirty old part of the city,' I began with a strength in my voice that had been missing when I had sung in previous rounds. 'Where the sun refused to shine, people tell me there ain't no use in tryin''. I closed my eyes and envisaged Hannah in my mind as I sung and my voice cracked when I reached the final chorus and I sang, feeling every word deep within, 'We gotta get out of this place, 'cause girl, there's a better life for me and you.'

The music faded and an ear-piercing howl of noise struck me as the audience started clapping and screaming. I opened my eyes to see the audience and judges standing in unison applauding me. After a lot of gesticulating from Simon it eventually died down and the judges made their comments: Simon said it gave him goosebumps, the crowd applauded; Sharon said it made her nipples go hard, the crowd bayed with laughter; Nicole said she was speechless and Louis said I had made the song my own, but I was expecting that as he'd said it to me for the past four weeks.

Simon then asked me what it was like to go back to my hometown, I hesitated as I thought of the people I'd seen, how amazed I was to see my step-dad Carl at home instead of at the pub or in the bookies, how much had the producers paid him to be there I wondered; how different my mum looked without her usual black eye; how surprised I was to see Mr Jackson singing my praises after the pervert had felt me up in detention every fucking week, with Mrs Spencer being all buddy-buddy and fucking smiles with him after she had repeatedly refused my complaints of abuse and put me in detention over and over again for lying; seeing Linda, my boss, who had done nothing but complain about me constantly throughout the six years I had worked in that shitty store, always on my back, getting me to work extra shifts threatening to fire me if I refused, there really aren't many jobs in Kirkhead for someone with no qualifications; Granny Pam who had got her grown-up son and his mates to beat the shit out of me when I told everyone I had seen her spit in the tea of a black customer and fucking Kevin and Michael who made my life hell at school after I had caught them making out together, slapping me around, telling everyone I was gay and that I had sucked off the school's caretaker for a quid, so everyone at school treated me like I had aids or something, and had the caretaker winking at me at every opportunity; how isolated, lonely and depressed this had made me feel and how I couldn't even lift myself up to work at my exams, to get the grades I knew I needed to leave that shitty little town and shitty life.

I thought about saying that all, getting it all out, a catharsis of emotion and hate, to the nation and the town that failed me, however I realised that was the Kirkhead in me, trying to keep me there, trying to keep me down, keep me following my step-dad's path of self-loathing and violence, I often wondered what my mum had seen in him to move us up to fucking Rochdale after my dad died, leaving our friends and life and opportunities in London far, far behind. It is like Kirkhead has a life-devouring soul, thriving in misery, revelling in hate, like Stephen King's Castle Rock. I then pictured Hannah and me hand-in-hand along the Thames at dusk, walking past the sellers with their Union Jack hats and tea towels; opening the door to my pop star mansion, all windows, pillars and driveway; standing in front of the crowds at the V Festival in Weston Park ready to deliver my headline set.

I straightened my shoulders, looked Simon dead in the eye and said 'I won't lie to you Simon, the welcome I received in Kirkhead blew me away, makes me so proud to come from there. I want to say thank you to all my friends, family and friends I haven't met yet for their kind words and support. Vote for me Rochdale!' I finished with a flourish and felt the Kirkhead presence around my soul release its grasp for the first time.

A Plague on the Earth

Francis pushed open the thick wooden door. The sweet, but cloying smell of antiseptics filled the space and pushed past him into the hallway. He walked into the room and closed the door behind him. The room was dark. Francis could make out the bed in the centre. The white sheets were a lighter shade of black than the rest of the room. He walked to the window and pulled open the heavy drapes a fraction. Sunlight beamed into the room, and Francis had to close his eyes at the glare. He turned and opened his eyes. After-glare gave everything in the room a green tinge. There was a bright sunlit corridor stretching from the window to the door. It touched the corner of the bed.

Francis took a deep breath and walked to the bed. As he got there, the door opened. He lifted his head to see the visitors.

'How is he?' Raphael asked as he entered.

'I've just got here,' Francis said. 'I haven't looked yet.'

'He can't be worse,' Bernadette said, as she closed the door behind and moved to the bed. 'He must be getting better. They and we need him.'

'He's been getting worse for the past one hundred years,' said Raphael.

'Thank *Him* that he's immortal. Anyone else would have succumbed by now,' she said, her voice full of reverence.

'He's in so much pain,' Raphael's eyes filled with tears as he moved around the bed and stood next to Francis.

Francis placed his hand on Raphael's shoulder in comfort. 'There have been signs that parts of him are getting better, they seem to be figuring things out down there. At least in some respects.'

Bernadette reached for the top sheet covering the figure in the bed, 'Not quick enough, I don't think there's much longer left.' She pulled the sheet back.

The person on the bed was male with long brown hair, he was naked apart from a loincloth. The first noteworthy thing about him was how thin he was. His ribcage was pronounced, his abdomen shrunken. His hip bones stuck out like icebergs on the ocean. His cheeks hollow, his cheekbones prominent.

'He's wasting away,' Bernadette said. 'He wasn't as bad as this last time I was here.'

'That will be the cancers attacking his body. He has leukaemia, skin, and lung cancer. He cannot keep any food down. We're feeding him intravenously, but we're losing.' Francis said.

The man had weeping, bloody lesions across his body and limbs. Across his shoulders, the skin looked like it had melted in patches, as though it had been dipped in acid. There were pits and troughs of sores and redness, and the skin between these affected areas was bleached bone-white. His previously-handsome face was a mask of pain. Tears flowed from his closed eyes. If you look closer at his hair, you will notice clumps are missing, the scalp leaking pus and blood. The pillow underneath his head was coated in smeared bloodstains. His skeletal arms, bloody and sore, led to broken and busted fingers on each hand, like they had been shoved into a thresher machine.

'What can we do?' Raphael asked. He had moved away from the bed and was looking out of the window at the brilliant sky above.

'Sebastian took them the painting, but it hasn't helped,' Bernadette said as she replaced the sheet on the patient.

'We are going to have to try a more direct method. It's the only thing left,' Francis said.

Bernadette and Raphael looked at him, their faces were aghast at the idea. 'It is forbidden!' They both said at the same time.

'Desperate times call for desperate measures,' Francis said. 'I'll take full responsibility, but there is no other way. They are crying out for him to return, but he cannot while they continue their ways. There have been precedents in the past. We have to take action. They only have, at most, twenty years left. He, probably, much less than that.'

***

Captain Hubert J. Taylor stood on the bridge of the ultra-large crude carrier, *Druj Nasu*. The one thousand five-hundred-foot oil tanker was on route from the Persian Gulf to the United States. Taylor looked out of the bridge windows at the calm sea and clear skies before them. He knew from the weather chart that this was due to continue for the next two days as the craft left the shelter of Africa and ventured into the Atlantic Ocean. His bridge crew were at their stations, but there was an aura of relaxed professionalism about them. Talking about the gridiron games that were on that weekend.

'Captain, there's a large rain cloud on the radar heading towards us from the North West. Approximately forty miles away,' Officer Phillips called out.

'There was nothing on the chart for today, are you sure?'

'Aye, Captain. It looks to be a band about one hundred miles across and twenty miles wide,' said Phillips. The Scottish brogue was still prominent in his voice even though he hadn't been home for almost two decades.

'Okay, Phillips, we know the drill. We'll have enough of these in the next few days anyway. It'll be good practice for the crew before a big storm hits. Sound the weather alert and let's get everything tied down that needs to be. How long before it hits?'

'About an hour, Captain.'

Captain Taylor watched through the bridge's windows as the sky ahead darkened. The tanker was still in brilliant sunlight, but Taylor knew that could change in an instant on the sea. The clouds grew closer, but the sea remained calm, there was no increase in the outside wind levels.

The clouds grew closer. Taylor began to feel a sense of unease. He asked for and received a pair of binoculars from the bridge crew and held them up to his eyes. The cloud was dense, dark and foreboding. He increased the magnification of the binoculars. The cloud was strangely shaped. A large mass led by a smaller mass. It looked like a sideways funnel aiming directly at his ship. He zoomed in as close as he could. The sight made his blood run cold.

'Sound the alert. Inform all crew members to stay inside the main structure and lock all doors and hatches. It's not a cloud. It's a swarm,' he shouted at his officers.

The swarm moved ever closer, and the first fringes reached the oil tanker. The windows of the bridge turned black as the insects coated them with bodies.

'It's okay,' Taylor said. 'As long as we stay in here we'll be fine.'

He walked over to the windows to get a closer look. *Locusts.* He shivered at their ugliness. 'They're locusts,' he told the bridge crew. 'They are looking for food and will fly off when they don't find any. We just have to wait them out.'

He watched the grasshopper-looking creatures scrabble over the windows looking for a feast. Taylor watched in fascination at the bugs. It wasn't until he noticed that they had started to eat away at the thick Perspex windows that he began to get worried. It started off slowly. Little chips were taken out of the shatter-resistant plastic at random points across the surface. It wasn't long before he was backing away. Unable to look away he backed into the bank of instruments behind him, jolting his lower back.

The first locust broke through the window and headed straight for Taylor. The inch-long insect avoided Taylor's swatting motions and landed on the binoculars still strapped around Taylor's neck. It started to eat the plastic housing as more came through the hole in the window. More holes appeared, and more bugs came through. It wasn't long before the bridge was overwhelmed by the creatures as they ate anything plastic they could find. The crew were on the deck of the bridge trying to keep the mass of insects from suffocating them. Not all managed to.

When there were no more plastic surfaces for them to devour the locusts left through the now open windows to join the ones who couldn't get into the bridge and were forced to scavenge on the superstructure and deck. Polymer fibre ropes, hoses, cable insulation and anything else plastic they could find were gone.

On the bridge, Officer Phillips lifted himself from the deck. Locust carcasses dropped from his hair and shoulders as he stood up to survey the damage. There were so many in the swarm that often the bugs fought over the plastic they could find.

'Captain, Captain, they've gone. Thank fook,' he said.

He walked around the smoking instrument bank to where he had seen Captain Taylor. Taylor was on the ground, unmoving. Phillips turned him over. Squashed locusts stained the Captain's white shirt. A locust wing was trapped in the Captain's closed mouth. Taylor's eyes were glazed and unfocused. Phillips heard other crew members starting to move about behind him. He felt Taylor's neck for a pulse. Nothing. He opened the Captain's mouth and stepped back in shock at the mass of unmoving insects squashed in there. Going for the Captain's dentures? Phillips' head started to spin, a rushing sound assaulted his ears. *Don't ye dare faint, ya ninny.* He shook his head to clear the noise when he realised it was coming from outside. He looked up as a massive wave hit the bow of the ship and flooded over the thousand foot plus main deck and swamped the bridge.

The wave dragged the *Druj Nasu* below the surface and pushed it to the sea bed floor. The tanker stopped with a little impact. Drowned but intact. The wave carried on as though nothing happened. Hitting ports down the African and South American coasts, swamping the offshore oil rigs in the Gulf of Mexico, the large logging camps in the Amazon, and the massive open-pit mines in Chile and Peru. It overtook the swarm as the insects headed to their next target, the Great Pacific Garbage Patch, the 100,000-tonne mass of plastic between California and Hawaii.

At the Cape of Good Hope, the wave met it's Indian Ocean twin. The resulting clash of waves resulted in a four-hundred-foot upsurge the size of Seattle's Space Needle, before dropping back. The Indian Ocean wave had devastated Australia, South Asia and the Middle East, wiping out the oil refineries and rigs in the Persian Gulf. The water mass reversed its course and headed back into the Indian Ocean overwhelming Indonesia and striking the countries in the Pacific Ocean. Japan's nuclear reactors were buried under fifty-foot waves. The water cooled the reactors' cores and stopped the reaction. Clouds of steam marked the graves of the sites. The surge continued its journey wiping out the nuclear reactors dotted along the east coast of China.

***

The man on the bed coughed. He pushed himself up to a sitting position, the sores on his body cleared as he moved. The open wounds closed. The pitted skin on his neck and shoulders straightened taut and smooth. He opened his eyes for the first time in a year. His irises were a deep golden colour, the usually white sclera was still blood-red from the illnesses and diseases he had suffered, but it too was in the process of clearing, milky white swirls washing away the contamination. He opened his mouth, a dry rasping voice cried out, 'What have they done?'

Don't Always Trust the Street Food

He woke suddenly. A tremendous pain behind his eyes, pulsating with every heartbeat, travelling from the front of his head to the base of his skull. Quickly, new agonies revealed themselves as his brain caught up with the messages sent from a thousand tortured nerve endings. His scalp and forehead felt like there was a cut, or ten, the blood already thickened into molasses, slowly drying. His neck and shoulders were screaming, his lower back competing in volume. Struggling to open his eyes as the drying blood had sealed them closed, he did not feel the eyelashes ripping out, the pain drowned out by the rest.

With his eyes finally open, he tried to see where he was. It was very dark with a skinny strip of light coming slightly above him. Beside his head was a small rectangular object, light reflecting off a dead glass screen, he reached for it, gritting his teeth against the pain as the muscles stretched. He grasped the phone in his hand, feeling the sharp ridges of the cracks in the screen against his fingertips. Praying the phone still worked, he pressed the power button. Instantly he was blinded by the glare of the screen, stabbing deep inside his head. He slammed his eyes shut with a curse and waited for the red tinted after-image to diminish. Squinting, he aimed the phone away and looked around, immediately he saw a door where the strip of the light was coming from. It was beige with a slide lock midway up; there were streaks of blue liquid and smears of blood, partially covering upside down signs indicating no smoking and which way to slide the bolt. He lifted his head slightly and saw his bloodied blue jean-clad legs and then his battered Converse trainers aiming towards a smoke detector and a dead light fitting. He dropped his empty hand below him and felt smooth cold metal.

The realisation that he was in a small toilet cubicle hit him fast, quickly followed by the knowledge that he was sprawled above the toilet pan, head down to the side, his neck and shoulders taking the rest of his weight, legs propped inverted against a wall. Deciding a short, sharp shock would be better in the long run and would at least alleviate the pressure, he pushed his legs against the wall and screamed as his muscles and joints awoke, forcing through the pain. Lifting up, so his right shoulder was taking all his weight and pushed off from the wall. He collapsed on the floor like a bundle of rags, wedged in with his face hugging the side of the toilet bowl, like a teenager regretting their first night of excess. Its coolness gave a small relief as the pressure from being upside down subsided. At some point during this, he must have dropped the phone, and everything went black as the screen automatically turned off.

He stayed there on the floor, jeans wrapped around his ankles, sobbing as the blood flowed from his head and neck around his veins, burning as it went, like a thousand needles pricking him all at once. Eventually, it faded, and he groped around for the phone, scraping his fingers on the rough textured metal flooring underneath him. Where can it be? He thought to himself. He reached into the bowl and felt it sitting there. With a heavy sigh of relief that he hadn't accidentally kicked the flush button during his rapid, ungainly descent, he closed his eyes, directed the screen away from him again and pressed the power button. He gently opened his eyes and took stock of his situation.

The cubicle was approximately two foot by three foot. Fortunately, he hadn't started his business before he blacked out, so he didn't have that to deal with. There were bits of toilet paper lying all around, dirty, and crumpled; there was no power or light apart from the 30 seconds or so burst from his phone's screen. There were several bulges to one wall, which looked like a monster had bludgeoned the outside trying to get in. Physically, he was in a state, most parts of his body were alternating between aching and screaming, depending on movement. Mentally, he felt that his facilities seemed intact; however, due to the bashes to his head, he thought he had better check to see if there were any memory issues.

My name is Jonathan Spiers, I usually introduce myself as Jon; I'm thirty-four years old, He remembered. *I've been married to Kayleigh for coming up to seven years now; her Dad was a big fan of Marillion, an Eighties rock band whose lead singer was called Fish; their biggest hit was the song 'Kayleigh', and she was named after that. Fish? That couldn't have been his real name, surely? I'll have to Google it later if I can. We have a child on the way, it's early in the pregnancy, so the sex is unknown, Kayleigh believes it's a boy though, a mother's intuition, I suppose. I co-own a business called Advanced Software Solutions with my business partner, and best friend, Darren Reynolds. A tall, gangly man with unkempt hair and a beard; over-sized, thick-lensed glasses and a never-ending supply of obscure band t-shirts. We've known each other since school; he is the brains of the operation. Darren decided on the business name and insisted we stuck with it, even after I pointed out the obvious problem we would have with the initials.* Jon suppressed a grin at the memory of the argument and continued checking for gaps. *We have created a software package which is selling very successfully in the UK. I am currently presenting it to companies in various European cities. This morning, I was in Seville, Spain, taking a later than planned flight to Lyon in France; having spent a long night with clients watching the local football team lose. On the way back to the hotel, I stopped for a bite to eat at a street stall, whose gambas ajillo, a spicy seafood dish which, while very tasty at the time, didn't agree with my stomach. After a torrid night, the airline was good to let me get on a later flight without too much hassle, or so I thought.* Jon concluded with a rueful smile.

His legs started cramping, curled underneath him, his blood being cut off; there was no way he could stretch them. He placed his hands on the toilet pan rim and pulled his body up. It felt like how he imagined a pensioner feels after a fall, every slight upwards movement a triumph and a battle of will against gravity trying to return him to the floor. Jon managed to raise high enough to shuffle his arms onto the bowl's edge and rested there for a moment; his weight supported by the strength in his forearms and his knees. With his body and thighs no longer trapping his feet and calves, he felt the now familiar surge of blood rushing to them. Jon planted his feet on the floor and pushed his body up using his legs, putting him into a very rough version of the 'downward dog' yoga position – legs reasonably straight, bent at the waist, head down and elbows and arms resting on the toilet. After the deadened feeling left his feet and legs, Jon stood upright for the first time and put an arm out to steady himself. His hand slipped a little in the blood and liquid on the wall, and he staggered into the edge of the toilet bowl, bashing his shins. The unexpected pain made him curse aloud. Still muttering to himself, Jon placed his hand on the door slide lock; remembering to close his eyes as tight as he could to block out the light and slid the bolt open; he slowly pulled the door open towards him.

Gradually Jon opened his eyes, his vision slowly adapting to the glut of light, expecting to see rows of passengers looking back at him with differing expressions of disgust, pity and amusement at his condition. Instead, the cabin of the plane had been sheared away; leaving a two-foot wide ledge. Where the seats and passengers were supposed to be, Jon could see blue sky with slight wisps of clouds. The jagged-edged peaks of a mountain range in the distance hazy from the sun, a vast forest of dark green conifer trees reaching to the snowy alpine summits – a beautiful postcard image. In the middle distance, he saw an earthy plateau covered in wreckage. A long straight gouge scoured in the earth like a child's finger across a carton of ice cream. The fuselage of the plane, in pieces. Scattered. Spilling seats, luggage, and debris like confetti at a wedding. Jon stared, mouth open wide, as his gaze brought in details closer to his field of vision. A drinks cart dented and upended, its wheels pointed to the skies, miniature bottles of spirits, mixers and overpriced snacks dispersed around it, a crude imitation of the tableau before him. Banks of seats tossed aside with unmoving passengers still strapped in place, limbs in unnatural positions posed like mannequins abandoned in a warehouse, their faces thankfully blurred at this distance. There was no noise coming from below, and there wasn't any wind buffeting him; the silence gave the scene an unworldly, but not inappropriate, solemn feel.

Jon grimaced at what he saw and turned away. Facing the cockpit, he was stunned to see the door wrenched open by dark grey rock like a shark's fin cutting through the ocean as it chases down its prey. The metal opening bulged outwards as the pressure of the impact moulded it like a metallic second skin. Next to the doorway were the plane's galley lockers, which always reminded Jon of the banks of morgue lockers in American crime movies, only containing blankets, food and pillows instead of refrigerated corpses. Opposite the lockers, Jon saw his metallic, filthy sanctuary and fought the urge to retreat inside, to close the door and hide away until help came. He went to the edge of the cabin to see how high up he was and whether he could make his way down to the plateau. He got down on all fours, *no need to risk falling out*, he thought. With his body still aching and fragile he shuffled across and looked down. He was at least twenty feet off the ground with jagged rock and thick brambles between the cabin and the ground. It would be impossible to get down there, so he was stuck where he was.

Not knowing how long he would have to wait to be rescued. Jon decided, while it was still daylight, to see what was in the lockers and settle down as comfortably as he could. There were two rows of three cabinets, he unclicked the fasteners on the one closest to him and pulled it out. It was reasonably heavy, stainless steel and covered in various semi-peeled sticky labels, in it were several travel bags of different shapes, some featuring the airline logo, presumably owned by the cabin crew, a creeping chill travelled up his arms, making his hairs rise, and Jon decided to leave them out of respect. He moved on to the second one. In this there were some flattened pillows in cellophane and a couple of worn orange blankets, he removed these and placed them to one side. The last locker was missing; Jon figured it was probably the one he saw in the field below and reached for the locker above it in the next row. This was smaller than the bottom ones. He placed it on the floor and opened it, inside was perfumes, aftershaves and watches. He closed the door and slid it across the floor, he must have used too much force as it teetered on the edge and fell onto the rocks below. The crashing sound loud and harsh in the still air. Guiltily, he moved to the next locker, he left the locker in place and opened the front.

Inside were stacks of cardboard boxes with 'tasty snack box' in fancy print on the lid. *This is more like it*, he thought. Inside the box were: a packet of plain crisps, a small pack of crackers, and an even smaller foil-wrapped portion of soft cheese. Crushed with disappointment, Jon opened the final locker. This only contained sheets of paper; the top one read 'Toilet Sanitation Checklist'. Jon closed it and pulled it out of the row. He carefully placed it on the floor against the side of the cabin, sat down on it, and put his head in his hands.

After a while, Jon looked up, tear streaks ran down his face, blood and blue smears smudged by the wet and his hands creating a ghostly sheen to his cheeks and forehead. He shivered and reached for a blanket. As he wrapped it around his shoulders he jolted as he realised in the far distance he could hear a mechanical noise, like a far-off neighbour mowing their lawn on a sunny weekend morning, slowly and steadily, get closer.

At Night

I t's time. I dragged myself out from underneath the bed; my nails gripped the fluffy pink carpet. Through the gloom, I saw the dolls and teddy bears lying misshapen on the floor looking like bloated, discarded corpses from the Soul Eater, their limbs and heads at unnatural angles. I licked my lipless mouth and smiled. *This is my favourite time.* I savoured the moment; the smell of innocence surrounding the room: that delicate perfume before the children become cynical and sullen teenagers, the perfume of dreams. I rose up from the floor; my long spindly legs placed either side of the bed. I pinched the duvet cover between stretched fingers and lifted it up with delicate care.

'Where is she?' I roared.

This doesn't happen. This is not right. I feel cheated, my heart torn to shreds. I need to breathe the child's slumbered breath to give me life. I need to stroke the child's straw-like hair to feel alive.

'Blade! Rot! Come out here now!' I shouted.

A creak from the wardrobe, a foot appeared, toes like talons. The rest followed slick and sleek like a falcon through the air. A face from hell emerged, a mouth with razor sharp teeth and piercing silver eyes. From the chest of drawers with raspberry handles the middle drawer opened an inch. A fetid smell emanated and filled the room, removing the innocence. Twisted hands clutched the drawer edge, the reddish-brown skin skewbald and oozing in places, the nails black with grime. The drawer fell to the piled floor with a muffled thump, followed by a creature from Hades, deformed and demented, a wicked hunchback with bulbous veined eyes and long, dank, dark hair.

'Spider, what's up?' Rot asked.

I could smell his foul breath from across the room, as he spoke I could see the blackened remnants of his teeth. I felt my gorge rise. I held my nose with my thin fingers. It's not just his stench that offends. His use of everyday vernacular instead of the, oh so much, better traditional speech patterns of our kind grated my insides.

'It's not our time yet,' Blade hissed his voice a rasping whisper sawing through the air.

'Which one of you has taken her?' I asked.

'She's gone?' A screeching wail from Rot. It feels genuine, *I have a sense of these things.* We both looked at Blade.

'Hey, don't look at me. I haven't taken her,' He raised his arms and opened them wide in innocence, the sharp dagger-like fingers spread out. 'Why would I after all these years?'

'I know what happened,' A small voice from above called out.

We all looked up at the lampshade, my neck creaked at the unfamiliar action.

'Who the fuck are you?' Rot asked. I'm sure Blade was thinking the same thing. I know I was.

168

'I am Murk, the Night Terror,' The tiny figure looked at us like we were supposed to be impressed. 'I steal the dreams of children, feast on their fear, and ravish their hopes.' He added.

'   I'm Spider, this is Rot and Blade,' I said.

'Where is she and what have you done with her?' Blade's voice rustled the still air with menace.

'I didn't take her,' Murk protested.

I reached up with one long arm and plucked him from the rose-coloured shade. I held him between my fingers and peered at him. My eyes are not what they used to be. I squinted and could make out a six, no seven, armed creature with tiny fangs.

'Put me down!' He squealed.

I flicked him onto the duvet cover; he landed next to the purple pony's mane. He scrambled to his feet and started scurrying away. Blade reached down and trapped one of Murk's arms under a fingernail.

'Not so fast. Little man. Where is she?'

'I... I... don't know where she is, but I know what happened,' Murk stammered.

'Tell us,' Rot said as he leant into to look at the creature.

'Okay, okay, back off, please. I can't breathe. I'll tell you.'

'Make it the truth or Blade here will disarm you, piece by piece,' I threatened.

'It was a few hours ago. She had just been tucked in by her parents and I was waiting for her breathing to change. I heard some loud thumps coming from the other room and in burst two men waking her. She cried out and one of the men slapped her. The sound was awful.' Murk started crying.

'Keep going,' My voice was flat and calm, even though I was boiling inside. How fucking dare they touch her. I will rip them to shreds. I will gorge on their guts. I will bathe in their blood.

'They tied her up and carried her out of the room. I don't know what happened next. I stayed up there,' Five of his arms pointed at the lampshade in unison. 'I didn't know what to do.'

'How long have you been here?' Rot asked, his putrid breath reminded why we had banished him to the last shift. A decade of decay. *It's just too much, brush or even bleach once a while. I've got to get out of here.*

'I've been here coming up to five years when she was moved out of the cot into the big bed,' Murk said.

'How come we have never seen you?'

'I visit her after you guys. It's not the nicest time thanks to that guy,' His free arms pointed to Rot. 'But, if I used one arm to cover my mouth and another to hold my nose it's bearable.'

'Come on fellas, enough about our newest neighbour we have to get her back,' I said in pain, my body ached from her absence already.

I strode to the door and turned the handle. This was new territory for me. I was born under her bed, a result of her sister's first nightmare, ten-twelve years ago. I had never left the bedroom before. *Why would I? Her sister moved into the other room when my angel was born, since then the girl has been mine.* I pulled open the door and was immediately hit with the metallic stench of blood. The hallway was dark, through the gloom I could see three doors and stairs leading down. I went to the door closest to me and pushed it open, I saw my visage reflected in the bathroom mirror and I smiled, enjoying the view of the perfect fangs smiling back at me. No child though. Blade and Rot had followed me and they opened the other doors. The odour of blood was stronger now and had mingled with the lingering malodour emanating from Rot. I couldn't bear it and vomited onto the tiled bathroom floor. Dark bile splattered up the side of the bath. I spat into the toilet and wiped my mouth with my arm. I closed the door.

'Rot, get back in there,' I pointed a long arm at the child's bedroom. 'I can't be around you anymore. If we need you we'll call.'

Rot, to his credit, did as he was told. I went over to Blade and looked past his shoulder in the room. The sister. She looked peacefully asleep in bed, only the thin red line across her throat indicated otherwise. I felt a pang of loss. I had, after all, enjoyed many nights of terrorising her until she became too old to fear "the monsters".

'This shit is fucked up,' Blade's voice was a harsh slither. His fingers clinked together as his hands opened and closed. *I know how you're feeling, I want to tear someone, anyone. Wrench their soul from their body, taste their tears.*

'Yep,' I say. What else can I say?

I walked over to the final doorway. The smell of blood was far stronger here. I could sense Blade follow behind. I looked

171

around the room. *Wow, they really went to town in here, didn't they?* Blood covered every surface. I saw what was left of Mum and Dad, their bodies split and open to the world. I thought of all the times I've spent with them, the nursery rhymes and the lullabies to the sister and the child. I vomited for the second time of the night. Black tar spewed from the very depths of my stomach. Blade didn't say anything. When I was done I coughed and spat until my mouth and throat were clear.

I looked back at Blade, he raised a hand and mimed slitting his throat with his razor-edged finger. I nodded and said, 'That, and worse.'

He shook his head, a deep frown on his face. 'Downstairs?'

'I can't sense anyone down there. No movement in the air. I think whoever the men were they've gone and so is the child.'

Blade punched the wall beside him, again and again. He made deep grooves in the plaster that quickly filled with blood from his knuckles. I placed a hand on his shoulder.

'I know,' I said. 'I know.' My voice wavered, I removed my shaking hand.

'Spider, what are we going to do now?' His voice was full of anguish. 'What are we going to do?'

I don't know how to continue without the child. My hunger for her terror is what keeps me going. Night after night I feed. The thought of not having that anymore filled me with despair. I cried out, the sound echoed through the house. I came to a decision.

I looked at Blade and pointed behind him. 'What's that?'

He turned his head to see and I closed my eyes. I pictured the child snuggled up tight in her purple cover, a gentle smile on her face. My eyes opened, and I grabbed Blade's hand, oblivious to the cuts it made in my hand. I brought the hand with its cutthroat fingers up to the side of my head. I paused for a fraction of a second. A heartbeat of time. *Goodbye my love.* Then rammed the sharpened digits into my temple. They sliced through the thin bone like a samurai's katana and I dropped to the floor in a shapeless heap.

The State of Prolonged Mutual Hostility

The car sped up to eighty-five miles per hour as Jeff undertook the blue Nissan Micra, it had been in front of him for the past eleven miles, his frustration at the delay the slow vehicle had caused was exacerbated by what was happening in the back seats.

'Jeff, aren't you going a little fast?' Sandra asked from the passenger seat beside him, her hands tightly clasped together, the knuckles white.

'I just have to get past this Sunday driver; he's been driving me mad going so slow for so long,' Jeff said. 'I'll slow down in a second or two. Have to get away-'

'Boys, quiet back there!' Sandra shouted, tilting her head, 'Sorry darling, you were saying?' Sandra brushed a lock of blonde hair away from her face which had come loose from the movement.

'Don't worry about it, I've slowed now. Boys! Your mum has just told you to stop, listen to her!'

'Michael pinched me,' Thomas said, his voice whiney and tight.

'You punched me first,' retorted Michael. 'Mum! He's doing it again, make him stop!' Michael started screaming with rage, banging his head against the car seat headrest, fighting the seat-belt restraint for freedom from his tormentor beside him.

'Shut up, both of you! Any more and I'll take away your iPads,' Jeff threatened. It was a hollow threat as the tablets were the only thing that gave Jeff and Sandra a momentary pause from the chaos behind them. Michael stopped screaming instantly.

'Mine isn't an iPad,' said Michael, with a matter of fact tone. 'It's a Kindle Fire.'

'At this minute I don't care, Michael. I am trying to concentrate on driving.'

'You haven't got an iPad because Mum and Dad don't love you as much,' said Thomas. Jeff heard a mouthed raspberry from behind him and then a wail from Michael.

'Boys, let your Dad drive, it's been a long day already and we're nearly home.'

***

Thomas and Michael were twins, and had been together for the past six years, even in Sandra's womb they bickered and fought, kicking her bladder, her ribs, her stomach and her spine. They never let up. Sandra had to be hospitalised twice due to their violence. Once born, the boys were identical in both appearance and in their hatred for each other. As babies they fought in the twin buggy meaning Jeff and Sandra had to buy them individual ones, they slept in different cots and refused to feed or sleep at the same time. As they got older the demands increased: their matching sandy coloured hair had to be styled differently from each other. They refused to wear similar clothes to each other, refused to eat the same foods, never wanted to be read the same story at bedtime, never wanted to watch the same programme on television. When they started school two years ago they were separated into different classes within a week. With the arguing, and the fighting, they were lucky not to be excluded from the school.

Jeff and Sandra had tried everyone: Their health visitor, the local GP, Social Services, even child behaviour experts. No one could help. Individually, the boys were the sweetest, most loving children you could ever meet. They were polite, helpful, very bright and well-read for their age; even their social worker praised their charisma and charm, she soon changed that opinion when she met them together. Together they were chaos.

This trip to Great Yarmouth was a chance for Jeff and Sandra to try and regain some control, taking the boys out of their environment. Somewhere new. Hoping the boys would be too excited to be their normal belligerent selves, but it had turned into a disaster. They had started before they had even left their street. Michael deciding that he wanted to sit behind his mum, where Thomas was sitting. Jeff pulled the car over and swapped the boys over. Thomas was so annoyed at being moved that he kicked the back of Jeff's chair the entire length of the journey. Two hours later they arrived at the holiday camp, rows and rows of caravans of differing sizes greeted their arrival. They stopped outside reception and upon leaving the car to check in and get the keys Jeff felt a twinge in his back, his knees buckled and he had to sit back down, Sandra went to the reception and got the keys, she took Thomas and decided to leave Michael in the car to keep Jeff company. Thomas was, of course, a delight without Michael; the staff in reception loved him and treated him to extra games vouchers and money off tickets for the camp's restaurant. It seemed to Sandra that she spent more time apart from Jeff, separating the boys, than they ever spent together. Surely, parenthood shouldn't be this hard. She thought.

The holiday went the way everything did with Michael and Thomas. The enclosed space of the caravan seemed to aggravate their worst qualities even more, resulting in each boy being banished to separate ends of the caravan. The sea air and running around the beach, instead of tiring them, seemed to give them an energy of malevolence they never had at home. There were instances of sand thrown in each other's faces, driftwood fights, cold, wet seaweed down the back of each other's t-shirts. The parents were exhausted. The children didn't stop during the night either. Lying in bed, praying for sleep, they could hear the boys through the thin caravan walls sniping and shouting at each other. Jeff and Sandra had a frank and earnest discussion during the early hours about how they were going to continue. They couldn't go on like this. Their relationship had deteriorated so much, they were almost strangers, and it was not good for the boys to grow up in this environment either. They decided to cut the holiday short and return home early, they had some serious discussion to do when they got home.

'Mum, Thomas won't let go of my hand,' said Michael.

'Thomas let go of your brother's hand. Just leave each other alone,' Sandra said.

'I'm not doing anything,' Thomas said. 'It's Michael who won't let go. He's pulling my arm.'

'Mum, he's pulling my arm. Stop it Thomas.'

'Owwwww it hurts, Mum, help,' said Thomas.

'Jeff, I think we need to pull over to deal with this. I'll swap with one of them.'

Jeff indicated and slowed down waited for a gap in the traffic and moved to the inside lane looking for a layby where they could stop. Sandra undid her seat belt and turned around in her seat to look at the children.

'JEFF STOP NOW!' Sandra screamed.

Jeff pulled the car onto the hard shoulder of the road, the tires crunching through the rough stones, the car slowed to a stop. He undid his belt and turned to see what was happening behind him. He couldn't understand what he was seeing. The twins' arms were joined together, flesh and bone fused into one limb connected at the wrist, their hands slowly melding into one. The boys were straining against their seat belt restraints, their bodies arched towards each other, the fabric strap dug deep into their chest. Jeff leant forward, reaching into the back seat to undo

Thomas' seatbelt. Following his lead, Sandra opened her door and went to Michael's side, she opened the door and reached around Michael, trying to avoid looking at the horror unfolding, she undid the clasp and he was free. At the same time Jeff undid Thomas'. Clear of the restraints the boys flew out of their car seats, as though propelled by an immense magnetic force. Their forearms, stomach, chests and legs were touching, Thomas' left joining with Michael's right and vice versa. Their clothes tearing at the seams as their bodies joined.

Sandra was screaming, Michael was screaming Thomas was screaming, Jeff was screaming. The inside of the car was a cacophony of noise. The boy's faces edged closer together, their noses touched and stuck together, an unknown force pushing them together, their chests together. They stopped screaming as their mouths dissolved into one. Sandra turned away and vomited to the side of the car. Jeff shut his eyes to spare him from the terror he was witnessing. All screaming stopped; the sudden silence was punctured by the occasional wretch from Sandra.

An angelic voice came from the back seat, 'Mum, Dad, it's ok, we're together now, this is how it was supposed to be.'

Jeff slowly opened his eyes; he blinked a few times and shook his head.

'A- a- are you Thomas or Michael?' Jeff asked.

'We are both. We are us… Please don't cry Dad, it's good. We're not fighting now.' the dark haired boy sitting on the back seat, between the car seats said, with a kind smile on his lips.

'We love you, Mum and Dad.'

Thoughts and Prayers

Officers Carl Jenkins and Richard Mullins entered the school building with their guns drawn. Jenkins crossed the familiar threshold of the main entrance. He had been here countless times: first with a backpack strapped to his back, then as a parent attending PTA meetings and basketball games. Mullins was ahead checking line of sights.

'North corridor, clear,' Mullins said, stopping at the junction with the east corridor.

'Check.' Jenkins overlapped him, staying outside his range of fire. He turned into the east corridor, his eyes searched for threats, near and far. 'Clear,' he said.

'Check.'

They made their way along the corridor, checking in classrooms as they went. Any cowering teachers and children were directed to exit through the main entrance and stay at the gate for assistance from paramedics and officers when they arrived. The officers went into Jenkins' old homeroom, where Mrs Miller was standing against the far wall away from the door and the windows. Fear had made her look completely different to the woman Jenkins had known for over twenty years. He only recognised her when she spoke. Her voice was so familiar to him that it was eerie to hear it come from a stranger's face. Jenkins told her which way to take the half a dozen children hunkered in the corner of the room, and she stroked his face as she passed.

'Thank you, Carl. Be safe.' Her touch was cold, as though the fear had drained her of blood.

'You too, Miss Miller,' he said. Even after all these years, I couldn't bring myself to call her by her first name.

His shoulder radio squawked for an update. As he answered it, he shooed Mrs Miller out of the room, gesturing for them to stay low.

'Officer Mullens and I are clearing the east corridor, directing survivors out the main entrance. No shots heard. No contact with the shooter and no victims seen. Is there an update on backup?'

'Backup is arriving on scene now; paramedics are on their way, in case,' Margery, the dispatcher, said, her voice an octave higher from the stress of the situation. *I didn't blame her; my heart was racing too.*

He heard a muffled crack of a shot. Both he and Mullins instinctively ducked at the sound. Jenkins informed dispatch, and they left the classroom. They headed further down the corridor past the rows of red lockers and locked classroom doors. Another shot sounded out. It echoed down the halls.

'I think it's coming from the cafeteria,' Jenkins said.

'It's your home ground. You take the lead,' Mullins said. His breathing was heavy and rapid.

'Thanks,' Jenkins attempted a smile of reassurance; but stopped as he realised it was more of a grimace. 'Stay frosty,

Rich,' I had brought the phrase to the partnership as a throwback to my high school football days. Even at the state final, I don't think my heart was beating as fast as this, my mind kept wandering. Jenkins could see some of the tension come out of his partner's posture.

'Ice cold, Carl, ice cold.' Mullins finished the expression with a smile.

They used this as a way of lightening the mood and to keep each other focused and calm. *Focus*, Jenkins told himself. It didn't work. *This was my school. I know, at least by sight, the entire faculty and many the students. My son, Spence, is a senior here.* At the thought of his name, Jenkins felt sick. He felt the same as when dispatch had said the name of the school over the radio, he had put the feelings away, locked them up, but now they had returned with a vengeance: A ball of ice in his stomach that froze his heart, and shrivelled his balls. He momentarily closed his eyes to regain control. Images of Spence flashed before him. *In the hospital, in my arms, the first day of kindergarten, his refusal to let go of my hand, his first catch, fingers clawed on the ball.* His thoughts went back to the night before and the argument they had had. The last he had seen his only son. The last words they said to each other.

Spence had come through the back door with a scowl on his face, he closed the door with force and stomped straight through the kitchen without a word to Jenkins, sitting at the breakfast nook with a sandwich.

'Hi, Spence!' Jenkins called after him. Nothing, apart the sound of his bedroom door slamming. This was unusual behaviour for him, normally an outgoing child. Jenkins still thought of Spence as a child, but his son was already eighteen and taller than him. Spence was the star athlete at Newton High. *In far better physical shape than I'd ever been at school.* A thought flashed through his mind, *steroids*, but he quickly dismissed it. *Spence is fully aware of the dangers of those things. I made sure of it.* Jenkins went upstairs to see what the matter was. He knocked on the door, 'Spence? Is everything alright?'

'It's fine Dad. Just give me some space, please.'

He would have entered if it wasn't for the pleading nature of the 'please'. *Give him space; he'll talk to me later once he's calmed down.* They had a close relationship, made even closer since the death of Marie, four years ago. Cancer. It had been quick, *thank God.* Jenkins didn't think he could have coped with a long drawn out decline, watching the woman he loved wither and decay. They found out in April, just after Easter and she was gone before Independence Day. He stayed strong for Spence. He only let go one weekend and allowed himself to grieve. It was four months after Marie had passed. His brother, Jerry, took Spence hunting and Jenkins stayed home with a couple of bottles of Jack Daniels for company and drank the pain away. He wasn't much for hunting anyway. He liked the outdoors, the quietness and the clear air. But the guns he could do without. Unusually for the area, he didn't keep guns at home, save for his service revolver which was kept locked away. *I've seen what they can do to people.* Jerry was the opposite: a complete gun nut, a card-carrying NRA member, with bumper stickers on his car.

He left Spence in his room and went downstairs. Later, Jenkins heard him come down and cornered him by the fridge.

'Is everything alright, Spence?'

'Yeah, Dad. Just leave it, ok.'

'You sure? Coach treating you ok? I know he thinks he's a badass.'

'Yeah, it's nothing.'

'Have you decided on college yet? The deadline for acceptance is coming up.' Spence had been accepted to every college he had applied for. Recruiters had been making the trek up here all year offering sports scholarships and the occasional illegal kickback.

'God Dad, just leave me alone. Everything is fine.'

'Is it to do with Adrienne?' Adrienne Kirkland was Spence's girlfriend; they had been together since they were sophomores.

'Leave. Me. Alone.' Each word was said with a fist slammed to the countertop, making the stacked crockery jump, then pushed past and stormed upstairs. Jenkins took a step to follow him, but something held him back. Maybe, it was the look in his son's eyes. A look of pain, hurt, and anger that Jenkins had not seen in him before. Maybe it was the sudden violence. *I don't know. I wish now I had gone to him and held him. I may never see him alive again.*

Another shot, then a second, woke him from his thoughts, he opened his eyes.

'Come on Rich. Let's get this guy.' He left the classroom with purpose and headed down the corridor in the direction of the gunfire.

As they got closer to the cafeteria, Jenkins saw children lying on the ground, some were moving, too many were not. The air was heavy with a smell of cordite and blood. Mullins called into his radio for backup and paramedics. They quietly told the children to move down the corridor to the main entrance. *Thankfully I don't recognise any of them. Not one of them is Spence. I'm not sure what I'll do if...* He shook his head at the thought. *Enough of that. You have children to save. That is your duty. They need your protection.*

Another shot. Jenkins heard screaming coming from the cafeteria. It was a horrible sound. Children's screams that climb in the ear and gnaw at the brain. It made thinking hard, and adrenaline kicks in. The urge to protect, the impulse to rush in, was too strong. Jenkins felt his body moving. Mullins placed his hand on Jenkins' chest, stopping him. Mullins knew what Jenkins was thinking. He bent to his ear.

'We do this by the book. Cover and back each other up. It's for our safety and the safety of the kids in there.'

Jenkins nodded his agreement and took point. He pushed the heavy door of the cafeteria open with care and entered, his heart beating fast, a tremor in his hands. The cafeteria was large and L-shaped, sunlight streamed in through the large windows at the far end of the hall. Jenkins took immediate cover behind a wide pillar to his left. Mullins took the one to the right. Jenkins noticed blood on the floor, drips, splatters and occasional pools. He looked around the pillar and saw the rows of tables and benches. They stretched out in three straight lines the length of the hall. There were children slumped over at random intervals, their heads in their trays blood pooling underneath. Children were laying in the aisles between the tables. He looked to the centre of the hall where the popular kids would be. Where everyone could see them, and where Spence would be. He felt sick; there were bodies around there, more there than anywhere else in the hall. Letterman jackets, school books, and pompoms lay abandoned on the table, and on the floor.

Another shot and screaming. Jenkins gestured for Mullins to move up along his side of the cafeteria. Jenkins stalked the other. The bend of the 'L' was to the right of the hall, where the kitchens and food serving stations were. The officers used the tables for cover, their shoes slipping in the blood. Jenkins came alongside the popular table and looked for Spence. He couldn't see him. Instead, he saw Brad Nicholson, the massive linebacker, face down, head in his food tray, blood dripping into the pudding cup. He'd been accepted to Cal Tech. Next to him, Leshawn Johnson, the fastest running back in the school's history, would have been going to Penn State. Now a ragged line of bullet holes across his chest. Spence's friends. *Where are Spence and Adie?* He moved past the table and saw her. Laid out on the floor, a dark red stain on the cream cheerleading outfit, shot through the heart, shot in the face, her arms and legs at strange angles like an abandoned marionette. *Oh, God.* He retched, feeling the bile burn his throat. Tears came to his eyes. *She is like a daughter. I know her parents Mitch and Tammy, I go drinking with Mitch each week. How can I face them if Spence lives and their beautiful daughter has been slaughtered?*

Jenkins shook his head and continued. *I must find the shooter and stop him.* He reached the point of the cafeteria where he could start to see the rest of the 'L'. He would be more exposed to the shooter here. He ducked down lower using the tables as cover. Along the far wall he saw a line of children sat against the wall, he looked for Spence. He wasn't there. The children, aged between fourteen and eighteen, sat there in tears or with their faces held in their shaking hands. The cafeteria doors opened, and Jenkins looked back, seeing that backup had arrived, *finally*. He looked at Mullins and mouthed 'cover me' to him. He popped up from behind the tables and ran to the column in front of him. It was in full view from the kitchens. Shots sounded out, and Jenkins felt the passage of the bullets behind him as he ran. He reached the pillar and shrunk behind it, minimising his profile.

'Can you see him?' Mullins called out.

Jenkins risked a glance, prayed the shooter wouldn't fire. He saw bodies in front of the man, seven, eight, maybe ten. He saw a young girl knelt in front of the shooter, crying and pleading for him to let her go. He saw the AR-15 assault rifle, black and sleek in the shooter's hands. He saw the man's black jeans, maroon Newtown High sweatshirt. He saw tears running down the face he seen every day for the past eighteen years, changing from a baby into the young man he was now. It was Spence. He couldn't tear his eyes away. *Spencer? No, no, no. This can't be true. My baby.*

'Dad?' he heard him say.

'Mullins, it's Spence. My God. It's Spence.'

He heard Mullins ask him to repeat. He was unable to answer him. Unable to process. *How could my boy be capable of such a thing?* His radio crackled, and it woke him from his stupor.

'Spence,' he called out, 'put your gun down, and we'll talk. It's not too late to sort this out.'

'Oh Dad,' his voice broke as he spoke. 'I killed her. She cheated on me, so I killed her. I was so angry. She cheated on me with Brad last summer while I was at camp. Everyone knew; they were laughing at me.'

'Put the gun down, let the children go. We can talk about this.' Mullins called out.

'Uncle Richard?' Spence had called Mullins 'uncle' since Jenkins, and he had become partners eight years ago.

'Spence?' Mullins said, there was a touch of incredulity in his voice. 'Come on let's talk about this. Put the gun down.'

'No, I can't. The SWAT team will kill me if I do.'

'There is no SWAT, it's just your Dad and me.' Jenkins could see Mullins waving to the officers making their way down the hall. Telling them to hold up.

'Spence, where did you get the gun?' Jenkins asked.

'Uncle Jerry.'

'He gave you the gun?'

'No, I asked him, and he refused. He said he was going to tell you. I stopped him before he could. I'm so sorry Dad.'

My brother? His lopsided grin and stupid face flashed before Jenkins' eyes in the blink of an eye. Jenkins felt rage building inside him, twenty-thirty-forty voices, one of them his brother's, screaming for vengeance. He saw his child holding a baseball bat – he saw his child holding a rifle. The image kept switching between the two. He stepped out from the pillar, his gun aimed at Spence.

Mullins stepped out too. 'Let them go, Spence. Drop the rifle. It's over.' His gun was also aimed at Spence.

Jenkins moved closer, and he saw the rifle in his son's arms lower, its muzzle pointed to the ground, away from the girl in front of him, and away from the children against the wall.

'Drop it, Spence,' Mullins repeated.

Jenkins heard the clatter of the rifle on the tiled floor of the cafeteria. He saw Mullins spring forward and kick the rifle away. He heard Mullins tell the children to go. Jenkins was focused on Spence. Peripherally he watched the children stream past him to safety, a blur running to freedom, His son the constant. Standing in front of the kitchen with his hands up, palms bloody, like a surgeon. Jenkins saw he was still aiming the gun at Spence. He saw his brother, Adie, her parents, Spence's friends, and classmates. He saw his wife, Marie. She serenely nodded to him, the slightest movement. His hand began to shake. He brought his free hand up to support his hold on the gun, to steady his aim. *I love you Spence, but I cannot bear to see you live, not after this, may God have mercy on me.* Jenkins pulled the trigger, once, twice. He then collapsed in a ball on the ground, mirroring his child, not hearing Mullins calling to him, or his radio screaming for updates.

Gang Aft A-gley

*T*he meteoroid streaked across the twilight sky, a dark smoky trail following, stretching across the horizon, breaking up the orange, red, blue and purple shades of the setting sun. Vehicles stopped, and people left their cars to watch it as it passed, they would be talking about this to their partner and children when they got home, and it would be the hottest topic on the nightly news shows and be on the front page of all the newspapers in the morning. It was already the trending subject on Facebook, and #asteroid had rocketed its way to the most used hashtag on Twitter for the year so far, as pictures and videos of the meteoroid were shared across social media platforms worldwide.

At the Planetary Defense Coordination Office in Washington, D.C., they were overseeing the path of the meteoroid.

'At current, the object is following the prearranged path with only a 0.015% variance, which is within parameters, speed is at 9.6 km per second and slowing,' Eddie Howes, the technician watching the progress on his monitor, said nervously into the microphone dangling from the ceiling.

The event was broadcast to, not only, the audience in the gallery: an intimidating spectrum of politicians, both domestic and foreign, and military dignitaries, but also via the internet to the President and various Heads of State across the globe, and their advisors.

'At projected rates, the time of impact will be in six minutes thirteen seconds,' Eddie's supervisor, Liz Kendall, said clearly and confidently into her microphone. 'This tallies with the estimated impact time given by NASA, allowing for a tolerance of plus or minus five seconds.'

'Speed is down to 8.4 km per second, variance 0.018%,' Eddie intoned as he tried to keep the excitement and nerves out of his voice, on this momentous occasion. It would not be a fine image to send to future generations listening to this moment to have his voice quavering all over the place for posterity.

'Time of impact: five minutes thirty-five seconds,' Liz said, apparently effortlessly, much to Eddie's dismay.

'Speed is reduced to 7.5 km per sec…,' Eddie hesitated, suddenly thrown by the information displaying on the monitor, '…ond, variance 2.05% and rising.' His tone and pitch rising.

In the gallery, above the control centre, there is sudden consternation and what had been a respectful silence, almost akin to a congregation at a sermon, changed as hushed tones of disbelief getting louder as the realisation of a possible catastrophe occurring before their very eyes struck.

Back in the control centre, telephones were ringing; their insistent calling ignored as the various technicians were frantically taping away at their keyboards, running diagnostics and replaying the last minute on their systems, trying to determine what had happened. Mission Controller Joseph Canton from the back of the room was asking what happened, but no one gave him an answer. Eddie could only continue his litany as the meteoroid veered off course. 'Speed 6.6 km per second, variance 10.5%.' He risked a glance at Liz and was unsurprised by the lack of emotion shown on her face, always the cool professional, he thought, with admiration, and strove to match his delivery to hers.

'Impact in four minutes and fifty-seven seconds,' She said assured and unperturbed. As she said this, she looked at Eddie and with a supportive nod urged him to continue.

'Ummm…' Eddie temporised. 'Speed reduced to 5.3 km, variance at 17.65% and growing.' He continued with more confidence in his voice.

'Where is it going to hit?' Caton asked, his voice rose to be heard above the cacophony around him.

'Current projections are that the meteoroid is heading to Europe. We are trying to narrow that down further,' A technician further down the line, spoke up.

'Come on people,' Caton cajoled. 'We need to know this immediately.'

'Speed reduced to 4.6 km, variance at 23%,' said Eddie.

'Time to impact four minutes three seconds,' Liz added.

Eddie and Liz continued their readings on the course of the meteoroid at regular intervals. Aware of the commotion behind them, trying their best to block it out as they kept to their tasks.

'Time to impact two minutes sixteen seconds.'

'Mr Caton, we estimate that the meteoroid will impact with 5688.54 joules energy which is equivalent to 1.36 megatons. This is based on the diameter of the meteoroid, the assumed density of the rock and the estimated speed of impact,' said Professor Robertson, of MIT. He was hunched over a table covered in sheets of paper with rough calculations scrawled over them, surrounded by the rest of the mathematical boffins, invited to attend this historic event, 'depending on where the meteoroid strikes the casualty count could be enormous,' he concluded.

'Speed reduced to 3.2 km per second, and variance is at 27%,' Eddie said shocked at what he had just heard.

'Time to im…impact one minute and twenty-six seconds,' Liz slightly stuttered as she too reacted to what she had just heard.

'Where is it going to land?' Caton demanded.

'We're working on it,' Professor Robertson said.

'Speed reduced to 1.6 km per second. Variance has slowed to 28%.'

'Time to impact fifty-six seconds.'

'France… it's France,' Robertson called out.

Eddie and Liz looked at each other, their eyes wide, mouths open. Mirrored expressions of terror. 'Oh God,' Liz said.

Eddie could no longer read out the numbers; his vision blurred with tears. He wiped his eyes, blinked a few times. He looked over at Liz, her shoulders were shaking, and tears were streaming down her face. He took off his headset and walked over to her. He placed an arm around her shoulders, and she buried her face in his chest. He held her tight, watching the digits reduce.

***

The meteoroid passed over the Casbah in Agadir, the illuminated inscription "God, Country, King" in Arabic on the hill was obscured by smoke. It carried on its journey, flying over Marrakesh and then on to the European mainland. It flew past Malaga, Zaragoza, and crossed the Pyrenees mountain range. Hopes were raised that it would crash into Aneto, the largest peak but the meteoroid passed by twenty-two miles to the west. It crossed into France on a curved northerly trajectory, its altitude swiftly dropping as its speed fell away. It passed over the *Cité de l'espace* theme park, dedicated to the space and the conquest of space, just outside of Toulouse, It flew three hundred and fifty foot above the proposed site of the *Occitanie* Tower, and if construction had been completed to schedule, it would have smashed two thirds up the building, spreading debris for miles around. The tower would have offered as much defence against the mass of the meteoroid as a blade of grass does against the plastic line of a garden strimmer. The meteoroid continued its way through the French countryside. It reached the eastern apex of the curve within sight of Lyon and continued its inexorable journey. It passed over the woods and lakes of the *Parc Naturel Régional du Morvan*, swinging its way round to its ultimate destination.

It ripped through the trees in the *Forêt de Sénart*, the ones it didn't tear out of the ground were set alight in its path. It struck land just outside of the Orly district. Four kilometres from the *Aéroport de Paris-Orly*. The impact of the 1.3-kilometre meteorite caused a seismic blast that was felt in the centre of Paris, sixteen kilometres away within three seconds. The blast caused buildings to crumble into rubble, shattered all windows in a twenty-five kilometres diameter, including the stained glass windows of

Notre Dame Cathedral, and the glass pyramids of the Louvre museum. The Pont Neuf bridge, with its railings adorned with thousands of lover's padlocks, broke up and fell into the river below. The same fate happened to its brothers. The statue of Henry IV on horseback slid off its plinth and charged, echoing scenes from the Battle of Arques and the fight against *La Ligue Catholique*. The Eiffel Tower was jerked out of its foundations and crashed down bridging the Seine, its tip ending up in the *Jardins du Trocadéro*. The Arc de Triomphe sheared into twelve great pieces crushing the vehicles around the *Place de l'Étoile* that were already being tossed around like hot wheels cars by a toddler. The giant domes of the *Sacré-Cœur Basilica* tumbled down the Montmartre Butte, or hill, crushing the bodies of pedestrians, and vehicles already devastated by falling buildings. The immense 360-foot cube, *La Grande Arche de la Défense*, toppled and crashed through the ground into the A14 tunnels that ran below. The 14th and 15th arrondissements collapsed into the catacombs beneath, severing water pipes, gas mains, and electricity cables. One of the countless sparks caused by the blast – vehicles crashing together, cut electricity cables, and a thousand other possible reasons – ignited the leaking gas and caused a forty-foot-high fireball to briefly illuminate the Paris skyline before the air blast of the impact struck the city, winds of up to 2000 miles per hour tore through crumpled streets still reeling from the waves of the seismic blast. This was followed by a great dust and debris cloud from the impact that shrouded the city in a layer up to eight metres deep in some places; the coating was higher closer to the impact zone. Anyone that survived the seismic and air blasts slowly asphyxiated under the blanket of dirt, rock, and stone.

Paris, the City of Light, now just a mass of rubble and dust.

The impact was felt up to three hundred kilometres away from the impact zone, from Rennes to the west, Luxembourg, and Belgium to the east. The Channel Islands of Guernsey and Jersey were struck by metre high waves that swamped the smaller islets around them. The south coast of the United Kingdom received waves of two metres in height, caused flooding across Kent, Sussex, and Hampshire. The Isle of Wight protected the port towns of Portsmouth and Southampton as it took the brunt of the damage to its southern end. The waves reverberated up the English Channel into the North Sea and struck Antwerp and Rotterdam in the Netherlands.

***

'Ladies and gentleman, the President of the United States of America,' announced Simon Feldmann, the White House Press Secretary. He left the podium, with the Seal of the President of the United States of America displayed front and centre. The Stars and Stripes flag of the USA was hung behind alongside the blue, white and red of the French Tricolour.

The hulking form of President Dwayne Johnson stepped out from the wings of the stage to a riot of flashing lightbulbs from the world's press assembled before the stage. The former WWE wrestler and movie star walked to the podium and stood behind it. He gripped the stand with both hands, his face ashen underneath his natural tanned colouring, the result of his Samoan and Black Nova Scotian heritage. The trademark Hollywood smile absent from his face. President Johnson had recently celebrated winning his second term. He ran as an independent candidate in 2020, giving voters a 'third option'. He ran against the incumbent President Donald Trump and the Democratic Nominee of … well, that was the problem, no one can remember. Their candidate was chosen to be as inoffensive to as many people as possible. However, by being so, they didn't inspire many people either. Trump's support faded when the much-rumoured Russian urination videotape was released. The tape showed Trump being urinated on by two black Russian pre-op transgender prostitutes. He may have survived if they had been post-op, or white, or not 'goddamn commies'. The trifecta of colour, nationality, and penis was too much, even for his base support to argue against. For the rest of America, the sight of Trump's Viagra-engorged raisin was enough to make them lay their vote elsewhere. President Johnson joined the race late on and swept America with charisma and charm. His first term as president was considered a success, and under his guidance America was returning to its former position as the world's leading superpower. Unemployment was at its lowest point since World War Two. Crime, especially gun crime, was lower than it had been in decades. The National Debt clock on 44th Street and Sixth Avenue in New York was actually running backwards as National Debt was reducing, albeit slowly. For his second campaign, he looked to build on this success and expand his purview to fixing the world's problems.

President Johnson looked directly ahead towards the main broadcast camera with its teleprompter.

'Ladies and gentlemen, it is with profound sadness I stand here tonight in front of the world and lament the loss of one of the great cities of the world. A city that inspired love and creativity throughout the ages. Its iconic skyline with the Eiffel Tower pointing to the heavens. My heart is torn with grief at its loss. Not just for the city, but for the whole of France. The devastation caused by the meteorite is unprecedented in the history of humanity. It is something that I am profoundly sorry for.

'The meteorite was supposed to land in Jackson Lake in Grand Teton National Park in Wyoming. It was supposed to be the greatest achievement of modern science and technology. It was supposed to be the start of a new era. An era that ended man's dependence on fossil fuels and nuclear materials. Clean, free and renewable energy for the whole of humanity, not just those countries that could afford it, those countries that could exploit their natural resources the most efficiently. Free clean fuel for every country. An era that would have propelled humanity to greater heights. Together.

'The minerals and metals in the meteorite would have powered the New Earth for millions of years. Now, however, the price has been too great. Over four million lives have been extinguished, millions more injured and in pain. A nation gutted of its capital, a continent gutted of its jewel, a world gutted of its hope.'

President Johnson paused and took a deep breath. He wiped a hand across his brow, smearing the makeup there. He didn't notice.

'So what went wrong? The world's greatest minds planned the mission. A global effort. We took samples from the asteroid Akiyama as it came into range of our planet. These samples were tested, and the discovery of unknown substances, metals, minerals excited the scientific community. A plan was put in motion to break off a chunk of the asteroid and guide it to the planet's surface.

'The asteroid was scanned, and a fault line within it identified. A series of holes were drilled into the asteroid and nuclear charges inserted. When detonated these split the asteroid causing the meteor to head towards earth, the remaining, much larger section of the asteroid was sent out away from the planet.

'Through the use of rockets dotted across the surface of the meteoroid its trajectory and rotation were calculated and guided, allowing the air resistance of the atmosphere and liberal use of retrograde rockets to slow the meteoroid to reduce the impact when it hit the planned landing site in an uninhabited area.

'The mission was proceeding as planned until five and half minutes before landing. A series of directional rockets received the command to engage three seconds after they should have. This interruption was caused by a solar flare that caused an atmospheric disturbance that temporarily affected the radio waves to the rocket series. A freak event. This delay caused the meteoroid to spin out of the pre-planned path and the computers that controlled the rockets couldn't keep up with the information quickly enough to correct its path.

'The meteorite landed near Orly, a suburb of Paris, creating a seismic blast rated 7.4 on the Richter scale. The devastation caused by this was compounded by 2000 mile per hour winds and a vast debris cloud. The crater caused by the impact is almost eight kilometres in diameter and five hundred metres deep.

'My thoughts and prayers go out to the people of France who have lost so much. Their capital city. Their countrymen. Their families and friends. Much work will be needed to help these people over the coming months and years. I pledge to the French people that the United States of America is in your corner. We will take whatever means necessary to restore your country to its rightful place in the world. A place of Liberty, Equality, Fraternity. I pledge to you that the City of Light will shine again.'

Cloaked and Shattered

Alec Foster was at his desk reading the *Iraq – Its Infrastructure of Concealment, Deception and Intimidation* report. The report had been issued to journalists the day before by the UK Government. As part of the MI6 Russian Section in Berlin, it was way out of Alec's purview, however, with it looking like the country would be going to war soon, he considered it useful to be on top of things in case he was transferred to the Middle-East section. As he looked around the office, he could see his colleagues all doing the same. He reached the end of the document. *No sources for the information. It reads like it was written for a school project.* He shook his head and turned to the front page, no author name on there either. *I bet whoever wrote that got a decent sum for it, far more than I get.*

He dropped the report in the small dustbin beside his desk. *To be burnt at the end of the day along with actual intelligence documents.*

"Alec, can you come in here a sec?" Arthur Newbury asked. Newbury was Alec's boss, Head of the Russian Section.

"Sure thing, Arthur."

Alec entered Newbury's office and closed the door. "Just been reading that Iraqi report. Did they get Claudia and Roger's son Chris to write it?"

Claudia and Roger Hamilton were Alec's, and Arthur's, friends. Claudia worked with Alec and Arthur in the Russian section. Roger worked under the Berlin Ambassador. Chris was their eight-year son.

Arthur laughed, "Probably. It does read like it was taken from Encarta."

"Encarta?" Alec asked confusion showed on his face.

"Really? When are you going to start using computers? For Christ's sake, Alec. It's 2003, not 1983. Encarta is an online encyclopaedia. You know what online is, don't you? The internet."

"I know what the internet is. I'm not that bad."

"You are. I'm going to have to send you on a course. It's going to be a vital tool in the future."

"We'll cross that bridge when we come to it. What did you want to see me about?" Alec asked, changing the subject.

"Oh yes," Arthur said. "Amsterdam."

"Amsterdam? Don't you get enough with Lesley?" Alec pointed over his head with his thumb at the secretary's desk outside the door. Lesley wasn't there at the moment. She was a young, attractive blonde hired more for her looks rather than her skills. "You're going to have to end that. If Julia finds out, you'll be history. I keep telling you 'don't shit on your own doorstep.' Seriously, end it before it gets out of hand."

"I'm not going to Amsterdam," Arthur said, dismissing Alec's advice. "I need you to go. We've been asked by the Ukraine Office. One of their guys takes regular trips to

Amsterdam, and they are worried that he's using the trips to meet a contact and pass over information and secrets to the Russians."

"Why can't the Ukraine guys send one of their own?"

"The guy is the Russian section head there, and will recognise anyone from that office, I know I would. It needs to be someone he doesn't know, and someone who knows Russian. You fit the bill."

Alec thought for a moment, "So it's a surveillance job then? Not looking for me to 'take him out'?"

"No, simply surveillance. He stays near the Grand. That's where they think he passes the information. So, unfortunately for you, you'll be far enough away from the red-light district. You may be able to stay out of trouble, for once."

"The red-light district?" Alec repeated. A wide smile crossed his face.

"You keep away from the windows there, I know about your history with prostitutes. Oh, and keep away from the cafés, too. You'll be no use stoned."

"Arthur!" Alec exclaimed with false shock in his voice. "Weed? I wouldn't dare, not with the 'random' drug tests we have to do each month. And besides, the only prostitutes I see are purely information sources. It's strictly professional."

"What about that red-haired busty one you're always with?"

"Brigette? She's the best. She got me that information last month about the SVR guy in the Russian Embassy who likes young girls to take a dump on him, I've contacted him already, and he's looking like he'll be giving us some good stuff about their activities in Europe." The SVR or Foreign Intelligence Service of the Russian Federation succeeded the First Chief Directorate of the KGB in December 1991.

"That was from her? Okay, I'll back off. I still need you to go to Amsterdam though."

"When do I leave?"

***

Alec arrived at Amsterdam Centraal station just after nine p.m. on the Friday after the meeting with Arthur. He'd been on the train from Berlin Hauptbahnhof, or Berlin Central Station, a little under seven hours. During the journey he had been studying the street map of Amsterdam from the *DK Eyewitness Top 10 Travel Guide Amsterdam* travel guide he'd picked up from his favourite bookshop in Berlin, the *Marga Schoeller Bücherstube* on Knesebeckstrasse, just around the corner from Claudia and Roger's apartment. Other people in the train carriage looked amused at him trying out the Dutch phrases in the travel guide. Alec was good with languages, fluent in both German and Russia, able to speak like a native with the dialects from the different regions of each country. It was one of the reasons he had been hired by MI6 back in 1987. Dutch wasn't a language he was familiar with. He could follow the words fine in the book, thanks to their similarity with German, but the pronunciation caused him difficulty. At least, until a fellow passenger took pity on him and moved to Alec's section of the carriage and spent the rest of the journey helping him.

Alec stepped on to the platform of the station and thanked the man for his patience. He looked for the station exit and took the tunnel to the *Centrum*, or centre, side. Alec had a small suitcase with him, which was quite light. The suitcase contained a change of clothes, some toiletries and Alec's surveillance equipment: discreet binoculars and camera, and a voice recorder to record any eavesdropped conversations. He exited the station onto the large pedestrianised square. The cold February air made him do up the buttons on his jacket. Amsterdam was a few degrees colder than Berlin had been. Alec stood still for a couple of minutes tuning in his senses to the different sounds and smells of the city.

Each city has a unique presence and feel to it. Alec had found that these first few minutes acclimatising to the regular running of city-life made it far easier to notice changes to the atmosphere and vibe of the place. London was all bustle, people and traffic rushing from one place to another. Berlin was more relaxed than London, but with an edgier feel to it. The people stand-offish and private. Here, Alec could feel Amsterdam was different. There was little traffic noise, plenty of trilling bicycle bells. A lot of people with backpacks. The city had a slight musty, damp odour. *From the canals, I suspect.* He reached into his jacket pocket and took out his cigarettes and lighter. He lit one up and enjoyed the first hit of nicotine. Out of respect for his tutor on the train, he had refrained from smoking during his journey. He remained in place while he smoked and then stubbed the butt out on the side of a nearby waste bin and dropped it in the receptacle.

Alec picked up his suitcase and headed down Sint Nicolaasbrug to go to his hotel. Alec made sure to keep out of the tramlines on the ground, having on a previous visit to the city narrowly avoided getting hit by one of the near-silent trams. At the junction of Damrak and Prins Hendrikkade Alec turned left and crossed the bridge over the Damrak canal with its famous six, and seven story crooked, multi-coloured 'dancing houses' which lined the far side of the water. He took a right on to Warmoesstraat and headed down the narrow road past many restaurants, hotels and bars. He soon reached the Hotel Old Quarter where he was staying. It was Alec's preferred hotel when staying in the city due to its closeness to the station and to the main entertainment areas of the city. Back in the office, it had taken a little sweet-talking to get Lesley to book him a place there, rather than cheaper hostels the bean counters prefer officers to stay in.

He entered the hotel and in front of him was the *receptie*, or reception desk, and hotel bar. The desk was part of the bar. The bar was loud, with Avril Lavinge's 'Complicated' playing on the speaker system. Alec recognised the song from going to bars with Brigette. To the right of the bar—slash—reception booths were against the far wall, and small tables and chairs were dotted here and there between the booths and the bar.

Alec walked up to the reception desk and stood there while the receptionist poured a customer a pint. When she finished, she spotted Alec and walked over.

"Hi," he said in German-accented English with a smile. "I have a room booked for tonight and tomorrow."

She reached for the booking's diary and asked Alec for his name.

"Stefan Duquesne." Stefan Duquesne was Alec's cover name. He'd chosen Duquesne as Fritz Joubert Duquesne was a famous German spy in the Second Boer War at the beginning of the 20th Century.

She traced her finger down the list of bookings. "I can't find Dookane on here."

Alec told her how to spell the name, and straightaway she found the booking. The difference between the spelling and the pronunciation of Duquesne was another reason for his choice.

Lesley had paid for the hotel when booking, so the receptionist—bar lady gave Alec the key and directions to the room and ran over the house rules.

"Thank you," said Alec as he picked up his suitcase. He headed to the back of the bar where the doors leading to the rooms were. He opened the door and walked up the staircase to his room on the fifth floor, the staircase was narrow and squeaked with every step.

He reached his room, opened the door and stepped inside. The room was very constricted, about six-foot-wide and fifteen foot long. A bed along one wall, and a sink and mirror in the middle of the opposite wall. Alec dumped his suitcase on the floor, took off his jacket and shoes and lay on the bed. *The Ukraine guy isn't coming in until tomorrow. A night in Amsterdam? If I weren't on a job, the possibilities would be endless.* He smiled and closed his eyes for a moment.

***

Alec woke two hours later. A little after midnight. He yawned and stretched while lying down. *A little power nap does the world of good.* He sat up and shook his neck from side to side the joints creaked as he did so. *You're getting old,* he told himself. Alec was thirty-seven and in relatively good shape. He maintained his physical conditioning through regular workouts and martial arts training, combined with limiting his drinking sessions to once a week. *I'll have to quit smoking soon though.*

He stood and took his suitcase and laid it on the bed. He unzipped it and removed the manila cardboard folder from the elasticated pocket in the roof of the suitcase. He pushed the suitcase to one side and sat back on the bed. He started reading about his quarry for tomorrow.

Andrew Marshall had been Head of the Russian Section in Kiev for the past five years. A year and a half ago he had started taking regular trips to Amsterdam, every three to four weeks. His superiors were concerned that he was leaking material to the Soviets. *Russians, Alec. They're Russians and have been for the past twelve years.* The report didn't specify what material Marshall was supposed to be leaking. There was a bit about Marshall's personal life that Alec quickly skimmed through. Marriage in trouble, wife considering divorce, no kids, no untoward activity with regards to finances. *Blah, blah, blah. If he were good enough to be Head of Section, he'd easily be able to find inventive ways to hide extra funds. I know I've put some aside for emergencies.*

Alec looked at the pictures of Marshall. There were his standard MI6 headshot and some blurry discreet long lens surveillance photos. He was in his late-forties, grey hair, double chin, and from the full-length photos about three stone overweight and not wearing it well. He wore an ill-fitting off-the-peg suit that did little to hide the growing belly. *That'll be all the Ukrainian varenyky he'll be eating in Kiev.* Varenyky are the Ukrainian version of pierogi. Dumplings filled with meats, vegetables, and other fillings. In Ukraine, they are served with sour cream and fried bacon and pork fat.

Alec then looked at Marshall's schedule for the day. Or at least the one he'd submitted. He'd arrive by plane at Amsterdam Schiphol at 4 p.m. *Train would probably take a day and a half.* Marshall was booked into the Hotel Fita for the night. The hotel was just outside of the rings of canals that made Amsterdam famous. South-west of the main city centre. About a fifteen-minute walk to the British Consulate General building, where Marshall was supposed to be going. He'd told his bosses that he had a source in the Russian Embassy in The Hague, and they met every few weeks in Amsterdam at the British Consulate General. *We'll see.*

Alec decided that rather waste the night sleeping or experiencing the city's drinking establishments. He'd familiarise himself with that part of the city and check out Marshall's hotel. He had already decided he'd start his surveillance on Marshall at the airport and follow him throughout the day and night

Alec put the folder back in the suitcase and slid the case under the bed. He put on his shoes and jacket. He had a second thought and removed the suitcase, opened it and took out the grey woollen knitted beanie hat and camera. He replaced the suitcase, put on the hat and put the camera in his jacket pocket. He wasn't armed on this trip. The point of it was to be discreet and not be spotted. *Holland is a friendly country after all.* He did miss the comforting weight and presence the firearm afforded him. He did take his travel guide though. He'd circled the location of Hotel Fita on there, as well as his hotel. He left the room not bothering to leave any tell-tales, *that's for the movies,* he thought. *If anyone were after me a hair across the door wouldn't stop them.*

***

Alec left his hotel and turned right to walk down Warmoesstraat until he reached the junction with Oudebrugsteeg. *Only a ten minute or so walk to the bus stop.* His stomach growled at him. He hadn't eaten since picking up a snack in the bistro car on the train. He walked past the quiet restaurants that were soon to be closing, and the loud bars that lined the route. As he turned on to Oudebrugsteeg, a narrow side street. Alec noticed a small queue outside Vlaamse Friet, the small take away storefront very popular with tourists and locals. He joined the queue and soon reached the front. The restaurant was only wide enough for three people to stand there. He ordered a cone of fries with mayonnaise. On the menu boards, there were around twenty other sauces he could have chosen including cheese, tartare, and piccalilli. The mayonnaise was thick and plentiful. Alec paid and left the shop. He continued along Oudebrugsteeg waiting for the piping hot fries to cool enough he could eat one without burning his mouth. He continued past The Grasshopper restaurant and bar, and Oudebrugsteeg opened wider. The Damrak canal was to the right, and behind it, the view of the Centraal station all lit up in the distance. Alec leant against the small wall of the bridge over the canal and ate his fries. He swirled the mayonnaise to coat more fires than the initial dollop given had done. The warmth was welcome on the cold night. The fries were much better than ones he had last time he was in Amsterdam from the Manneken Pis restaurant on Damrak. Alec looked in the direction of Damrak and could see the supposed number one fry still open. Much larger queues were at this restaurant, but that could well have been down to it being located on a main thoroughfare in the city.

Alec crossed Damrak, watching out for the tram lines in the road, and continued onto to Oudebrugsteeg on the other side. He was still eating his fries. Most of the mayonnaise had gone now. The street narrowed to match the close confines opposite. Alec walked past the Coffeeshop de Kroon, the air thick with the cloying, acrid smell of weed from the coffee shop. Alec paused for a moment and took a deep breath, enjoying the illicit nature of his actions. *Drugs test be damned. They wouldn't be able to detect this.* Satisfied with his actions. Alec dropped his now empty fries cone wrapper in one of the street bins and continued his journey. He lit up a cigarette to finish his meal off. Oudebrugsteeg ended at the junction with Nieuwendijk. Alec turned left as he recalled from his travel guide. Nieuwendijk is one of the major shopping streets in Amsterdam. At this time of the night, all the shops were closed, their shutters down and lights off. Alec took a sharp right onto a very narrow side street, Dirk van Hasseltssteeg. The street was barely wide enough for two people to walk side by side. Alec stopped at one point to let a party of English men past. The biggest and loudest one was telling the others of the girl he had just been with, forgetting that they had all seen her in the window too. The low-spoken comments from the last of the party as they passed Alec, made him smile, as they mentioned dentures and a gummy blow job.

Alec reached the end of the street as it met Nieuwezijds Voorburgwal. This had a much wider pavement area and both vehicle and tram lanes. Nieuwezijds Voorburgwal runs from north to south. Alec crossed over and waited at the stop for the route 288 *nachtbus*, or night bus, to Nieuw Sloten to arrive. As he waited, he lit another cigarette to while away the minutes. It didn't take long for the bus to arrive. Alec signalled he wanted the bus to stop and boarded when the driver opened the doors. Alec paid the driver the fare and received a paper ticket in return.

Alec took a seat near the middle section doors, and the bus set off.

It only took twenty minutes or so for the bus to reach Alec's stop, Rijksmuseum. The Rijksmuseum is a Dutch art and history museum. It is the third busiest museum in Holland, after the Van Gogh and Anne Frank museums. During the journey, Alec refamiliarised himself with the street map for the area. He disembarked on to Hobbemastraat, opposite the museum. He walked up the street until he reached and turned on to the junction with Jan Luijkenstraat. It was a wide road with buildings on either side and large leafless trees lining the route waiting for spring. Cars parked in angled bays and of course, the ubiquitous bicycles mounted on pavement racks on either side. The Hotel Fita was down here. He started walking down the road. The difference in this road compared to the ones in the Centraal area where he had come from was stark. *These are more like the roads in Berlin.* Alec made his way to the hotel. As he drew near, he started looking for areas where he could stand watch for his prey unseen, or at least obscured. The Hotel Fita was a four-storey building on the corner of Jan Luijkenstraat and the pedestrianised van de Veldestraat. Opposite the hotel was a walled open concrete playground for a nearby school.

Not much chance of not being noticed hanging around a kid's playground. Just past the playground, Alec spotted the upmarket designer stores of Philipp Plein and Max Mara that he recognised from the *Ku'damm* in Berlin. Both stores were closed for the night, faint spotlights in the windows displaying the latest fashions. The presence of these stores and the wealthy appearance of the buildings around him told Alec that he'd need to look reasonably smart tomorrow to avoid drawing attention to himself. *Makes sense to have the consulate and embassies near the money.*

Alec walked back to Jan Luijkenstraat and the hotel. There were no apparent places he could hide. He moved further down the road.

The houses to the right had alcoves with steps leading up to the front doors. Alec walked up one set of steps and sat on the top step. He looked towards the hotel. The entrance was lit, and he could clearly see the doors of the hotel, themselves at the top of a set of steps. Alec calculated the distance between the two buildings as around one hundred foot. *This is a possibility.* There was a tree on the pavement in front of him that would help conceal him from across the street. He stood up and walked back towards the hotel. He stopped outside, walked up a couple of the steps and turned and looked over at the alcove. In the street lit darkness, he could barely make out any features of the building, the tree helped break up the outlines too, drawing the eye to where the trunk and branches caught the streetlight. *Perfect. It'll start getting dark around 6 p.m. so by the time Marshall gets here so this will be hidden.* Alec looked at his watch. It was a little after 2 a.m. *It's getting a little late. I could be out all night later, depending on what Marshall does. I'll head back to the hotel. I've seen the Consulate building before there's plenty of cover around there.*

Alec took a final look at his hiding place and retraced his walk back to the bus stop on Rijksmuseum. He lit a cigarette at the bus stop and waited for the bus. It wasn't long before the bus arrived. Alec got on, paid and found a seat.

***

Alec disembarked the bus at Nieuwezijds Voorburgwal and began the reverse journey he had made earlier. The streets were much quieter than they had been earlier, no throngs of people enjoying the nightlife and excitement of Amsterdam. Just the occasional pissed up pack of lads. Alec gave each one a wide berth. He crossed Damrak on to Oudebrugsteeg, where he had the fries and mayo earlier. The dimly lit narrow street made him wary. A small group turned onto the street, coming from Warmoesstraat. They were loud, swaying with the unsteady and overcompensated steps of the intoxicated. Alec counted four guys. From their braying noise, he figured they were no strangers to the moneyed, arrogant City of London area he always tried to avoid whenever he was back in London on a night out. Their wealth making them confident and rude.

They walked in a single wide group blocking the whole street. As they moved closer to Alec, he moved to the right-hand side and stopped to let them pass. Despite the cold February night, they wore thick cotton shirts of varying hues. Paul Smith, Ralph Lauren, and Stone Island were all represented. Red, blue, green, and mustard yellow. Each shirt them costing more than the flights out to Amsterdam would have done. Alec gauged the men: all were over six foot and looked gym fit. All were in their twenties. Despite their night's activities, they walked with a swagger. *They look like a scrap would top their night off. Something to boast to their colleagues about after the weekend.* Alec shook his head and started inhaling deeply, increasing the oxygen to his muscles.

As they passed Alec, the mustard shirted one on the end of the line dropped back slightly to allow room. Not enough. But adequate to serve the illusion. His shoulder hit Alec's with force. Enough force to knock a man to the ground if they were not expecting it. Alec saw the other end of the group swing round to start to give him a kicking on the floor. Alec was waiting for the move. He'd braced himself and placed all his weight on his leading left foot. The man's barge had the opposite effect he'd been expecting. As his shoulder struck Alec, Alec pushed back. The man's face was an 'O' as he fell to the ground. Alec stepped forward and kicked him in the face as he dropped. A satisfying crunch. Alec took another step and turned to face the others. He shifted his balance to go on the attack. Green and Blue watched their friend fall. Red, the closest one, was already in position to stamp on Alec's prone body. Alec launched his foot at the man's unprotected groin and spun with an elbow at Blue's head. Alec's foot connected with force, as did the elbow. Both men fell to the floor to join their brother. Green swung a wild haymaker as Alec ducked. The blow went over Alec's head, and Green stumbled over Blue. Alec took advantage and sprung up with an uppercut, using the base of the palm of his hand, which connected with the lower jaw and uprooted the man. All four men were down and out, and Alec was breathing heavy.

He took the time to go through each man's pockets, removed their wallets, passports and mobile phones. He stuffed them in his jacket pocket. Took a final, satisfied look at his handiwork. *Still got it.* He smiled. As he stepped around Mustard, he felt the man's hand reach for his trousers. A weak attempt to restrain him. Alec dipped down and batted the man's hand away. He stood up again and walked to the end of the street.

His hotel was a minute to the left. His warm bed was calling him. *Better not make it easy for the Police.* He sighed at the delay. Instead of heading left to perceived sanctuary Alec crossed over onto Lange Niezel and with long strides escaped the scene. Past the closed bars and restaurants. He continued on Korte Niezel before turning left onto Oudezijds Achterburgwal. This was one of the most popular streets in Amsterdam for tourists. The street was bisected by a narrow canal which reflected the red neon of the prostitute windows lining the streets on each side. Most windows had the heavy red curtain drawn to indicate they were closed or in use. There were more people here, pockets of men and women talking and drinking. Alec slowed his pace. As he strolled alongside the canal, he kept dipping his hands into his jacket pocket and dumping the wallets, passports and phones of his assailants in the dark water as he went. He walked past the Moulin Rouge Live Sex Show on the opposite bank of the canal.

The sight of it made him smile as he remembered Brigette taking him there and pushing him to join in with one of the performances much to his protestations. Alec went on stage with a performer who wrote in marker pen on his chest. *She was very talented; she didn't even use her hands.* Alec turned on to Armburg and walked through onto Oudezijds Armsteeg. It wasn't long before he reached Warmoesstraat and entered his hotel. The detour had taken him twenty minutes but wouldn't give the police or any witnesses a direct route to him.

He reached his room, entered. *No one there.* He shrugged and removed his clothes. Alec removed his toiletries bag from the suitcase, brushed his teeth. Then turned off the lights and got into bed. *Busy day tomorrow,* he thought as he closed his eyes.

***

Alec woke, his legs felt heavy and his back a little tense. He looked at his watch. 10 a.m. *Plenty of time to get in position. Marshall gets in the airport at 4 p.m.* Alec's stomach rumbled. He got up; his bare feet sore on the carpeted floor. Alec stretched out his back slowly, working each set of muscles, his arms reached up to the ceiling. Satisfied he had started the blood flow moving across the muscles. Alec set about doing his morning yoga routine. He had been introduced to yoga about three years previously. His advancing age and the impetus of the new millennium had pushed him to make changes to his lifestyle so he could keep doing the work he loved. After thirty minutes he switched up the exercise to one with more intensity. Push-ups, sit-ups, planks and holds. The jumping jack squats caused the floor to squeak alarmingly. At the end of the routine, Alec was sweating freely and breathing heavily. He smiled at the feeling. He walked to the sink and turned on the cold tap and drank directly from the tap, the cool water drenched his thirst and from the excess, which had run from the side of his mouth, along his neckline and down his chest, and a bit of the carpet around the sink. Alec brushed his teeth and wrapped a hotel towel around him and left his room to go to the communal shower. There he washed away the sweat and the small amount of sleep remaining. When done he returned to his room and got dressed. Put his surveillance gear in his jacket pockets. Ready for whatever the day would bring.

Leaving the hotel, Alec spent a lazy morning eating at various small restaurants. Starters and street food. He didn't know if he'd get the chance later. He slowly wandered around the De Wallen area killing time and admiring the women in the windows. When he first visited Amsterdam the women in the windows had startled him. They were like the store mannequins in the windows of the stores in London's Oxford Street or Berlin's Kurfürstendamm. At least until they moved. Beckoning passers-by with their flirty gestures, scantily-clad bodies, and suggestive poses. *Damn them for being so beguiling.* Alec smiled as a beautiful woman in lingerie looked at him. She raised her arms over her head; hands entwined at the wrist and deliberately bit her lip at him. Alec blushed slightly and forced himself to carry on walking rather than giving in to the urge of knocking on her door. *Time to head for the airport, I think.*

Alec walked to Centraal Station and bought a return ticket to Schiphol airport. *I might not need it, but it's better to be prepared.* He got to the platform and boarded the train when it arrived. Twenty minutes or so later he was at Schiphol airport. The train station was underneath the main airport. Alec walked up the stairs to the Arrivals floor. The flight was due in an hour. Alec looked at the arrivals board to see if they had allocated a gate for the flight. At Schiphol, there are four arrival gates. The board hadn't been updated, so Alec bought a coffee and sandwich from one of the eateries. He sat on a bench facing the arrivals board and waited. *Will Marshall go to his hotel first, or will he head straight to the consulate? He's only here for one night so won't have much in the way of luggage. That'll mean he'll skip the baggage reclaim section and head straight through customs after immigration. Will he get the train to Centraal Station or bus to the hotel? If he gets the bus how can I remain inconspicuous?* Alec mulled over varying scenarios, mapping out routes in his head. Sipping poor airport coffee and eating a bland, lifeless sandwich. The arrivals board updated and showed the passengers on the 4 p.m. flight from Kiev would come in through Arrival Gate 3. Alec saw that he had thirty minutes to kill so decided to head outside and have a cigarette.

When he had finished, he disposed of the butt and walked to Arrival Gate 3. It was on the same floor as the terminal entrance. He got to the gate and headed over to the nearest wall to wait. *I'm not sure how good Marshall is. He's Head of Section in Kiev so he must have been pretty good back in the day, but he'll be out of practice and hopefully not too switched on.* Alec put on his woollen beanie and

218

removed a pair of plain glass spectacles from his inside pocket. *Not long to go now.* Alec expected Marshall to be one of the first through the gate. He waited.

Marshall wasn't the first one through the arrival gate, but he was part of the initial pack. Alec was looking for passengers with grey hair, as it was unlikely that any would don headgear until they hit the outside. He spotted Marshall immediately. He walked with a slight waddle, his thighs catching as he strode. He was wearing a nice blue suit very badly. Over his shoulder was a brown leather strap attached to an old-fashioned brown leather satchel style bag with double clasp fastenings. He had a grey woollen overcoat folded over one arm. Alec looked at the man's face. It looked tired, skin sagging and pale. Black circles under the dark eyes. The eyes were, however, darting around the arrival hall scanning people waiting there. *Still a little of the old instinct there.* Alec aimed his gaze to the good-looking blonde walking a few steps behind and to the right of Marshall. He could still see Marshall but tracked the woman, *just in case.* She was worth tracking though, wearing a tight skirt and top that emphasised her curves. Alec saw Marshall head towards the steps to the train station below and reluctantly followed, stealing a final gaze at the woman as she was swept up in the arms of a man Alec had spotted pacing apprehensively. *Lucky fella.*

With Marshall in front of him, Alec removed his woollen hat and glasses and stashed them away as he walked. Marshall was two-thirds down the staircase when Alec reached them. *I'd prefer to be a little further away. You know where he's headed so take your time. He doesn't look like he's the type of guy to exert himself to lose a tail.* Alec walked down the stairs at a slow pace. There were times he lost sight of Marshall but soon picked him up again as they headed to the platform for the train to Centraal Station.

At the platform, Marshall stood about a quarter of the way down. Alec walked past him and stopped midway along. He turned to face the direction the train would be coming from. Marshall was facing the same direction, obviously doing the same. Alec saw that the hems of Marshall's trousers were frayed where they hung down over the heel of the shoe. *Trying to lose weight, that in-between phase where your trousers hang looser on you, so you have to hitch in your belt a little more and before you have to buy a new pair. Good on you mate.* Alec's attention was drawn to the sound of heels click-clacking along the platform and saw the woman from the arrivals gate with her partner. They reached Marshall and stopped to wait for the train. Marshall didn't even turn around to look at them. *Interesting.* The train then approached the platform. Marshall moved closer to the platform's edge. The train stopped, and Alec waited until Marshall had boarded the train. Alec let other passengers get through his carriage door on before him watching in case Marshall played the traditional on-off move to lose a tail. The good-looking woman followed Marshall, helped up the train step by her partner. The platform quickly emptied as passengers boarded the train. Alec heard the guard's whistle and stepped onboard at the last minute. *Ready to jump out if necessary.* When the train started moving, he relaxed. *Marshall wasn't fit enough to jump off out a moving train.*

Alec stood in the doorway of the train, watching the scenery as it passed. He thought about the routes Marshall could take from here. *If he gets off at Amsterdam-Zuid, he'll be getting a bus or tram to Rijksmuseum to go to the hotel. If he stays on to Centraal Station, he'll probably take the same bus I did last night to get to the hotel. If he decides to head into town before going to the hotel, well I'll follow.* It was only a few minutes before the train started to slow as it approached the first stop, Amsterdam-Zuid. Alec prepared to exit the carriage as soon as he could. He opened the door before the train had fully come to a stop and hopped off. He moved the centre of the platform where there were benches were for waiting passengers. He watched Marshall's carriage to see if he was disembarking. It didn't take long. The man's bulky frame exited the train and made its way down the platform to the exit and the tram stop. Alec followed.

Marshall paid for the tram at the ticket machine next to the stop. Alec let a couple of passengers go ahead of him and then used the machine himself. He stood a little away from the tram stop on Marshall's blind side. The tram arrived, and Alec moved in close to Marshall. He intended to follow him directly on to the tram working on the assumption that Marshall wouldn't notice someone directly behind him. The tram doors opened. Marshall was at the front of the queue and boarded. Alec followed him. Marshall took the first seat available, and Alec walked past a couple of rows directly behind him. He sat and took out his travel guide and pretended to read. The tram filled up and then set off. Marshall pressed the bell to disembark as the train entered Paulus Potterstraat. Paulus Potterstraat was a wide avenue with museums along the right-hand side, including the van Gogh Museum and the Stedelijk Museum of modern design. Marshall got off from the tram and began to walk down van de Veldestraat and towards the hotel. It wasn't long before he was on Jan Luijkenstraat and walking up the hotel's steps. Alec followed and crossed the road to the surveillance spot he had identified the night before.

Alec stood on the top step and looked towards the hotel entrance. He lit a cigarette. If Marshall made a sudden entrance, Alec was ready to step back into the shadows. Alec stood there for about twenty minutes looking at the entrance. He started to get bored. *This is the worst part. Just waiting around. There's only so many cigarettes I can smoke.* Alec removed the surveillance camera from his jacket pocket. MI6 produce tiny handheld ones, but this wasn't one. It was a standard off the shelf model digital camera. A sticker on the front proclaimed 3x optical zoom and 2.0 megapixels, *whatever that means.*

Alec powered on the device to check it was working. There was a lot of buttons that Alec had been trained on and promptly forgot. He remembered how to make sure the flash was off. There was a handy slide button on the top of the camera, next to the shutter button, with two options: On and Off. The button was on the off slide. *It is best not to have the flash going off if I'm trying to be discreet.* Before he had left the office, Alec had persuaded Claudia to turn off the shutter noise for him. She didn't even mock him too much. The camera silently powered up and the small preview screen lit up and displayed the manufacturer's logo. After a few seconds the logo vanished, and the preview screen showed a blurry image of Alec's thumb. Alec adjusted his grip, and the screen cleared and showed the concrete step Alec was standing on. He checked the battery level indicator and was relieved to see it was full. He left the camera on and placed it back in his pocket. Alec went back to waiting for Marshall.

***

Darkness fell, street lights came on, windows lit up behind drawn curtains, Alec still waited. He'd gotten so bored of sitting on the step he had scampered down and snatched a stone up from the pavement. He returned to his surveillance spot, he began to whittle his initials into the brickwork of the house he was loitering against. By the time Marshall finally showed at 9 p.m. Alec had added the date and thrown the stone away in impatience. Marshall had changed into a grey suit. This one tailored much better, cut to suit his size. Alec slowly crept back into the shadows of the alcove. *Now let's see where he is going.* Alec watched waiting for Marshall to head left past Alec to the Grand Consulate. Instead, Marshall went in the opposite direction towards Rijksmuseum. He was on the other side of the road from Alec so following him was easy. Alec maintained a fifty-metre distance, taking care to watch where he was walking to avoid kicking a bottle or can or jutting out bicycle wheel and giving away his position.

Alec thought about where Marshall would be going. *He must be getting the bus from the Rijksmuseum. There's not much else that way at this time of night. If I get to the bus stop first, it may help to cover me. He'll be following me.* Alec crossed the road onto Marshall's side and took the turning at Hobbemastraat. Alec sprinted down the road and turned on to Paulus Potterstraat at speed. The street was empty of pedestrians. He passed the Stichting Diamant Museum and a couple of jewellery shops on that side of the road. He turned the corner. Marshall was not in sight. Alec ran to the bus stop and bought a ticket from the machine. He stood at the bus stop and gulped down oxygen to control his breathing before Marshall came. It didn't take him long, even with the cigarettes Alec had smoked that evening. Alec was breathing normally by the time he saw Marshall out of the corner of his eye. Marshall headed towards the ticket machine and purchased his ticket. He stood away from Alec facing in the direction the bus would be coming from. There was only Alec and Marshall at the bus stop.

Do I let him get on first? That may involve talking to him. Or being English, even the old 'after you—no, after you—I insist' tussle.

223

Certainly, he'd remember me. The bus approached, and Alec positioned himself to get on first. He turned away from Marshall, trying to limit how much of his face could be seen. The bus stopped, and the doors opened. Alec got on. There weren't many passengers on board, so Alec walked straight to the back of the bus, hoping to put some distance between himself and Marshall. When he sat down, he saw that Marshall had already taken a seat at the front. The bus started off and followed the same course it had done when Alec returned had to his hotel earlier.

Marshall pushed the bell to stop the bus on Nieuwezijds Kolk, *I'm getting a sense of déjà vu here,* and stood up. He moved to the front of the bus. When the bus stopped, and the doors opened, he stepped off. Alec got up and hurried to the front.

"Sorry, I was miles away," he said to the driver.

He hopped off the bus and saw Marshall heading towards Dirk van Hasseltssteeg. Alec followed. *He's definitely following the same route I took this morning.* Alec held back as the street narrowed. *I can catch up with him when he reaches Damrak. That'll be crowded this time of night.* Alec stalked his prey through Nieuwendijk and the west side of Oudebrugsteeg. Marshall walked without hesitation. He knew where he was going. Marshall reached Damrak, not stopping at the coffee shop Alec had the night before. Marshall turned left, instead of carrying on straight across Damrak to Oudebrugsteeg. Alec picked up the pace to not lose him. Alec saw him enter a restaurant. *Is he meeting his contact in there?*

Alec reached the restaurant, a standard touristy pizzeria steakhouse type of place. Empty tables outside. Looking through the windows, the restaurant seemed reasonably busy for a Saturday night. Alec saw Marshall being guided by a waiter to an empty table set for two. Marshall removed his coat and hung it on the back of his chair. The waiter retrieved a menu and removed the second place setting. Marshall picked up the menu and started flicking through. *It looks like he's dining alone.* Alec backed off and stood at the perimeter of the restaurant on the pavement. He could still see inside. He took the opportunity to remove his camera and take a few photos of Marshall sitting alone. He put the camera away and lit a cigarette to while away the time. Marshall's food arrived. He started eating, and from the look on his face, it looked like it was more Michelin tyre than Michelin star. After a few minutes, he called the waiter for the bill. Alec could see him apologising for not finishing his meal. Pointing at his stomach and miming pain. Alec smiled. *An argument in the middle of a city centre restaurant is not ideal for someone looking to sell secrets to the Russians.* As Marshall put on his coat, Alec moved away from the restaurant, crossing the road so he'd be in a good vantage point to see where Marshall went next.

Marshall exited the restaurant, doing his coat up against the chill. He looked behind him at the restaurant and made a look of disgust. His tongue came out, and he shuddered. He shook his head. Marshall lifted his head to gather his bearings before he set off again. Marshall crossed the road towards the impressive looking Beurs van Berlage building across the road to Alec's left. The former stock-exchange turned events building covered over four hundred foot. A stark contrast to the rest of the typical narrow buildings along Damrak.

Marshall turned on to Oudebrugsteeg where Alec has eaten his fries and mayonnaise the night before. Alec set off after him. Marshall continued through Oudebrugsteeg to Warmoesstraat. The road Alec's hotel was on. *He's not going where I think he's going, is he?* Instead of going left to the hotel Marshall turned right. *Yep, he is. The only question left to ask is which one he is going to. He looks like a man on a mission. I'm sure he's got a destination in mind.* Marshall headed down Warmoesstraat. Alec narrowed the distance between them. The large groups of people walking the streets giving him plenty of cover. He followed Marshall onto Enge Kerksteed. He could see the Oude Kerk ahead. The Old Church was the oldest building in Amsterdam and dominated the red-light district in which it stood.

Marshall ignored the few red-lit windows in Enge Kerksteed. Walking by without even a glance at the ladies. Alec made up for the man's neglect. *Purely to maintain my cover, of course.* When Marshall reached Oudekerksplein, the square containing the church, he turned left. Alec tore himself away and continued. As he turned the corner, he saw Marshall at one of the windows speaking to one of the ladies. Alec drew in closer. Close enough to watch their exchange while pretending to be thinking about visiting the lady in the window next to Marshall. The woman in Alec's window was wearing lingerie that barely covered her ample chest, and as she turned for him, he saw the panties didn't cover much of the impressively-sized bottom either. Her deep brown coloured skin glowed in the red lights either side of the window. Marshall and his lady concluded their doorway talk, and she let him into the room and drew the curtain behind them. *I must hear what is going on in there. She could be the contact.* Alec thought for a moment. Working out the different options. In the end, he went with the one that could cause the greatest trouble, but if successful would get the best result. Alec approached the window in front of him. The lady opened the door a little with a beaming smile.

"Hi, I'd like to come in," Alec said in his German-accented English. *Not the smoothest opening line, I know.*

"Sure baby," her voice was like velvet. "Forty euros for twenty minutes? I will treat you good." She was shorter than Alec even in her heels. She squeezed his bicep with one hand as she spoke. "I like your muscles."

"Err... Thank you. Yes, twenty minutes should be fine, maybe longer if necessary."

She opened the door wider for Alec to enter. She closed the door and drew the curtain as he entered the room. The room was darkly lit. A narrow bed lined one wall. A sink, the other. *Looks like my hotel room.* Alec smiled.

"What is your name, handsome?" she said behind him. Her hands stroked his back.

"Er... Stefan." Alec said turning around.

"Where are you from Stefan?" the stroking continued on the front.

"Berlin."

"You here for fun?"

"Business, I suppose," Alec said. "What's your name and where are you from?"

"I'm from the Dominican República. You can call me anything you what, honey. Shall we get started?" She moved her hands to the lapels of Alec's jacket and pushed it backwards.

Alec held up his hands to stop her. *This is going to be awkward.* "When I said business. I meant it. I'm working now. I need to listen to them next door. I'm an investigator."

"An investigator?"

227

"Yes, the man's wife hired me to catch him cheating on her. I have a recording device to tape them."

She looked at him closely. "You're not creepy man, are you?"

"No, not creepy. I can pay more." Alec took out his wallet and took out some Euro notes and passed them to her.

"You not want sex?" she looked disappointed. Or, at least Alec's ego thought so.

"Not while I'm working, but I may come back another time when not working."

"It's not because I'm ugly?" she pouted.

"No, really. You're lovely. I have to record the man though."

"Ok, creepy man. You do your work."

"Thank you." Alec removed his tape recorder with its microphone and cable wrapped around it. From his inside jacket pocket, he took out a pair of inner-ear earphones and plugged it into the socket on the device. He unwrapped the cable and placed the microphone against the wall. He put one of the earphones into his ear and turned the tape recorder on. He winced at the resultant feedback and turned the volume down. He could hear murmuring and a rhythmic thumping.

"What are they doing?" She asked after a couple of minutes, leaning against the bed.

"Umm... you know. What people normally do in these rooms."

"You like to listen?" She started to make fake orgasm noises, then laughed.

"I'd rather not. It's like going to a restaurant and just standing there looking at the food." The thumping from next door continued. "So, what's your name?"

"Alaia," she said.

"A beautiful name for a beautiful woman. Does it have a meaning?" *Arthur would have a fit if he could see me small-talking a prostitute wearing next to nothing while I'm on the job. How will I explain this one away?*

"In English, it means happiness. I think."

"Well, I'm sure you bring that to your customers."

"Maybe you not a creepy man, after all. What they doing now?"

"It's gone a little quiet. Maybe he is having a breather."

"Can I listen?" she said, moving away from the bed over to the wall Alec was standing against.

"Sure," he said holding out the spare earphone.

Because of the cable length, Alaia had to stand very close to Alec. The closeness made Alec very aware of the subtle perfume she was wearing, and even more aware of the unsubtle clothing. Or lack of it. The room started to get a little hot. Alaia moved closer to the wall and to Alec to hear better.

"I can hear their voices. They are talking," she said.

"Can you make out what they are saying?" the blood rushing around his head had made it hard for Alec to concentrate.

"The man is telling Ruth, that he had a great time. As always. He must be one of her regular customers."

"Ruth? Not as nice a name as Alaia."

"Shhhh," she scolded. "I'm trying to listen. He is now saying that he loves her. He'll leave his wife for her. Move to Amsterdam to be with her."

Uh-oh, that is a reasonable explanation for these visits every month. He is infatuated with her. Well, I know what that is like. Brigette's face came to his mind. *Although I never acted on it.*

"Why do men do this? They know what we do,' Alaia asked. 'It's not like *Pretty Woman*."

"Don't ask me. I'm just a creepy listener, after all."

Alaia smacked his chest and laughed. "No, you, I think are different. You think like us. Work and life are different." She looked up at him. Holding his eyes in hers.

From the other room came shouting, loud enough that Alec could hear without the earphones. He took his earphone out. "I think our time may be over soon."

Alaia took her earphone out too and held it out to him. "I think you're right."

Alec took the earphone from her, their hands touched as he took it. He looked at her and smiled. "It's been a pleasure, Alaia. Maybe next time I'm in town."

230

She put her finger on his lips to quiet him, "Don't spoil it, creepy man."

Alaia walked over to the curtain and opened them, then the door. Alec turned off the tape recorder and wrapped the cables around it and stuffed it in his pocket. He walked to the door.

"Thank you," he said when he was beside her.

Alaia reached up and pulled his face towards hers. She kissed him on the lips. "You go now. You don't want to be caught." She smacked his bum for emphasis.

Alec left into the icy cold air, lips burning. He turned, but Alaia had already shut the door and drawn the curtains closed. He moved away from the window and into the shadow of the church. He was barely there when the curtains at Marshall's window were opened at the door flung open. Marshall was forcibly expelled from the room in a state of partial undress.

"Do not come back!" the woman screamed at him as she slammed the door shut. Hard enough to rattle the glass in the frame. She closed the curtains, leaving Marshall sobbing in the street.

***

It was a good few minutes before Marshall pulled himself together. Oblivious to the laughter and pitiful stares of passers-by. He stopped crying, tucked in his shirt, and pulled on his suit jacket. He looked down at his unlaced shoes, shrugged and left them as they were. He looked around for the first time, now aware of where he was. He took a final look at the closed window of his dreams. Took a deep breath, turned and walked away, his stride broad and purposeful.

The suddenness took Alec by surprise, and he hurried to catch up with the big man. He followed him up Enge Kerksteed and Warmoesstraat. Marshall bundled through groups without stopping. Ignoring the shouts of protest and curses. He turned on to Oudebrugsteeg. Alec's progress was blocked by one of the groups Marshall had infuriated.

"Excuse me, excuse me, excuse me," Alec said as he gently pushed through the mass. He reached Oudebrugsteeg and saw Marshall ahead. He broke into a run.

His quarry was standing on the stone bridgework Alec had leaned against the day before. Marshall's suit jacket was neatly folded beside him on the bridge, his shoes resting on top. Marshall stood there looking at the Damrak canal below him. He was deep in thought and didn't turn at the sound of Alec's running footsteps on the pavement. He bent his legs and pushed.

Alec jumped up and grabbed the man's belt. He planted his feet on the edge of the bridge, his legs apart for support. There the two men balanced, held in place as gravity and momentum decided which way they would fall. It didn't take them long to make up their mind. Alec felt himself being dragged forward by Marshall's greater weight. Alec reached inside himself and pulled hard on the belt yanking the man backwards. Alec fell too. His body hit the pavement hard. His body softened Marshall's fall. He protected Marshall's head from hitting the floor by using his neck as a firemen's air cushion. The air left his lungs in a whoosh and stuck in his throat.

"You bastard!" Marshall shouted at him. "Do you know what you've done?"

Alec floundered gasping for oxygen while trying to push the larger man off him. Marshall rolled to his side and off Alec. He looked at Alec.

"Do I know you? I've seen you before, I'm sure."

With Marshall's weight off him, Alec started to breathe. He didn't answer until he could.

"Marshall, you prick. What the hell were you thinking? You dumb shit."

"How do you know my name?"

"Idiot."

"Were you following me?"

"Shut up for a second."

"Who are you?"

"Shut up."

Alec got to his feet. He heard the tinkle of glass from his jacket pocket. *There go my glasses.* He laughed as the relief hit him. He took a deep breath. He looked around at all the people surrounding them. "Come on, Marshall, get up. You've caused enough of a scene. Let's get a drink. I think we need one or two."

Alec held out his hand for the man.

A few minutes later Alec and Marshall were on the terrace of the Grasshopper restaurant and bar overlooking the Damrak canal that Marshall had wanted a closer look at. They had a pair of whiskies in front of them. Alec was smoking a slightly crushed cigarette.

"So, are you now going to tell me who you are?" Marshall asked.

"My name is Alec Foster, I'm from the Berlin office."

"Berlin office? You're MI6?"

"Man, she's messed you up bad. Yeah, I work under Arthur Newbury in the Russian section there. I was sent because your office thinks you're selling secrets to the Russians."

"What? That's crazy. Why would I come to Amsterdam for that? We're right next door to the Russians. I could do that a million different ways in Kiev."

"They had suspicions about your behaviour. Rightly so, by the looks of things, but for the wrong reasons. You should know better."

Marshall had the grace to look ashamed. "She said she loved me," he said weakly.

"Of course, she did. They all do. That's their job. Make you feel good, so you keep coming back. I bet after the first couple of visits she even refused to take your money, but you insisted and gave her even more, and that became the going rate."

"She said she'd save it for a deposit for a flat for us. How comes you know so much about it?"

"I have a friend in the business. She's taught me well. Hopefully, you'll learn from this lesson." Alec drained his whiskey and lit another cigarette.

"So, what happens now?"

Alec looked at the canal, at the lights reflecting on the surface. "The way I see it, it can go two ways. One, you come clean. Tell your boss what your trips have been about, you'll probably have to tell your wife as well. You'll be demoted and probably sent back to London to live at a desk in a basement for the rest of your days."

Marshall made a face. "And the other way?"

"I could have followed you for your whole trip, and you only went to the Holland Casino on La Guardiaweg. There you won and lost a load of money. Then headed home slightly ahead. There was no prostitute or canal incident, and no Russians."

"Why would you do that? We don't know each other."

"We all do stupid things for love."

Alec thoughts turned to a woman he'd known a long time ago. How the light in her grey eyes faded as life left her. The floor of the café covered in broken crockery, and an expanding pool of blood. Alec picked up his second glass of whiskey. "All of us." He raised his glass, silently toasted the night and the past, and swallowed the lot.

Acknowledgements

I would like to thank my wife, Helen for all her incredible support and patience. I couldn't have done this without her. Helen, I'm sorry for constantly boring you with my writer talk. I'm not going to stop though lol.

I'd also like to thank my three boys, BeeBee, Lunicorn, and Dilly. They are great kids in their own unique and special ways. It's a hell of a buzz hearing you guys say 'My dad's an author'. I love you little guys so much.

I'd like to thank Katie Hagaman for designing the awesome cover for this book. Any authors reading this needing a cover made contact her, at katiehagaman.wixsite.com.

A lot of these stories were written for the monthly writer's competition on the Football365 Forum. I'd like to thank my fellow writers on there for inspiring me to improve my writing and their incredible feedback on each story, which has made revamping and remastering the stories for this book a heck of lot easier than it could have been.

Thank you to the Thunder Team Alpha Force for the unbelievable support and friendship you guys have shown. Gil, Sean, Katie, Sarah, Corry, Kenny, Marnye, you are all incredible, and Jordan, you're okay too. :wink emoji:

I would also like to thank you, the reader, for buying this collection of short stories. I hope you enjoyed the stories as much as I enjoyed writing them. Can I please ask you to review this book on Amazon or Goodreads when you've finished it? Reviews are the main way Indie Authors can get exposure. Each review adds to Amazon's bizarre algorithm lifting each book further up the search results page. As well as gaining exposure there isn't an author in the world who doesn't love getting a brilliant review. It seriously makes their day; I know it does for me.

Finally, feel free to add me on Twitter @paulblakeauthor and say 'Hi', you can also, if you were so inclined, check out my website http://paulblakeauthor.com.

Paul Blake, London, 2019

About the Author

Paul Blake started writing in 2016 when he took a creative writing module to complete his Bachelor of Arts (Honours) degree after failing far too many programming modules. He discovered a passion and has been writing since.

His first novel, A Young Man's Game was published in 2018. He is currently outlining the sequel to A Young Man's Game and also working on a ninja based novel, tentative title Revenge of the Ninja.

He has also had a short story published in the March 2019 issue of Kyanite Press.

Paul is 43 and lives in London, England with his wife and three boys.

Also, By Paul Blake

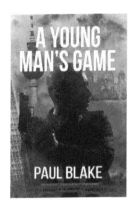

A Young Man's Game: A spy thriller novel. Set in Berlin, 2017. Alec Foster (from the story Cloaked and Shattered in this collection) is Head of Section of MI6 in Berlin. This man is no Jason Bourne.

He is fifty-one, and a borderline alcoholic counting down the days to retirement. Alec is told of a plot to assassinate a British Minister and that there is a traitor in MI6.

As he tries to uncover the traitor, Alec is chased around Berlin by the assassins, the Russian SVR, and the Berlin Police.

He must use his long-forgotten skills and push his body to the very limits to survive. He comes face to face with actions from his past, as everything and everyone he cares about is threatened.

Love in the Mind: A short story collection. Contains two exclusive sci-fi short stories showing the sacrifice women will make for love. These are only available in this volume.

* Don't You Forget (About Me): An alien object has landed on the earth, and is offering untold knowledge. Will Isabelle Bennett give up her memories to help the human race?

* Jumping Someone Else's Train: Two women try the new legal drug, Mind, for the first time. Can their friendship survive?

Racing Vengeance short story in March 2019 issue of Kyanite Press magazine.

All are available in ebook or paperback format on Amazon.

Indie Books Recommended By the Author

Over the past year, I have read many books written by Independent Authors. It's my way of giving back to the writing community on Twitter that, on a daily basis, inspires me and cheers me on.

Each of these books I have loved, as much, if not more than the traditional books I've read over the same period. Each book contains vivid characters, well-realised settings, compelling plots, and are simply a joy to read. They wouldn't be out of place on a rack in Waterstones or on the bestseller lists.

I highly recommend each of these books, they cover a range of genres and styles so you'll definitely find something you'll cherish.

Fir Lodge (Book 1 in the Restarter Series) by Sean McMahon

The first novel in The Restarter Series.

If time shattered, taking away everything you loved, how far would you go to get it all back?

Arriving at a lodge in Norfolk for a long weekend retreat, a group of friends meet for a thirtieth birthday celebration. Before the weekend is over, five of them will die. Trapped in a thirty-three-hour time-loop, only Hal and Kara have the ability to alter fate, and prevent the deaths of their friends.

But in order to unravel the secrets hidden within their own past, they must first learn how to adapt to the new rules of their reality. Time, however, is a relentless force.

One which will stop at nothing to ensure that events unfold exactly as destiny dictates. With time no longer on their side, Hal and Kara will have to decide just how far they are willing to go to free themselves from their perpetual prison, and exactly what they are prepared to sacrifice to defeat an enemy that has already won. Only one thing is certain... Every action has a consequence.

The second in the series The Dark Restarter is one of the best books I've ever read.

The Unfortunate Expiration of Mr. David S. Sparks by William F. Aicher

 Who is David S. Sparks? Where is David S. Sparks? When is David S. Sparks?

In the aftermath of The Chemical Wars, nature has reclaimed humanity's infrastructure. This world, lush with life – yet dangerously uninhabitable for mankind – houses the remaining population who ekes out an existence in quarantined cities anchored off the mainland.

David S. Sparks awakens into the chaos of this future world, unsure of his place in a reality wildly different from his fragmented memories. As the desire to retake the planet swells, so too does the question of how. Will the same mistakes be repeated? Can technology beat nature, or is it time for another approach? And what is David Sparks' role in it all?

Dive into a wild, mind-bending journey as one man chases the ultimate question of self, discovering the truly illusive nature of reality.

Demon's Destiny (Book 1 in the After Dark series) by Sarah Bailey

Walking home at night in the back streets of London was never a good idea.

When her life is threatened, Ella is saved in the nick of time, only to find Lukas is a bounty hunter from Hell. Trusting the enigmatic demon with her darkest secret, Ella Ward is inexplicably drawn to Lukas. Fighting a mutual attraction, she accepts his offer of protection, only to be dragged headlong into a world she barely knew existed. A world where demons tangle with vampires and shifters and Hell literally breaks loose.

Together they hunt down an artefact stolen from Hell. Close on their tail is the vampire Mistress of London, bent on tearing apart the mystery surrounding who Ella really is. Without warning, Ella's unknown powers explode.

Can she survive the ensuing storm? Or will she lose her heart and soul in the process?

Bits and Pieces by Dawn Hosmer

A chance encounter with a stranger traps Tessa within the mind of a madman.

Tessa was born with a gift. Through a simple touch she picks up pieces of others. A "flash" of color devours her—the only indication that she's gained something new from another person.

Red equals pain; purple, a talent; yellow, a premonition; orange, a painful memory; and blue, a pleasant one.

Each flash blurs the lines between her inherent traits and those she's acquired from others. Whenever she gains bits of something new, she loses more pieces of herself. While assisting in search efforts for a local missing college student, Tessa is paralyzed by a flash that rips through her like a lightning bolt, slicing apart her soul. A blinding light takes away her vision. A buzzing louder than any noise she's ever heard overwhelms her, penetrates her mind. As the bolt works its way through her body, images and feelings from someone else take over. Women's dead eyes stare at her as her hands encircle their throats. Their screams consume her mind. Memories of the brutal murders of five women invade her. Will she be able to find the killer and help save the next victim? Can she do so without completely losing herself?

Flicker of Shadows by M. N. Seeley

In 1890, a remote mountain castle in Eastern Europe is host to two conflicting realities.

In one reality, a Police Inspector and a lunatic approach a crime scene from opposing ends. In the other, a bat has succumbed to delusions of grandeur and plans a life beyond the bounds of his supernatural world.

When the bat claims the abandoned mountain castle for himself, he sets the two realities onto a collision course.

Within that impact, a creature is forged and unleashed upon the mountain communities. Not only are lives at risk, but so too is the light of childhood innocence within the minds of the Inspector (Murnau), the Lunatic (Onno) and the Bat (Morton).

Their understanding of reality will be irrevocably corrupted among the flickering shadows cast by the castle creature.

Told in the epistolary format of letters, journal entries and interview transcripts, A Flicker Of Shadows is a psychological mystery with a slow burn. It is written to appeal to New Adult and Adult audiences by purposely mashing what appears to be a children's story with an adult tale of folklore monsters and classic horror beats. But, do not let that fool you.

Fragments of Perception (Short Story Collection) by C. R. Dudley

Fragments of Perception will take you on a roller coaster ride through the depths of the psyche.

In these imagined versions of our world, future technology meets metaphysics, quantum theory blurs with spirituality, and insanity becomes a friend.

Here you will see through the eyes of personified thoughtforms, people who worship black holes, and individuals exploring planes of shared consciousness. You will encounter guardian angels who feel misunderstood, meditating robots, and mythical species sending advice to humanity in unconventional ways.

Whatever your perspective, this is a book that will stay with you long after you turn the final page.

The Awakening (Book 1 of The Awakening series) by K. L. Hagaman

As their territory is thrown into chaos, princess Lilja and her keeper, a unique guardian by the name of Kaden, must find a resolution and return peace to a people driven by fear.

But how does one exactly restore a fallen kingdom if they can't even remember it?

After an incident of war, Lilja has found herself just there—lost inside her own mind and a stranger to her very existence.

Their destinies entwined, Lilja and Kaden's only hope rests in the hands of a magic wielder whose price for salvation may just be more dangerous than the war itself.

Together they must forge a path to save their civilization, but first they will need to come to terms with who they both truly are, because the past is always just around the corner.

The Little Demons Inside (Book 1 of the Eudimonia series) by Micah Thomas

This is not a love story, but there is love.

This is not a horror story, but there are horrors.

This is not a true story, but there is truth.

In 2017, something went wrong with the world. Or, at least, in 2017, everyone finally saw it.

Henry needed to get off the streets to avoid the heat and volunteered for an experimental drug trial. The permanent side effects made his life dangerous and unpredictable. Henry doesn't know what to do, doesn't know his place. He's a broken version of a wandering superhero. Then he meets Cassie. Their connection is brief and intense.

These two lost souls are propelled together, apart, and together again in a mind-bending adventure that challenges them to face their demons.

Margot by Lisa De Castro

 Margot has gifted herself with a vacation to Corsica—the fulfilment of a promise made to herself long ago. She must admit she's enjoying the solitude that traveling alone brings, even if the indulgence prompts a guilty twinge or two.

Exploring Corsica's shoreline, museums, and churches, Margot finds herself reflecting on her life and her mortality. Her daughters are grown, and her marriage at this point is best described as comfortable. As she looks back on her past through a series of revealing flashbacks, Margot realizes she's come to a pivotal moment in time.

A chance meeting with an old boyfriend complicates matters further, igniting half-forgotten passions and memories of her own father's infidelity—and pleasure, temptation, and guilt combine for her in equal measure. Will these stirrings change the course of Margot's life, or will they simply ruin the stability she already has?

A delicate unfolding of one woman's life, Margot is like the sea surrounding Corsica: beautiful, seductive, and capable of dragging the reader into unexpected depths. Author Lisa De Castro brings both Margot and Corsica to vibrant life, seamlessly blending evocative descriptions of Corsica's weathered, ancient landscapes with Margot's bittersweet memories—and her possible future.

Trumpland (Short Story Collection) by M. D. Parker et al.

November 8th, 2016. A new President was elected, and the United States was forever changed.

Now 8 authors have come together to share the alternative facts of the dystopian futures we have yet to witness.

From the schoolboy romanticizing delusions of grandeur to nuclear Armageddon; from civil wars to the diseased undead; from walls isolating nations, to trade agreements, to environmental disasters – will any of the signs be bright enough to be seen?

Will we heed the warnings before Lady Liberty's torch is extinguished? Can we write a new future for a nation, for the entire world, before it is too late?

Trumpland's stories present a speculative inquiry into the fallout from the most consequential election of our age. All artists donated their contributions with proceeds from the sales being donated to charity.

Time, For a Change by Adam Eccles

Terry's dead-end IT job is about as much fun as an internal cavity search.

Chances of promotion? None. Chances of a raise? Not happening. Chances of romance? Nada.

It's time for a change, but that's easier said than done when your prospects are as dismal as the Irish weather in January. Enter stage left a gorgeous young girl who inexplicably finds him interesting. Toss in a mysterious wooden box hidden in his late father's workshop and the dull monotony of Terry's life is broken.

But will it stay that way? What is in the wooden box? Can love conquer all – even the terrible tedium of a dead end job?

This is for all the office workers, all the cynics, all the souls who look into their future with nothing but dread.

Map of the World (Short Story Collection) by Zev Good

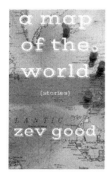 In this debut collection of stories, Zev Good takes the reader into a world he knows and illuminates so well: the middle-class American South.

In the opening story, "The Sweet By-and-By," an inexplicable tragedy brings to light the cracks in a family's foundation.

In "Had," a man recalls his youth and must, at last, come to terms with the one love he could never have.

The title story alternates between the present and the past, and tells us a truth we all know but find hard to admit: that to rescue ourselves, we sometimes have to leave others behind.

These stories, populated with mothers and children, friends and lovers, the living and the dying, reveal the intricate and tenuous bonds that unite us all.

Preservation Protocol by John Prescott

Currently not for sale, but there is a new edition coming on August 23rd, 2019, published by Kyanite Publishing. I was lucky to get this book before it was removed from sale.

Definitely, one to look out for, an excellent sci-fi thriller. A cross between I, Robot, Bladerunner, and the TV show Almost Human.

Max Kincaid, a police detective from the 29th precinct of New Wave City was working another case against the mob when Daryl Marston walked into his life.

Both soon find themselves entangled in a far-reaching conspiracy involving the mob, the government and Synthetics: artificial humans designed to be nearly indistinguishable from the genuine article.

Max must fight his prejudices against Synthetics while helping Daryl, an innocent victim of a secret organization's darkest machinations.

The lines between right and wrong, human and machine, friend and foe soon become blurred. Will Max unravel the conspiracies whirling around him in time?

Inn Spirits: Tales of the Folsom by C. M. Harris

Like Preservation Protocol, this has been re-released under the Kyanite Publishing family.

I read the original version and loved it.

They said the supernatural wasn't real, that it couldn't hurt you. They've never been to the Folsom Inn, a place where the dead do more than talk. They touch, they scream, they kill. Come stay for the night, won't you?

From my review: 'A very creepy book along similar lines as the Puppetmaster and Annabelle movies. Creepy little dolls, blood, and violence. Very Richard Laymon, but with creepily awesome dolls.' I think I need another synonym for creepy but man, what a creepy book.

Colour Me Confounded by Poulomi Sanyal

In the first of two stories, teenagers Rupa and Minerva think they will be friends forever.

The two high school girls are virtually inseparable, despite their many differences. Years later, Rupa looks back on that relationship and the dramatic incident that ended their friendship. While she writes her memoir and travels the world, she comes to a realization about her connection with Minerva and the experiences they shared.

The second story centers on Ariana, a Canadian Iranian engineer. She is happy with her work in Toronto, but a friend's surprise career move brings back old memories of a previous job in Montreal. She hated that job and felt isolated and unappreciated. There was one person, however, who made it worthwhile.

As both Ariana and Rupa look back on their pasts, they come to startling discoveries about their current lives. Will these insights lead the two to choose different paths—or just fill them with more regret?

Machine Gun Jesus by Dean Tongue

In this hilarious off the wall comedy, Jesus is sent by God to modern day Earth to try and make a difference in the world.

Not fancying being nailed to a damn cross again, Jesus agrees to do it with one condition – That he can do things a little bit differently this time!

So join Jesus (or Jay Cee as he likes to be called these days) as he embarks on a rap career with his D-Cyplez – Honkey Killa and Suicide Bob.

Join him as he tells amazing stories about how his mother got pregnant and Adam and Steve (Eve was a printing error apparently). Join him as he swills beer, smokes drugs and gets into fist fights on live television. Join him as the world slowly starts to turn against him – again! Join the second coming! Will Jesus die for our sins again? Or will he make us die for his?

Dancing at Midnight (Book 1) by Rebecca Yelland

 After a fifteen-year absence, Carolyn Graves has returned to her childhood home following the death of her mother.

With the purpose of settling her mother's estate, Carolyn attempts to push past the emotions of their strained relationship – and her own anxiety issues – to quickly complete the process and be on her way.

But as Carolyn begins to sort through her mother's private documents, she discovers a disturbing history behind her mother's early life.

As a result, Carolyn learns the truth about her parent's relationship and the secret they have kept hidden for decades

.

Ferryman by Michael Blaylock

Some people can fly. Some can see impossible distances.

Some can change their appearance, control the elements, or run at incredible speed. Charlie Ferris can kill with a touch.

Contrary to what the superhuman government believes, Charlie has no dreams of world domination or mass murder. Neither does he wish to pretend his powers don't exist. He wants to use his abilities for good, but how?

As the immortal years pass, Charlie fears that villainy is the only option for the master of death. But when an undying army appears at their doorstep, the superhuman authorities have no choice but to call on a professional killer.

Charlie wants to believe that this is his chance to prove he's a good guy, but sparks fly at every encounter. When harassment mounts and prejudice backs him into a wall, The Ferryman must decide what is more important: a good reputation...or goodness?

Kiss Me When I'm Dead by Dominic Piper

 The stunning debut thriller by bestselling author Dominic Piper, Kiss Me When I'm Dead introduces the enigmatic, London-based private investigator Daniel Beckett.

When Beckett is offered double his usual fee to track down Viola Raleigh, the missing daughter of a billionaire arms dealer, he has no reason to believe the assignment is not as it seems.

But his investigation is hindered as he discovers he's being stalked by a professional surveillance team.

As he learns more about Viola's life as a drug addict and high-class call girl, he starts to realise that his wealthy client has been economical with the truth.

It isn't long before Beckett himself is in danger, but his adversaries quickly discover that they are dealing with a formidable opponent with a far more sinister background than they might ever have imagined.

Crisis Point by James Kemp

Why is rolling news showing footage of US Marines holding off an armed assault on the White House? Where have the Secret Service taken the President and why has the Vice President invoked the 25th Amendment? Why has US Space Command mobilised its strategic reserve and put it into orbit?

Crisis point is a stand alone novella set in the same near future world as Perfects (published late 2016).

It tells the story of a military conspiracy reaching to the top of the US Military to subvert the democratically elected US President.

This is a future where some Americans have realized that spending their blood and treasure as the world's policemen hasn't been effective and have decided that someone else should take a turn.

In the middle of the 21st Century Mike Duff is a career officer of US Space Force. The military are getting cut, and the defense contractors aren't happy about it.

Mike is a patriotic American, loyal to the Constitution and proud of his country, but he doesn't like what he sees the politicians doing.

Copyright

Visit the author's website at www.paulblakeauthor.com.

Printed in Great Britain
by Amazon